'As I read I felt a storm gathering, a force, a reckoning started to hurtle towards me, and in the middle of this the importance of family sits centre stage. The violence is prominent, yet there is a subtle, thought-provoking energy that twists through this tale, and ensures that *The Mine* is an absolutely cracking read' Love Reading

'*The Mine* is another beautifully written and absorbing read from the Orenda books stable – it is not a long read but it is an extremely compelling one … I adored the sense of place that Antti Tuomainen brings to this book, descriptively speaking it is intense and gorgeous, one of those stories that absorbs you into its vortex for the time you spend reading it' Liz Loves Books

'This was a truly beautiful book – deliciously dark, thought-provoking, and gorgeously written. It gave me chills, and not only because of the endless snow and cold. I see why Antti is so revered in Finland' Louise Beech, author of *How To Be Brave*

'*The Mine* is a gripping and traumatic environmental thriller about how far people will go in order to hide the truth. The book is well written and it has been translated by David Hackston, so that none of the beauty and elegance of Tuomainen's prose is lost to the reader. *The Mine* is a thriller that shows off the best of Finnish noir and raises the question of why has it been hidden from the English reader for so long. I'm extremely thankful to Orenda Books for bringing Antti Tuomainen to my attention and I can guarantee this is a book you cannot put down' Nudge-Book Reviews

'I can highly recommend this fast-paced thriller with its sparse yet highly descriptive language. It works as an emotional thriller too as the reader is unsure of how Janne's actions will affect his delicate family situation' Shaz's Book Blog

'An excellent thriller with all the hallmarks of Scandi Noir, gripping, elegant and looks to the bigger issues that play an important role in society – in this case the environmental disasters surrounding the mine and the corruption in covering it up' The Quiet Knitter

'Antti Tuomainen's *The Mine*, set in snowy winter darkness in
northern Finland and amid a miasma of murky state corruption is
right up there with the best … offering a sympathetic, politically
engaged investigative journalist and a profound concern for the
environment' *The Times Literary Supplement*

'Tuomainen's spare style suits the depressing subject and raises a
serious question: how do you find hope when law and order break
down?' *Financial Times*

'Antti Tuomainen is a wonderful writer, whose characters, plots and
atmosphere are masterfully drawn' Yrsa Sigurðardóttir

'Tensely written, full of twists and sudden violence, this is nothing
less than the birth of a new genre: dystopian detection' *Sunday
Telegraph*

'This chilling novel compels … Clever, atmospheric and
wonderfully imaginative' *Sunday Mirror*

'*Dark As My Heart*, the most lauded Finnish crime novel of recent
years, lives up to its acclaim' *The Times*

'The sparse prose style suits the dark, treacherous, rain-soaked
environment of this dystopian vision of Helsinki' *Glasgow Sunday
Herald*

'Antti Tuomainen again creates a powerful book, set firmly within
the boundaries of strong themes and unforgettable characters, with
a huge dose of beautiful sensitive style, masterfully translated from
Finnish by David Hackston … The King of Helsinki Noir is a
writer of life. I cannot wait to see his atmospheric work appearing
on screen' Crime Review

'Topical. Frightening. Beautifully written, with a fast-moving story, which makes it almost impossible to put down. Plus it's a standalone, so you haven't missed anything up until now. This is another absolute belter from Orenda, but, really, you wouldn't expect anything less by now, would you?' Crime Worm

'Antti Tuomainen begins *The Mine* with an intriguing and enticing prologue. The reader doesn't know who the character is, but these couple of pages are written with such care and clarity that you are captured straight away … and then left wondering … *The Mine* is an excellent thriller that deals with extremely topical issues. The setting is perfect and the translation is so well done. Oh, and that ending…' Random Things through My Letter Box

'The writing is utterly compelling – I read this book in a sitting. I shivered at the bleakness and cold of a wintery Finland. The layers of Janne's character – his need to write, his desire not to let his family down, his demand for validation and support despite offering little in return – made for thought-provoking reading. It was hard not to sympathise with all concerned. The denouement tied up each plot thread whilst skillfully maintaining the bones of all that had gone before. Questionable decisions were made but they fit perfectly the characters and story. In many ways this is a straightforward crime thriller but the execution achieves so much more. It provides a dark and altogether satisfying read' Never Imitate

'Antti Tuomainen's skillful storytelling is as sharp as an ice pick, and I cannot wait to read more from him … If you like your thrillers to be peppered with a little bit of conspiracy and action, then *The Mine* is most certainly one to pick up!' Bibliophile Book Club

'Part crime story, part conspiracy, with a dash of mystery thrown in for good measure. It's a splendid concoction of beautifully evocative locations and compelling characters … Definitely a page-turner that'll keep you up into the wee small hours' Espresso Coco

'The pacing and style are brilliantly effective; calmly drawing you in until you realise you're practically up to your knees in Finnish snow and up to your neck in a complex mystery and there's no way you're gonna want to leave this story even after the last page is turned' Mumbling About

'*The Mine* is an emotionally charged, thought-provoking Finnish environmental thriller. It's stunningly written and translated seamlessly – no word is out of the place and the descriptions provide an amazing sense of the chilling frozen setting. I was totally gripped throughout and struggled to put the book down … This is a stunning book – yet another winner from Orenda. *The Mine* is a book that will stay with me for a long while' Off-The-Shelf Books

'The author's beautiful writing is one of the reasons I loved this book as much as I did because it played out like a movie in my mind and I could really buy into what was happening in the story because of that. The entire book had me gripped from start to finish and did not disappoint come the end' Reviewed The Book

'I could just picture the snow and hear the silence due to the fact no one was around. It was extremely atmospheric. More important, current topics are covered in this book as it touches on environmental activists and the damage that we as humans are doing to the world. It was very cleverly done and showed different ways that people go about raising awareness. Overall a great book and another one I have already been recommending' Life of a Nerdish Mum

'The book is really well written and the author painted such a vivid picture of Finland that I could imagine I was there. In fact, all the descriptions of the snow made me dig out my fleecy blanket and thermal socks as I really began to feel that cold … 4* out of 5*' Ginger Book Geek

THE MAN WHO DIED

Finnish author Antti Tuomainen (b. 1971) was an award-winning copywriter when he made his literary debut in 2007 as a suspense author. The critically acclaimed *My Brother's Keeper* was published two years later. In 2011 Tuomainen's third novel, *The Healer*, was awarded the Clue Award for Best Finnish Crime Novel of 2011 and was shortlisted for the Glass Key Award. The Finnish press labelled *The Healer* – the story of a writer desperately searching for his missing wife in a post-apocalyptic Helsinki – 'unputdownable'. Two years later, in 2013, they crowned Tuomainen the King of Helsinki Noir when *Dark as My Heart* was published. *The Mine*, translated by David Hackston and published in 2016, was an international bestseller. Several of his books have been optioned for TV/film. With his piercing and evocative style, Tuomainen is one of the first to challenge the Scandinavian crime genre formula, and *The Man Who Died* sees him at his literary best.

Follow Antti on Twitter: @antti_tuomainen, on Facebook: Facebook.com/AnttiTuomainen and on his website: www.anttituomainen.com

David Hackston is a British translator of Finnish and Swedish literature and drama. Notable recent publications include Kati Hiekkapelto's Anna Fekete series (which currently includes *The Hummingbird*, *The Defenceless* and *The Exiled*, all published by Orenda Books), Katja Kettu's wartime epic *The Midwife*, Pajtim Statovci's enigmatic debut *My Cat Yugoslavia* and Maria Peura's coming-of-age novel *At the Edge of Light*. He has also translated Antti Tuomainen's *The Mine* (published by Orenda Books). In 2007 he was awarded the Finnish State Prize for Translation. David is also a professional countertenor and a founding member of the English Vocal Consort of Helsinki. Follow David on Twitter @Countertenorist.

The Man Who Died

ANTTI TUOMAINEN

translated from the Finnish by David Hackston

ORENDA
BOOKS

Orenda Books
16 Carson Road
West Dulwich
London SE21 8HU
www.orendabooks.co.uk

First published in the United Kingdom by Orenda Books 2017
Originally published in Finland by Like Kustannus Oy as *Mies joka kuoli* 2016
Copyright © Antti Tuomainen 2016
English language translation copyright © David Hackston 2017
Second impression 2017

ISBN 978-1-910633-84-7
eISBN 978-1-910633-85-4

Typeset in Garamond by MacGuru Ltd
Printed and bound by CPI Group (UK) Ltd, Croydon CR0 4YY

Orenda Books is grateful for the financial support of FILI,
who provided a translation grant for this project.

FINNISH LITERATURE EXCHANGE

SALES & DISTRIBUTION

In the UK and elsewhere in Europe:
Turnaround Publisher Services
Unit 3, Olympia Trading Estate
Coburg Road, Wood Green
London N22 6TZ
www.turnaround-uk.com

In USA/Canada:
Trafalgar Square Publishing
Independent Publishers Group
814 North Franklin Street
Chicago, IL 60610
USA
www.ipgbook.com

In Australia and New Zealand:
Affirm Press
28 Thistlethwaite Street
South Melbourne VIC 3205
Australia
www.affirmpress.com.au

For Anu,
With love, once again

The author has taken considerable artistic licence with regard to geographical, medical, temporal and natural scientific details. In all other respects this story is factually correct.

'He was some kind of a man.
What does it matter what you say about people?'

– Marlene Dietrich, *Touch of Evil*

PART ONE
DEATH

1

'It's a good job you provided a urine sample too.'

The oval face of the doctor sitting behind the desk exudes seriousness and gravitas. The dark rims of his spectacles accentuate the blue, almost three-dimensional intensity of his gaze.

'This...' he stumbles. 'This requires a little background. I've contacted my colleagues in Kotka and Helsinki. They said essentially the same as what we've been able to deduce here. Even if we'd picked this up the last time you visited, there's nothing else we could have done. How are you feeling?'

I shrug my shoulders. I go through the same information I told the doctor the last time I was here and give an account of the latest symptoms. It all started with a sudden, powerful wave of nausea and vomiting that quite literally knocked me off my feet. After that my condition seemed to stabilise, but only for a while. Sometimes I feel so dizzy that I'm worried I might faint. I have coughing fits. Stress keeps me awake at night. When I finally fall asleep, I have nightmares. Sometimes my headaches are so intense it feels like someone is scraping a knife behind my eyeballs. My throat is constantly dry. The nausea has started again and it hits me without any warning.

And all this just when my business is getting ready for the most important time of the year, the greatest challenge we've ever faced in the short time we've existed.

'Right,' the doctor nods. 'Right.'

I say nothing. He pauses before continuing. 'This is not to do with prolonged, complicated flu symptoms, as we thought at first. Without a urine sample we might never have found out what was wrong. The sample told us a lot, and that's what led us to conduct the MRI scan. With the results of the scan we've now got a fuller picture of what's going on. You see, your kidneys, liver and pancreas – that is to say your most important internal organs – are extremely badly damaged. Given what you've told us, we can deduce that your central nervous system is severely compromised too. In addition to that, you may have experienced some amount of brain damage. All this is a direct result of the poisoning that showed up in your urine sample. The levels of toxicity – that is, the amount of poison in your system – would be enough to knock out a hippopotamus. The fact that you're even sitting here in front of me and still going to work is, in my estimation, due to the fact that the poisoning has taken place over an extended period of time and in such a way that the poison has had time to accumulate in your body. In one way or another, you've become used to it.'

In my gut it feels as though I'm falling, as though something inside me tears free and hurtles down into the cold abyss beneath. The sensation lasts a few seconds. Then it stops. I'm sitting on a chair opposite the doctor, it's a Tuesday morning and I'll soon be on my way to work. I've read stories of how people act with great clarity in a fire or of how they don't panic after they've been shot, though they're bleeding profusely. I sit there and look the doctor in the eyes. I could be waiting for the bus.

'You mentioned you work with mushrooms,' the doctor says eventually.

'But the matsutake isn't poisonous,' I answer. 'And the harvest is just around the corner.'

'The matsutake?'

I don't know where to start.

I decide to tell the short version: back in Helsinki my wife worked in institutional catering, and I was a sales officer. Three and a half years ago the recession hit both our workplaces, and we were made redundant at around the same time. Meanwhile Hamina – like dozens of similar small Finnish towns – was desperately looking for new commercial activity to replace the empty harbour and recently decommissioned paper factory. We had a series of quick negotiations, secured a generous start-up grant, acquired premises that cost next to nothing and staff who were well acquainted with the local woods and terrain. We sold our one-bedroom apartment in suburban Helsinki, and for the same money bought a detached house in Hamina and a small fibreglass boat that we could tether to the jetty a mere seventy metres from our post box.

Our business idea was simple: the matsutake – the pine mushroom.

The Japanese were crazy about it, and Finnish forests were full of it.

The Japanese would pay up to a thousand euros per kilo of mushrooms in the early, sprouting phase. To the north and east of Hamina there were forests where picking pine mushrooms was as easy as plucking them from a plate in front of you. In Hamina we had treatment facilities, a dryer, a packing area, chilled spaces and employees. During the harvest season we sent a shipment to Tokyo once a week.

I have to catch my breath. The doctor seems to be thinking about something.

'What about your lifestyle otherwise?'

'My lifestyle?'

'Your diet, how much you exercise, that sort of thing.'

I tell him I eat well and with a good, hearty appetite. I haven't once cooked for myself since I met Taina, and that was over seven years ago. And Taina's meals aren't the kind in which a teaspoon of celery purée stares dejectedly across the plate at a solitary sprig of wheatgrass. Taina's basic ingredients are cream, salt, butter, cheeses and plenty of pork. I like Taina's food, always have done. And it shows around my waistline. I weigh twenty-four kilos more than when we first met.

Taina hasn't gained weight; it might be because she's bigger-boned than I am and has always looked like a weightlifter in peak physical condition, ready for a competition. I mean that in the nicest possible way: her thighs are solid, round and strong. Her shoulders are broad and her arms powerful without being masculine; her stomach is flat. Whenever I see pictures of female bodybuilders who are not ripped and grotesque, I think of Taina. Besides, she exercises too: she goes to the gym, takes aerobics classes, and ever since we moved here she goes rowing out at sea. Sometimes I try to keep up with her, though that too is becoming a rare occurrence.

I don't know why I'm speaking so quickly, so effusively, why I have to talk about Taina in such detail. The next thing we know, I'll be giving the doctor her measurements down to the nearest centimetre.

Then, as it seems the doctor isn't focussing his healing eyes in the right direction, I ask him what we're going to do about it. The doctor looks at me as though he's just realised I haven't listened to a single word he's been saying. I notice his eyes blinking behind his spectacles.

'Nothing,' he says. 'There's nothing we can do.'

The overexposed room is so full of summer and sunshine that I have to squint my eyes at him.

'I'm sorry,' he says. 'Perhaps I wasn't clear enough. We can't say for sure what kind of poison has caused this. It appears to be a combination of various natural toxins. And like the poison itself, judging by your symptoms and the account you've given, the extent of your poisoning seems, from a toxicological perspective, to be an optimal combination of exposure over an extended period of time and exceptionally highly developed levels of tolerance. If this were a case of specific, one-off poisoning that we were able to attend to promptly, there are a number of measures we could have taken – antidotes we could have administered. But, in your case, I'm afraid there's nothing we can do. There is nothing that will return your body to its normal state or that will change the … how should I put it? … the direction of travel. It is simply a matter of waiting for the body's functions to shut down one by one. I'm sorry, but the condition will inevitably lead to death.'

The brightness of the summer's day streaming through the window only serves to heighten the luridness of his final word. The word must surely be in the wrong place. I must be in the wrong place. I came here with a simple bout of the flu, I tell myself, with a few stomach cramps and occasional dizziness. I want to hear him tell me that all I need is rest and a course of antibiotics; or that, in the worst-case scenario, I might need my stomach pumped. Then I'll recover and get back to…

'I might compare this situation to a patient with pancreatic cancer or cirrhosis of the liver,' the doctor continues. 'When a crucial organ exceeds its capacity, it never returns to normal but runs down, as it were; it burns itself out until it finally snuffs out like a candle. There's simply nothing to be done. An organ transplant would be out of the question, because the surrounding organs are damaged too and would be unable to support the new organ; on the contrary, they would likely cause the new organ to malfunction too, in my opinion. What's more, in your case every organ appears to be in an equally advanced state of degeneration. On the plus side, that might be the secret of your relative state of wellbeing – a balance of horror, if you will.'

I look at the doctor. His head is nodding, barely perceptible.

'Of course, everything is relative,' he says.

The doctor is sitting behind his desk. He'll be sitting there for the rest of the day, tomorrow and next week. It's a powerful thought, and a moment later I understand why it occurred to me.

'How…?' I begin. It hits me that this is a once-in-a-lifetime question. 'How … when … Should I…? How much time do I have?'

The doctor, who will help save lives for at least another decade before retiring for another ten, perhaps twenty years, suddenly looks grave.

'Judging by the combination of factors,' he begins, 'days; weeks at most.'

At first I want to yell, shout anything at all. Then I want to lash out, to punch something. Then I feel nauseous again. I swallow.

'I don't understand how any of this is possible.'

'It's a combination of everything that—'

'I don't mean that.'

'Quite.'

We both fall silent.

It seems as though summer turns to autumn, to winter, spring and back to summer again. The doctor casts me an inquisitive glance, all the while fiddling with the blue document on his desk bearing my name and details in large letters: JAAKKO MIKAEL KAUNIS-MAA. SOCIAL SECURITY NUMBER – 081178-073H.

'Do you have any requests?'

I must look confused, because the doctor continues his question. 'Crisis therapy? Psychiatric help? A hospice place or a home carer? Painkillers? Sedatives?'

I must admit, I hadn't thought about things like that before. I haven't exactly spent time thinking about the practical aspects of my final days, so there's no to-do list, as it were. Death only comes round once in a lifetime, that much I realise, and maybe I should have put a bit more effort into it. But I've always avoided the subject and everything to do with it. Now I understand quite how immense it is. Big questions, big decisions. And for the last seven years I've always made big decisions with my wife: the move from Helsinki to Hamina; from the mundane to the matsutake.

'I'll have to speak to my wife.'

When I hear myself, I know it's the only thing I can do: I must speak to her, and after that I'll know everything there is to know.

2

The asphalt seems to puff and shimmer. The wind has forgotten its only function: to create a breeze. Everything around me is so green and the air so stifling that it feels like I've been plunged into a bath of thick moss. I grip the sweaty telephone in my hand. I don't know why; I'm not calling anyone. You don't tell people these sorts of things over the telephone. I peel my shirt from my skin, but it glues itself back almost immediately.

I sit in the car, turn on the ignition and set the air conditioning to the coolest setting available. The steering wheel feels moist and limp in my hands. If my sense of calm is merely because I'm still in shock, that for the moment suits me fine.

I turn left out of the hospital car park. The most direct route would have been to take a left. I need a few minutes; I want to gather my thoughts.

Our premises are situated on the other side of the prominent water tower in the suburb of Hevoshaka. I drive as far towards Salmenvirta as the road will allow, take a left and follow the shoreline towards Savilahti. Flashes of police-blue sea glint between the trees and the houses. Someone is mending a series of already flawless garden paving stones; a woman with fluttering hair is returning from the market, the basket at the front of her bike laden with groceries. It's five to eleven. Morning in the town of Hamina.

I arrive at Mannerheimintie and turn left. From Mullinkoskentie I take a left onto Teollisuuskatu. The suburb of Hevoshaka is small and its vistas are staggeringly heterogeneous. There you can find all forms of business and dwellings of all shapes and sizes – everything from detached houses to blocks of flats, from fast-food kiosks to industrial warehouses.

Our business is located in a brownish-yellow, single-storey building with a small loading bay at one end and sauna facilities and a patio at the other. I can't see Taina's car in the forecourt. Perhaps she's still at home or gone into town for lunch. She does that sometimes. I don't like to go home in the middle of the workday. It messes up my internal clock. It's far easier, far more structured, to stay at work during the day and come home in the evening. In that way the two remain separate: work is only for work, and home feels all the more like a home.

I turn the car round in the forecourt and drive towards Pappilansaari. The phone is in my lap, between my legs.

Hamina is often called a concentric town. However, this is only true of the town centre: the Town Hall and the blocks immediately surrounding it. Otherwise its streets are every bit as angular as they are in other towns.

The market is bustling.

In addition to the local stall keepers, there are the trinkets common to every summer market square in the land: hardened strips of liquorice, unashamedly overpriced cotton sauna towels, stiff underwear in boxes of ten, twenty and a hundred.

I sometimes think about death, but even thinking about it is all but impossible – especially your own death. A second later I'm thinking about something different altogether: today's shopping list, the business's outgoings.

A few minutes later I reach the bridge across the Pappilansalmi strait. Hamina is a small town dotted across islands, peninsulas and heathland, in clusters of a few houses here and there. The sea reaches its long tentacles between the houses and their inhabitants, snatching up blue segments of the green landscape.

I see Taina's wine-red Hyundai from a distance. Behind that, one corner at a time, I make out the shape of a black, shining Corolla. It looks as though it has just been washed. Well before the end of our drive, I pull in by the side of the road and switch off the engine.

Had Taina said anything about Petri popping round?

Sometimes Taina stays at home testing new recipes, and Petri gives her a hand. Petri was our first full-time employee. He knows all our machinery and equipment and he can install and mend everything we need. On top of that he knows every road, and every hill and dell within a fifty-kilometre radius. He also helps to solve the company's various logistical problems.

Very well, I think as I step out of the car, I'll tell Petri to go back to the office, tell him the cleaning equipment won't start up. I'll think of something. Then I'll sit Taina down on the sofa and tell her … I don't know what I'll tell her. But you can be sure I won't have to make anything up.

Ours is the last house at the end of a narrowing gravel road. Its lively yellow front faces the street; behind the house there is a verdant garden decorated with currant bushes and age-old flowerbeds, which rolls down towards the reeds and bulrushes along the shore. In the middle of the garden is a patio ten square metres in size, where you can sit and look out at the sea in peace and quiet; only the opposite shore is visible, and that too is at a suitable distance.

I walk up the steps to the front door. These last few weeks I've felt constantly out of breath. I thought it had something to do with my flu, that it might be bronchitis or at worst a bout of pneumonia. I place a hand on the railings and steady myself for a moment. I hear the sound of an approaching hydroplane.

Affluent Russian tourists have bought up enormous fortresses along much of the local shoreline, and in addition to the yachts moored at their private jetties, many of them have their own light aircraft too. They roar around in the things, causing a nuisance for a few summers, before becoming bored and putting everything up for sale. Of course, it's impossible to sell villas that size, let alone hydroplanes. In a recessive and ageing community with high unemployment there are relatively few impulsive millionaires.

The hydroplane glides closer.

The railing suddenly feels cold. I pull my hand away, open the door and shout out a hello. Nobody answers. Maybe they're in the kitchen. I walk along the hallway to the other side of the house, where the kitchen is situated. The wooden floorboards creak beneath me.

The kitchen is empty, everything is spotless. No pots or pans bubbling on the stove. No smell of cooking in the air. The counters gleam, clean and empty. I call out Taina's name.

The hydroplane sputters directly above the house, its noise drowns out my voice. I move towards the back door, open the door and walk out onto the top step. The hydroplane masks the sound of the door opening – that and the inadvertent gasp that escapes from my mouth.

The patio sways.

Or perhaps it's me that sways.

No, it's definitely the patio that's moving.

Despite the roar of the hydroplane as it swerves through the warm, blue sky directly above me, my sharpened senses see and hear the cheap metallic sun-lounger creaking at the joints, the fabric of the red-and-white striped cushions rubbing against one another with synthetic howls, the wheels of the German gas barbecue standing to the right of the sun-lounger shunting closer to the edge of the patio one millimetre at a time, the garden swing to the left moving restlessly from side to side, the pots of geraniums that look as though, at any moment, they might burst into a sprint.

Petri is lying on the lounger, the soles of his feet facing the house – facing me. His neck is arched backwards in an almost unnatural position over the edge of the lounger. He is looking upside down at the sea – if his eyes are open, that is. I don't know if it's possible. Taina is doing her best to make sure he keeps his eyes shut.

Taina has her back to me. Her broad back is gleaming with sweat, her round, strong buttocks glow like a pair of ruddy cheeks. She is riding Petri as though she were trying to climb a mountainside on horseback: her feet are placed firmly on the patio decking and her hips are pumping, encouraging the horse to give all it's got. It's an impressive sight. Taina's face is angled up towards the sky. Perhaps we're looking at the same hydroplane.

The tempo increases, though such a thing ought to be physically impossible.

I see an iron bar leaning against the side of the woodshed.

At that point, vomit surges within me. The wave of nausea is so powerful that it almost floors me. I grip the railings with both hands. An arch of vomit flies through the air towards the patio.

The hydroplane shakes the entire house. Instinctively, as if guided by an inner power, I step back inside and pull the door shut behind me.

I can feel air filling my lungs. For a few moments I haven't breathed at all. I stand up straight.

The sound of the hydroplane has grown fainter, more distant, like a fly buzzing in the next room. I know now that what I came here to say cannot possibly be said – doesn't deserve to be said – and that what I need most of all right now is the air conditioning in my car.

3

Every now and then I drift into the lane of oncoming traffic and have to focus my eyes on the middle of the road. The road jumps, swerves. Thankfully the streets are all but empty; the tourists must be at the market or out at sea, while all the locals go about their business in the town centre either in the morning or the early evening. Midday is a moment of calm.

My mind, however, is anything but calm. My rage turns to shock, then colossal disappointment, then a hollow chill that encompasses everything, before the rage wells up again. At times I can hear the doctor's voice, see his serious face and white coat in front of me, then a moment later the sight of Taina's round thighs pumping like a rodeo rider.

The car's air conditioning is at full capacity. The cool air calms the tingling sensation on my skin and soothes the sting of the sweat in my eyes.

My face feels like it belongs to me once again.

And I seem to know where I'm going.

I see a parking spot outside the police station. The two-storey building looks quiet. It is the only modern building in the square. There are churches on both sides of the Town Hall: to the southeast one for the Orthodox congregation, to the northwest one for the Lutherans. Lining all sides of the square are rows of wooden houses, all a hundred and fifty years old – renovated, beautiful, ornate. If they were in Helsinki, you'd have to win the lottery to own one.

I've visited the police station only once before, about a month ago. It was to report a theft. Some packing materials left by a delivery firm we employ were stolen from the forecourt outside the company premises. I knew who had taken them. I'd done a bit of detective work myself. The problem was I couldn't prove anything, and the police didn't warm to my theories. So I kept my mouth shut, took my copy of the statement in which I'd reported the missing goods so that I could send it to our insurance company, went back to work and got a lecture from Taina, who told me I always give in to people far too easily.

Which makes the current situation markedly different from how I'd thought of it only a moment ago.

I've switched off the engine. The air conditioning's all-consuming vortex subsides and is replaced with a curious sense of calm. I am sure I can hear the sound of a girl in a summer dress cycling past, the breeze in her skirt, the tyres against the asphalt, the conversation about blue pansies taking place outside the florist's, the hum of the refrigerators at the ice-cream stall. I ask myself what has happened to me, and I know the answer.

The front door of the police station opens.

A man, approximately my own age, angrily looks around, gets in his car and sits down with a thump, as though he is determined to break the seat, and then, with a screech of tyres, he speeds off towards the Reserve Officers' School. *Precisely*, I think to myself. The mistakes we can make when we do things in haste, in a tantrum, a state of turmoil.

Only seconds earlier I was about to storm into the police station – and tell them what, exactly?

I'm dying, I might have been poisoned, but I haven't a shred of proof. My wife is in the garden right now, screwing our young employee, Petri. What are you going to do about it?

I realise all too acutely just how stupid and unmanly it would sound.

If I die – I can't bring myself to say 'when' – I don't want to spend my last days at a small-town police station revealing details of my private life to all and sundry. Especially as revealing such details won't achieve anything. What happens, then, if the conspiracy theories hurtling through my mind turn out to be true? What happens if my wife and her lover – ten years her junior, no less – really have decided to poison me?

The idea pops into my mind of its own volition, from where I don't know. I certainly haven't put it there. But there's a certain logic to it all: let's get the fat old git out of the way, then we can stop all this foreplay and get down to business. But why not just file for divorce? I don't know.

And if we assume that the two of them were to come under suspicion, how would the matter ever be resolved? In what time frame? And how would I benefit from it?

I wouldn't. I'd be dead.

I step out of the car. The midday heat takes me in its arms, the air is still. I glance around. The deep, bright, radiant green of the trees heralds the height of summer.

Two uniformed officers step out of the station, young men with weapons dangling from their belts. One of them looks over towards me. I smile and nod a hello. The officer looks as though he's wondering whether or not he knows me. He doesn't; he couldn't. He turns, looks ahead and continues listening to his partner. We pass one another, the distance between us a metre and a half at most.

There's a young schoolgirl working at the ice-cream stall. She has long brown hair and long brown arms. A friendly smile is her default expression. She's the embodiment of summer.

First I order a scoop of rum and raisin, then a scoop of liquorice and banana, and just as she's about to hand me the cone, I ask for a third scoop, this time of ye olde vanilla. The girl presses the scoops tighter against one another and hands me the cone, now standing over a foot high. I hand her a fifty-euro note and put the change in the little tip box on the counter. She thanks me in a bright, ringing voice, and I wish her a sunny life.

With the cone in my hand I sit down on a small, stone wall and lick the little melting streams running down the side of my ice-cream tower. I can't really feel anything. Here I am, right here. It occurs to me that's how it's always been, I just didn't understand it before.

Again I look over at the police station. I have to talk to someone. Not right this second, my mouth full of the delicious, sweet, creamy goodness – but soon. From now on, everything is soon.

My parents are dead. I was the only child of an elderly couple, I have no siblings or other close relatives. I haven't kept in touch with my childhood friends. I have no hobbies, no colleagues. I go through the faces that have populated my life – the sounds they make, their shapes. One after another, familiar people stand up to say something, walk towards me, touch me, look me in the eyes, then saunter away again all the more assuredly. Nobody stops, nobody remains, nobody waits to hear what I've got to say. I'm about to lose all hope.

The ice cream makes me feel better. The effect is like injecting a strong stimulant directly into my veins. At least it's what I imagine that must feel like. I might never have the opportunity to try intravenous drugs in what's left of this life, so the comparison will have to remain in the realms of supposition. But isn't that the same for everything? What else is our life if not a mishmash of assumptions, expectations, suppositions and conclusions pulled out of a hat?

I've never had thoughts like this before. I don't know if that's a good or a bad thing.

The ice cream feels good in my stomach. It's a small victory.

Once again I go through the people in my life and eventually come up with something that might yet prove useful.

The short car journey to the office goes far more smoothly than the psychosis of the previous drive. I steer with my right hand, hang my left out of the open window and let the summer air blow against my face.

The town is quiet and warm. I drive along Mannerheimintie and for the first time I notice the park that spreads out on both sides of the road. On the left it slopes down through the shade of the trees towards a pretty little pond, and to the right its green undulates across what is left of the town's old fortifications.

Eventually I turn onto Teollisuuskatu, but I don't pull up outside our premises. I can hear Taina's voice. There's a certain castigating tone to it, like when she told me that I never see things through, that I give in too easily. That voice merges with the sight I witnessed only a moment ago. I feel livid.

I drive on about seven hundred metres until Teollisuuskatu makes a ninety-degree turn to the left and changes name. I pass a dark-blue building.

The Hamina Mushroom Company. Three men who, six months ago, appeared out of thin air.

They've been in contact with our Japanese clients. I know for a fact they've promised our clients more competitive rates and higher quality. Of course, it's an empty promise because such a combination is completely impossible. But as a salesman I know a pitch like that is music to the ears of any importer. I don't know how they're planning to attract good pickers or how they're going to organise the harvest. It can't be a question of money, as the Hamina Mushroom Company doesn't have a client anywhere near the size of ours.

The forecourt is empty. There's generally a van decorated with garish signs parked outside. Sometimes one of the building's large lever-gear doors is open, through which I can hear the strains of the latest Finnish pop songs and see at least one of the company's owners having a cigarette on a couch carried out into the yard. This time, though, everything's quiet and the building looks deserted.

I drive on for a while and make a U-turn. I approach the blue building again and try to focus my eyes. Nobody. Nothing. I pull into the side of the road before driving onto the forecourt.

It's only midday, and I'm already here. The morning's events seem to have happened longer ago than is feasible. I take my foot off the clutch, steer the car round in an arc in front of the building, stop and step out.

In addition to the lever-gear doors, the building's long wall also features a standard door. Beside it is a buzzer; I press it. A moment later I press it again. Nobody opens the door, and I can't hear steps from inside. I give the door a try. I turn the handle and the door opens. I step inside and call out. No answer.

Immediately in front of me is some kind of office; I'll have to walk through it to reach the other areas of the building. I stop in the office, though. The tables and shelves are empty. A solitary laptop computer and an office chair facing the door suggest that someone might have been working here and has left in a hurry. The entire room is dominated by a portrait – a photograph blown up many times and then framed. President Kekkonen's eyes fix on my forehead and won't relax their grip, even though I turn and continue further into the building.

They've certainly made an effort with the kitchen and staff room. That is, they've made an effort in the way that men make an effort if they're given free rein over interior design. A tall bar counter and a large drinks cabinet with glass doors show that these men certainly like their beer. The selection is mostly Estonian, and there's plenty of it.

The kitchen is tidy. To the left of it is the staff room, complete with a couch, an enormous television and an impressive sound system. I look through the neatly organised shelf of CDs and DVDs. Soft rock and action thrillers; Arttu Wiskari and Vin Diesel. A punching bag hangs from the ceiling, a pair of red boxing gloves dangle on the wall, and beneath them is a selection of hand-held weights.

When I turn around, though, what I see on the opposite wall is something altogether different.

I walk over to take a closer look. I've seen Samurai films, and these swords are the same as the ones I've seen in the hands of those stern-faced warriors. I reach up and carefully lift one of the swords from its mount. I pull it from its sheath. The blade is long. The steel glints, the sharpness of its edge gives me shivers – cold, unpleasant shivers. I press the sword back into its sheath and replace it on the wall.

I still haven't seen anything remotely related to mushrooms. If I were to judge purely on what I've seen, I'd guess this was a cross between a sword-fighting club and an Urho Kaleva Kekkonen appreciation society. Still, the office, kitchen and staff room only cover a small amount of the warehouse's total area. I open another door and step onto the factory floor.

In less than thirty seconds I am both more envious and more taken aback than I have been in a long time. Or I would have been, if I hadn't already been taken aback twice today.

The equipment and machinery are better and more modern than ours. It all glows and gleams, and clearly hasn't once been used. There isn't a single scratch, a single speck of rust. I walk around the facility and swallow back my surprise. I wasn't expecting this.

It seems clear that

a) our competitors are serious;
b) they are something altogether different from what I'd imagined;
c) for the third time today I've been caught with my trousers down.

I take back that last metaphor. I haven't once been caught with my trousers down. Maybe that was my mistake.

We have a very real competitor.

I still think of the company in the plural – as 'ours'. It's hardly surprising. Taina and I own the company together, we founded it together, and together we have built up our little success story. It feels important; it is important. The business might just be the most important thing in my life right now. At the very least, it has remained constant and unchanged all morning, something that at this point can be considered a minor miracle.

Sunlight streams into the operations room through the only window in the wall with the doors. The air in here is cool. I've probably seen everything I came to see. I stand on the spot for a moment, then walk back the way I came. Kekkonen can vouch that I walk all the way out of the building.

I jump into the car, accelerate out of the forecourt and turn onto Teollisuuskatu, which runs straight along the back of the building.

It's a stroke of luck. The Hamina Mushroom Company van is coming in the opposite direction. All three men are sitting in the cab. They each look at me in turn as I pass them.

4

'A week,' says Olli as he spreads mushroom pâté on a slice of fresh rye bread. The pâté is a centimetre thick, the slice of bread is like an antique ski. 'Then the first batch will be ready to leave, if you ask me.'

Olli is a veteran mushroom professional, an expert on mushrooms and all aspects of their quality, packaging, drying, preserving, freezing and shipping. He is a fifty-one-year-old grandfather. He is someone I might be able to talk to, at least about some of my problems.

'So I can promise the Japanese a shipment next Wednesday?' I ask.

'You can promise anything you like,' says Olli. 'But the forest will decide.'

'Of course.' You have to interpret Olli a little, sometimes even translate him into plain Finnish.

'We won't know until we know.'

We are sitting on the patio outside the office. Olli begins tucking into a bowl of puréed meat-and-potato soup. Coffee slowly drips through the filter. I'm still full of ice cream. I have no appetite. Perhaps I can manage a biscuit. I take one from the bowl on the table, break it and put a piece in my mouth.

'Olli,' I say, 'can I ask you something?'

'You're the one that pays the wages.'

'This isn't to do with work. It's a … personal matter … and quite pressing. It's actually very pressing. From now on everything is pressing. It's best you know that.'

Olli looks at me with his brown eyes. He has thick, dark hair, combed back with gel, and an angular, friendly face. This is what George Clooney would have looked like if he'd been born in Hamina, eaten plenty of carbohydrates and spent his life working with mushrooms.

'My question is … well, it's to do with the opposite sex. Women.'

Good job I made that clear, I scoff to myself, in case he didn't realise I'm a man. Olli doesn't seem perturbed. He nods. I turn my head and look over towards the neighbouring plot. The grey industrial building is at a slight angle.

'I mean, you've got experience,' I say.

'Five decades.'

I'm about to say something but do a quick calculation and turn back to look at Olli. 'I guess, sometimes, you've been … how should I put it … disappointed…?'

Olli sighs. 'Five decades, mate. That's how long I've been disappointed.'

I can't conceal my bewilderment. 'I thought that…'

'That's right,' says Olli and leans a tanned elbow against the table. He too turns to look at the grey warehouse. In the sunshine it looks almost white. 'I've got plenty of experience. With women. I was nineteen the first time I got married. She left me five years later. The next one left after we'd been married for three years. The latest one left after only a year.'

'I'm sorry.'

'It's all right,' says Olli, looking wistfully into the distance.

This isn't going quite the way I'd planned. I imagined I'd be able to tell him, if not directly or in much detail, about my own disappointments. I can still see Taina's bouncing buttocks pounding against Petri's virile hips. But now I feel as though I ought to console him instead.

Olli turns his head. 'You were saying something?'

'Yes. I have a suspicion that … my wife has someone else.'

Olli slowly sucks air into his lungs. I might just be witnessing the longest inhalation of breath in the history of the universe.

'No,' he says.

'Yes,' I reply.

'Are you sure?' he asks.

The slapping of sweaty flesh, the taste of vomit in my mouth. I nod.

'Bloody women,' says Olli.

'That just about covers it.'

For a moment neither of us says anything.

'So what are you going to do about it?'

Olli's question takes me by surprise. I'd imagined he would give me the answers, not make me more uncertain than I was to start with. Surely that's the point of confiding in someone – a problem shared and all that.

'I don't know,' I answer honestly. 'I've never been in a situation like this before. I don't know what to think.'

'It's tough. Someone's been dangling his oar in your pond.'

'I haven't thought of it like—'

'He's been mowing your turf, mate, punting up your stream.'

'Right.'

'You know what I do to get over the worst of it?'

Come up with new metaphors, perhaps? I think, but decide not to suggest that, and shake my head instead.

'I lower the bar.'

'Excuse me?'

'I lower my standards,' Olli explains. 'I don't expect as much from the next one as I did from the last. If the last one was just about house-trained, I'll settle for one a bit rougher round the edges next time.'

'You just told me each of your marriages was shorter than the last, so I don't think you're onto a winning strategy.'

Olli looks at me as though I haven't understood what he's said; as though I haven't understood anything about anything.

'No plan is a hundred per cent foolproof.'

My stomach begins to cramp and I double over. A searing pain races through my temples, as though someone is pulling at my skull with a pair of pliers. The seizure lasts only a few seconds, and once it's passed the sun seems brighter than a moment ago. I glance at Olli. He looks worried, or at the very least somewhat startled.

'Are you all right?' he asks.

'Never been better.' I straighten myself and sit squarely on my chair.

'What about the business?'

This is a much easier question to deal with. That said, there are still lots of unresolved issues regarding the business, mostly due to my impending death. For the moment, however, I'm not going to breathe a word about that to Olli. I don't think I could deal with another mixed metaphor.

'This won't affect the business at all,' I say, and I know it's the truth. 'Business as usual, that's the main thing.'

Olli seems to accept this.

'But about our new competitor,' I say. 'Do you know the men over there?'

'More or less.'

'Have they got a history?'

'A history?'

I look at Olli. He was clearly thinking about a different kind of history. 'With mushrooms,' I say. 'The mushroom business.'

'None whatsoever.'

I think about this for a moment. I'm not about to tell Olli I've just visited the premises of the Hamina Mushroom Company either.

Visited? Wouldn't it be more truthful to say I was breaking and entering? I don't know. Something happened to me outside the police station. I can't exactly say I came to my senses, because I've subsequently broken into our competitors' premises and asked for advice from a man whose recipe for dealing with woman trouble is a steely determination to make things worse for himself every time.

I think about our competitors' shiny new equipment, their fantastic set-up.

'What do you know about them?' I ask.

Olli sighs, puts down his soup spoon and stares at me.

'Local lads.'

I say nothing.

Olli takes my silence as a sign to continue. 'Asko is the blond one

– the older bloke who's always driving their van. The guys in the passenger seats are Sami and Tomi. Asko has done all sorts: he's worked at the paper factory and at the harbour, processing and canning fish. Sami used to play baseball. Tomi's just got out of prison, killed his mother. Sami was the Hamina baseball club's best switch-hitter of all time, as well as playing thirteen seasons at second base.'

I look at Olli. He sees my confusion.

'Baseball's big in Hamina,' he begins. 'Besides…'

'Tomi killed his own mother?'

Olli nods. 'Over some herring. He used to live with his mother. She fried a lot of herring. The fat really stinks. The smell, the grease, it sticks to everything – curtains, clothes, you name it. When you go to bed in the evening, your pillow smells of herring. But she liked them.'

'So how did these guys decide to become … mushroom entrepreneurs?'

Olli shrugs at me. 'They probably saw how well things are going for us.'

5

I'm sitting alone in my manager's office, a computer and piles of papers in front of me. To the right of the computer is a picture of me and my wife, tanned and happy on a beach holiday in Phuket. I was still in pretty good shape back then, though you can tell I was pulling my stomach in. Not quite our honeymoon, but almost. The blue-green waters of the Strait of Malacca wash across our feet as we stand arm in arm. We're both wearing red swimsuits. I recall how they reminded Taina of *Baywatch*, but I can't remember whether she thought that was a good or a bad thing.

The moment captured in that photograph seems as distant in years as it does in kilometres. The Taina I saw today isn't the Taina in this photograph – the Taina who pressed herself so tightly against me that our suntan lotion all but glued us together.

A marital affair.

Taina's affair.

One or the other. I don't know what it was that made me back away from the top of the steps this morning, what power made me shut the door behind me. But I know I did the right thing. I would have looked like a pathetic cuckold if I'd rushed into the garden, feebly brandishing the iron bar.

I click the computer on.

Its low murmur is familiar and oddly comforting. Perhaps this is the voice of the earth, its ambient soundtrack.

I search online for information about the Hamina Mushroom Company. There's nothing to be found. Naturally there's an entry in the Register of Companies, but because their operations have only just begun, there is no financial statement or other information. Asko Mäkitupa is listed as the CEO, and the capital stock is given as the paltry sum of two thousand euros. When I think of their flashy equipment and facilities, I'm all the more baffled as to how a docker, a mother-killer and a switch-hitter have managed to secure such a flying start to their business venture.

A sudden wincing pain in my chest, and for a moment I see everything double. A cold sweat breaks out across my neck, my throat tingles. Again the turn seems to be over in seconds.

I google some information on poisoning and simply confirm what the doctor has already told me: sustained poisoning initially causes a rise in tolerance levels before ultimately leading to organ failure and total collapse – which will happen … when the time comes.

Olli walks past the open door. He looks pensive. It seems we all have our problems. Mine appear to be twofold: those affecting my life and those affecting my death. Until now I haven't realised how closely the two are intertwined. When it comes to the crunch, death is really a distillation of life: everything is condensed into the single, colossal question of how best to live it. Or how we should have lived it.

If you had only a day left, what would you do? And what if you had a week? A month?

I haven't thought about things like this. It seems I haven't thought about very much at all.

Something has woken me up.

Which is just as well, given what is about to happen next.

The van belonging to the Hamina Mushroom Company swerves onto our forecourt. I look out of the window and watch as the van bounces across the unpaved yard. The three men sitting in the small cab are so tightly packed together that they don't seem to move at all.

Olli puts his head round the door to my office and says something. I tell him I'll take care of it. He looks at me without answering and walks off.

The men are stepping out of the van as I open the front door and walk out onto the forecourt. The day is at its brightest; I have to squint against the sunshine. The dust whipped up by the van sticks to my face. I can taste it, a bitter blend of earth and petrol.

Once on the ground, the men take up their respective positions.

I remember what Olli told me about them, so I recognise Asko easily. He has stepped out of the driver's seat and he's obviously the eldest of the three – well over fifty; he clearly works out and is still in good shape. He has receding, longish blond hair, which he has combed back over his head, blue eyes, which shoot darts right into my own, dimpled cheeks, veins that stand out along his brown arms, and he is wearing a pair of trainers in bright neon colours at the end of his sockless, unnaturally tanned legs. The overall impression is of someone learned and experienced in the most primitive way. He is a hunter; ageing, yes, but uniquely skilled.

The two others – Sami and Tomi – stand to attention at Asko's side.

I'm guessing Sami, the baseball player, is the only non-weightlifter of the three. He's lanky and surprisingly pale. Even I've got more colour in my cheeks, I think, and I'm a dying man in sedentary work. A complexion like that takes hard work, as does the gleaming bronze of Asko's legs.

The other of the sidekicks – seeing them next to Asko it's hard not to think of them in those terms – is built like a barn door. That must be Tomi. He is big, in every respect. His head is three times the size of a normal man's. I don't know whether it's possible to body-build your head, but somehow it is bulkier than usual. His face takes up a few rugged square feet of summer landscape, and his expression would darken even the brightest sun.

'We came to give you a warning,' says Asko without any introductions or pleasantries. His voice is congenial, it's deep and soft. 'We've just watched a security video that shows you breaking into our premises.'

I should have realised there was a possibility this would happen. But I can't undo what's already done.

I raise both hands to accentuate what I'm about to say. 'I'm sorry. If you got that impression, I can assure you it wasn't my intention. I didn't break in. I came to say hello. The door was open, so I assumed you were indoors and I stepped inside. When I couldn't find anybody, I left.'

'Not before you'd conducted a spot of industrial espionage.'

I look at each of the men in turn and give the friendliest smile I can muster on a day like this. 'Like I said, it's easy to see things differently.'

'Want us to rough up the fat boy?' asks Tomi.

'There is, of course, a third way of seeing things, but I wouldn't go there,' I say. 'If I may say so, it seems—'

'We're here to give you a warning,' Asko repeats.

'Ask him why he was snooping round our warehouse,' says Sami.

'I thought you just asked that,' I say to Sami, then turn to Asko. 'Shall we start again? This is completely unnecessary. I made a mistake and I've apologised. Twice now.'

'Ask him about the Japanese,' Sami urges his boss once again.

His voice perfectly matches his appearance: it's limp and pale. I can't understand how someone with a build like that could hit a ball at all, let alone knock it out of the park.

'What about the Japanese?' I ask, and turn to Sami. 'And what's all this, getting someone else to ask questions for you?'

'You owe us,' says Asko. 'Compensation.'

'Compensation?'

'When are the Japanese arriving?'

To my knowledge the Japanese aren't coming at all this summer. If they were, I'd know about it. At least, I think I'd know about it. Having said that, this morning I thought I was going to live forever and still believed I was married to a faithful wife. The situation presents an unexpected opportunity.

'In a week and half,' I say. 'I see you're ready for the harvest.'

'Sod the harvest,' Tomi snaps. 'The fat boy's getting on my nerves.'

Fat boy? That's the second time now.

'What Tomi means is we're not involved in the picking,' Asko explains. It appears he's used to interpreting for the other two. 'We oversee operations.'

'Does that mean you've already employed your pickers?' I ask.

'Don't tell him,' Sami quickly interrupts.

Asko seems to breathe slightly more deeply. He knows I've got the answer I was looking for, and that means there might be even more questions to come.

'Are the pickers local or do you bring them in from further afield?' I ask. 'And, with the Japanese in mind, I assume your pickers have logistics experience – preserving, packing and exporting?'

Asko looks at me for a moment in silence. 'You've been warned.'

I say nothing.

Asko is about to turn away when Tomi pipes up. 'If you find a snapped bolete in your bed, you'll know what it means.'

Asko stops in his tracks. I stare at Tomi. He is so big that just looking at him is something of an athletic feat.

'A snapped bolete?' I enquire.

Tomi nods his enormous head.

'I don't know what that means, but if I do find a porcini sliced in two on my pillow, I'll think of you.'

Tomi shakes his head. 'Not sliced. Snapped.'

Asko raises a hand.

Sami and Tomi stare at me for a moment longer, then the three of them climb back into the cab. The van sways from side to side.

'We'll be on our way now,' says Asko from the window. 'But consider yourself—'

'Warned.'

The van first reverses then pulls away, its tyres crunching against the gravel of the forecourt. I turn and head inside. I think I see Olli at the window, but it might simply be my imagination, as a moment later the windowpane reflects nothing but clear, blue sky.

6

I close the office door behind me and take out a paper and pen. There are two tables in my office. On the desk there are a humming computer, tall piles of documents, and the general clutter of a small business. I sit down at the conference table.

I'm a man of lists. I like being able to see my entire life on a single sheet of A4.

As usual, I divide things into three categories. I write down the headings, leaving plenty of space between them for notes and comments:

1. ONGOING PROJECTS
2. PLANNED PROJECTS
3. TODAY'S TASKS

I once heard a principle by which there are only important matters and urgent matters. The principle suggests that important matters should be dealt with first. If I've understood correctly, this paradox is supposed to encourage a more effective use of one's time. With that in mind I write out another set of headings:

1. IMPORTANT MATTERS
2. URGENT MATTERS

I get started. Some of these categories simply require going through things I know already. Some things are still so fresh that I need to clarify them and put them into words in my mind first, before committing them to paper.

1. ONGOING PROJECTS
   - death (my own); cause: poisoning
   - ascertain source of poisoning ⇨ possible poisoners
   - Taina (& Petri)
   - harvest: go through issues with pickers and employees
   - find out what competitor is up to
   - reassure the Japanese
2. PLANNED PROJECTS
   - stay alive (for the time being)
3. TODAY'S TASKS
   - -

I glance through my notes. As so often when I write things down, this helps me to see connections between individual issues. I am dying of sustained poisoning, which has developed over a long period of time. Thinking logically – that's what lists are for – there are only two places in which I could have been exposed to such prolonged toxicity: either at work or at home. Someone must have poisoned me deliberately. I begin a new list:

1. WORKPLACE
   - NORDIC FOREST DELICATESSE EXPORT LTD
   - Taina (quality and tasting officer, chief recipe designer, ~~slut~~)
   - Petri (chief of machinery and deliveries, ~~playboy who can't keep his tackle to himself~~)
   - Olli (packaging, preserving, freezing)
   - Sanni (chief picker and harvest coordinator)
   - Raimo (purchasing manager)
   - Suvi (part-time office assistant)
   - me (CEO)
2. HOME – PAPPILANSAARI
   - Taina (wife)
   - Veikko (garden hedgehog)

For a moment, I wonder whether I might have vomited over Veikko the hedgehog. It's wholly possible, because one of his favourite hiding places is the tangle of bushes in front of the steps at the back of the house. I feel bad at the thought that I might have done something like that to poor Veikko and decide to look into it as soon as … It's not easy for me to say *as soon as I get home*. Home should be a place where we're protected from the evils of the world. It shouldn't be a place where we're forced to look on as the genitals of one's wife and one's employee whack against each other. Be that as it may, the wellbeing of Veikko the hedgehog is paramount.

At first the list seems surprisingly short, but a moment later it seems long. This is doubtless caused by the fact that I'm living, as it were, in two different time zones: the previous time zone, where I could put things off indefinitely, where there was always time tomorrow and where the future was a long, vague concept that essentially carried on forever; and the current time zone, where there's no time to do anything at all, a time that could end so suddenly that even the most basic tasks might be left undone.

It's a terrifying thought. It brings me back to the final section of my list:

3. TODAY'S TASKS
    – commence murder investigation (investigation into ~~my suic~~ my own murder)
    – commence investigation into infidelity (~~Taina riding Petri on the sun lounger~~)
    – in light of the above ⇨ hide my health issues from everybody

Again the pain hits me out of the blue. This time it's what I imagine an electric shock must feel like. My whole body quivers, the pain strikes each cell individually. It hurts, everywhere, in every part of my body. I sit down in front of the window as it darkens, as day turns to evening, and I lose my grip.

I don't die.

As with all these seizures, everything seems clearer once it's over.

The list is on the table in front of me. I look up. I am sure I see a human-shaped figure passing the window.

Just then my phone rings.

I answer, and at first I don't recognise the voice. The doctor gets straight to the point, and it doesn't take me long to get up to speed. I'm in a state of perpetual 'now'. I'll be in the present moment until I stop existing altogether. An aftershock runs the length of my spine.

The shadow of the human figure is seared onto my retinas, but a moment later the concrete wall, illuminated in the sunshine, is all I can see.

'You said you wished to discuss the matter with your wife,' the doctor is saying. 'Have you had a chance to talk to her?'

'I haven't found the right moment,' I reply. It's an honest answer.

'I understand. This can be a delicate situation for our loved ones too.'

'That's one way of putting it.'

'Excuse me?'

'Nothing,' I say, and at that the thought occurs to me that the doctor has called me because he's given me the wrong diagnosis, confused me with another patient, read the wrong papers, because this whole episode has been one big misunderstanding. 'Has there been a change in my condition?'

'I don't know,' he says. 'Has there?'

My hopes dwindle as quickly as they flared up. I'm on an emotional rollercoaster, that much is clear, but perhaps the continuing sense of shock prevents me from feeling the steepest of the ups and downs.

'Apparently not,' I say.

The doctor is silent for a moment. 'I'm calling about the results of your toxicological screen. The laboratory tests are still under way, so the situation is still live, as it were. But the good news is you don't have anything infectious.'

I'm in two minds as to whether to ask, *If this was the good news, what on earth is the bad news?* I say nothing, lean back in my chair.

'We've sent more urine samples to Helsinki. I imagine that by tomorrow or the day after we'll have a better idea of the make-up of the toxin – the poison, that is. As I said yesterday, we're probably looking at nature's own toxins. As things stand now it looks as though what we're dealing with are poisons that can be acquired from various plants and mushrooms through a process of—'

'I want to know everything there is to know. Right now,' I interrupt him. 'You have to call me as soon as anything comes to light. Promise me.'

The doctor clears his throat. 'Well, you see, tomorrow is the start of my summer holiday, but I'm sure my colleague—'

'No.'

'My colleague could—'

'No,' I repeat, emphatically, clearly, and without losing my temper. As I say it I look down at my list. What have I written beneath the heading 'TODAY'S TASKS'? 'Commence murder investigation'. This is where it starts. This phone call.

'Nobody else,' I say. 'Only you. This is a small town. I don't want anybody to know about it. Nobody at all. Nobody at your surgery; nobody anywhere. Medical confidentiality, right?'

'Of course, but with a view to your care and—'

'Precisely. We don't talk about this to anyone until I've established my wife's … position on the matter.'

I feel it's important that I tell him the truth. But maybe not the whole truth: I can simply leave out the parts of the truth I don't want to discuss.

'And,' I say before the doctor has a chance to get a word in, 'I want to be able to contact you at any time. I need a number. In case I need painkillers or something.'

I can almost hear the doctor cursing the incursion into his long-awaited holiday. But let's face it, I'll only be murdered once.

'Very well,' he says. 'But preferably only call during the daytime.'

The doctor gives me his mobile number. The figures come reluctantly from his mouth, but come nonetheless. I hang up and look down at my list. I read the names I've written down and head for the door.

7

I park at the edge of Kipparikuja, and the Saviniemi gravel crackles beneath my feet as I step out of the car. The row of hawthorns, as tall as me and as dense as a brick wall, hides from view the pretty green garden complete with its berry bushes and ancient apple trees. The house stands at the end of the garden.

It's a dark-blue wooden house, built before the advent of the pre-fabricated houses for veterans but in very much the same style. It is also a touch smaller than most veterans' houses, its habitable floor space probably no bigger than that of a modern one-bedroom flat. Everything is well looked-after, everything neat, tidy and ordered: the house, the garden, the shrubs, the flowerbeds.

Sanni is sitting on the steps of the porch, crouched over her running shoes.

Her long auburn hair covers her face and gleams in the sunshine like a new copper roof. As she ties her shoe laces her fingers are quick, agile, seemingly used to finding things, assessing and picking them. Sanni is the same age as me. She is our harvest coordinator; she knows the local terrain like the back of her hand and makes sure our pickers are efficient, able to exercise quality control by themselves, and that they work where they are supposed to. Sanni is divorced and now lives alone, and to my knowledge she is perfectly content with that situation.

She is wearing white running shorts, a small red bag, strapped round her waist, and a black, tight-fitting sleeveless top. I think it must be the first time I've seen so much of her soft, fair skin. She ties her shoes firmly, looping the yellow laces into neat double knots sitting upright on her new, red trainers. She looks up, notices me and gives a start. She hasn't heard me arrive.

'You crept up on me,' she says.

'Me?'

We stand a few metres from each other. Sanni's eyes are a mixture of green and blue.

'The way you just appeared out of nowhere.'

'I'd like to talk to you,' I stammer. 'I know you're very conscientious and everything's probably fine, but the harvest is due to start any day now, and I'd like to go over a few things.'

Sanni is small and delicate, about five foot four tall. Looking at her slender frame, I am suddenly reminded of the words Tomi used to describe me: fat boy. I instinctively pull my stomach in and puff out my chest, but straight away it makes me feel ridiculous. Here I am, a dying man, standing in the middle of the garden, and still I'm trying to make an impression on the opposite sex.

'Okay,' says Sanni.

I exhale and try to let my stomach sag back to its normal position naturally without her noticing.

'Let's sit down over there,' I suggest and gesture towards a set of green-and-white checked deckchairs. Before sitting down I double check to make sure I'm not sitting on any human excretions, fresh or otherwise. It's hardly necessary, but witnessing Taina and Petri's little moment together has destroyed any faith I've had in the general hygiene of sun loungers.

The sun has settled permanently in the sky. That's what it seems like, at least. A bright white glow that doesn't move, doesn't change, and that nothing can touch. The blue sky looks as though it has been wiped clean; it is empty and pristine. The air is still. Somewhere someone is beating a rug.

'I was just talking to the guys from the Hamina Mushroom Company,' I begin. 'I didn't get any straight answers out of them, of course, but judging by what I've seen and heard today, I think we have a competitor that we should take very seriously.'

Sanni says nothing.

'I happen to know that their packaging and preserving equipment is far more modern than ours, and it's ready to be switched on at any moment. I tried to ask them about pickers, but I didn't get an answer. There's something about this whole business that seems a bit off. To be honest, everything seems off. Everything, damn it.'

Sanni looks at me. I bat my final sentence away with a dismissive wave of the hand.

'Have you heard anything?'

Sanni hesitates slightly. It's a fleeting pause, short enough that if you blinked you'd miss it, and that's why I notice it. Her hesitation disappears, Sanni flicks the long hair from her face, but still she won't answer.

'Sanni,' I ask. 'Have you heard anything?'

She looks at me.

'They offered me a job. As head of the picking staff.'

Head? With us, Sanni is only a coordinator.

'When did this happen?'

Sanni turns to look at the bushes. The tangle of green is like a jungle.

'Just now.'

'And what did you say?' I ask.

Again she looks at me. She looks different from a second ago, her blue-green eyes now reflecting the white glare of the sun.

'I said I'd talk to you about it.'

I breathe in, breathe out.

'What do you know about them – about their business?'

'I know I'd get a significant pay rise.'

The distant beater continues whacking dust from the rugs. The sound seems to ricochet from the direction of the shore.

'You once told me you have a passion for mushrooms.'

'I do,' Sanni nods. 'I like them more than any human being. But with a raise and…' She turns her head, stares straight ahead.

'Did they offer you more than just a raise?'

Sanni is silent for a moment. 'They think our – well, *your* – company doesn't have a future.'

A profound, searing pain bubbles from deep within my forehead, and an electric eel slithers across my field of vision.

'In what way?' I ask. 'Why don't we have a future?'

Sanni looks at me. 'Because we lack courage and determination,' she says. 'Because we're not aggressive enough.'

'Is that their opinion or yours?'

Sanni purses her lips and glances down as if to check that her laces are still tied securely. They are.

'Sanni, I have to say this out loud,' I begin. 'The Hamina Mushroom Company doesn't inspire trust. On the contrary. With their background…'

'I know,' Sanni nods. 'But there are so many different sides to each of us. Just like mushrooms. A bolete that looks beautiful might be riddled with maggots. The milk cap is an ugly mushroom, but it's perfectly good to eat. Sami and I used to date each other.'

'You and the baseball player?'

'Yes, back in the day. When he stopped playing, we stopped dating.'

Sanni notices me watching her. My gaze is what you might call intense.

'Why are you looking at me like that?'

'You are…' I fumble for words. 'What I mean is, he seems so different from you, so completely…'

'…Like every time he tried to hit the ball he whacked himself round the head instead? In a way it's true,' she explains. 'Sami's last ever game, he was warming up before going out to bat for the final time. They were playing a team from Seinäjoki, and the mood in the stadium was tense. They were down by only a single run. The batters were swinging their bats around at the edge of the pitch, but Sami was completely focussed on the game. He was warming up, doing the low stretches he was famous for. A player was called out, but the call was unclear. Sami was stretched out like a panther ready to leap at its prey, so when he jumped to his feet Halonen's bat caught him round the head as it came hurtling towards the bench. Halonen was the wild-card batsman. He packed a real punch.'

We sit for a moment in silence. The sound of the rug beating has stopped. The garden is fragrant.

'What are you going to do now?' I ask.

'I'm going to run ten kilometres,' Sanni replies, 'in under fifty minutes.'

'I didn't mean that.'

'I know.'

Sanni runs her hand through her hair, slips a band from round her wrist and ties her hair tightly behind her head. Her ponytail is like a copper flag poised to flutter in the wind. She pulls a protein bar from her bumbag, tears open the wrapper and begins to eat.

'Sanni, what do you want?'

She swallows, then bites off another piece of her bar. 'That pay rise, maybe,' she says with her mouth full.

'In life, in general?'

There's a strength and brightness in the blue-green glow of Sanni's eyes, and something else too, something I've never noticed before.

'That's quite a question for a Tuesday afternoon.'

I look at her and say nothing. She runs her tongue across her upper lip, swallows the food in her mouth.

'I want to walk through the forest on a fresh, crisp morning. I want an SUV that isn't Korean, Japanese or Chinese. I want breakfast in bed, but never on my birthday. I want to get people round to fix my drains. I want to own underwear from Victoria's Secret at least once in my life. I want a new, high-grade shotgun. I want to run the Tokyo marathon in under three and half hours. I want to know everything there is to know about mushrooms and plants.'

Sanni stops and pops the final chunk of energy bar in her mouth. I think of my list, my investigation, my poisoning. This is what it's like to be human, to be surrounded by other humans: I know what Sanni wants, but I know nothing about her.

'What kind of raise are we talking about?' I ask.

'Fifty per cent.'

I almost choke, though my mouth is empty.

'They promised me even more,' she explains.

'I don't doubt it for a minute.'

I need Sanni, for so many reasons. More than anything, I have to keep her close to me. What's more, I know where to find the money she wants. Petri hardly needs a new delivery truck. He seems perfectly capable of getting anywhere and everywhere with his own equipment.

'Well, for a raise in that ball park ... if I agree to it ... I'll have to ask for something in return '

Sanni seems eager to hear my offer.

'I'd like you to play hard to get,' I say. 'Tell the guys at the Hamina Mushroom Company that you'll think about it carefully, that you have to weigh up the pros and cons. Tell them you'd like to know how they are planning on organising their harvest operation and who they are doing business with.'

The corner of Sanni's mouth curves into a smile. Not quite a smile, perhaps, but her lips give a small twitch that soon melts away.

'You want me to spy on them.'

I say nothing.

'Maybe I was completely wrong about you,' she says and manages to sound at once disappointed and excited.

8

I turn the car, the gravel crunches and sunlight glints against the bonnet as though someone is playing with an enormous mirror. Instead of turning on the air conditioning I roll down the window, slowly cruise along the gravel path and turn onto Kalastajankatu. I glance in the rear-view mirror to make sure I'm not slowing anybody else down. A dark-blue Ford Mondeo appears from around the corner. I increase my speed a little and look to the right.

I catch a glimpse of the garden outside a light-coloured detached house. I've seen the man in front of it before, he's always out working, from dawn till dusk – always doing something. This time he's chopping firewood, which can be seen around the garden, both in neat rows and in a pile the size of a small ski slope. The man is short, sinewy and ageless; with his weather-beaten face and perfectly fat-free body he reminds me of the guitarists from the Rolling Stones. He has the aura of someone who likes to get down to business – a humble fusion of ruthlessness, straightforwardness, mystique, and the sense that he gets things done. If I had to wage a war, I'd send that man and his chainsaw off to win it for me. Today it seems I can imagine doing all kinds of things.

At the intersection of the gravel path and the road I stop to let a truck drive past. In the rear-view mirror I see the dark-blue Mondeo gliding towards the edge of the path and staying there. It seems my thoughtful dallying didn't slow anyone else's driving after all. The indicator clicks as I turn and continue along the road leading towards the town centre. In my ears I can hear Sanni's steps as she runs further away from the car, I can feel the warmth and size of her palm as we shake hands on our little deal. I see her auburn hair, her white shorts – which look all the shorter when she's running. Sanni, my secret mushroom agent.

The dark-blue Mondeo.

Only once I've checked to see if it's still behind me do I even realise I'm checking for it. I instantly look away. Then check again. I decide to go for a little drive. I head downtown. The market square is almost empty. I twist and turn through the streets, heading towards the heart of the town, and then I have an idea.

Designed more than three hundred years ago, the concentric streets around the Town Hall are a divine gift to anyone being chased, or at least to anyone who wants to find out whether or not they are being chased. The largest circular road is only a partial circle: a ring road about a kilometre long and with the final quarter of its length missing. This is Isoympyräkatu, 'Big Circle Street'. At some point I lose sight of the Mondeo.

I drive along Isoympyräkatu for as long as I can, all the way to the Bastion. Built in the early nineteenth century, the Bastion was originally a military fortification. Nowadays its atmospheric central embankment, perforated with a series of brick casemates, hosts an array of public events.

Taina and I once visited the Bastion during the Hamina Tattoo. I banish from my mind the image of a sun-tanned Taina, her bare thighs tacky with sweat – dismiss the memory entirely. I turn onto Rauhankatu, head straight towards the Town Hall and again see the dark-blue Mondeo behind me. For a few seconds I'm convinced my imagination is playing tricks on me, but it isn't.

Very well.

The smallest of the circular roads is only two hundred metres long. The cobbled street runs neatly round the Town Hall, so neatly that the Town Hall itself, which stands some twenty metres taller than the rest of the town, looks like an island raised on its foundations at the meeting point of eight roads. As I glance in the mirror the thought occurs to me that all roads do not lead to Rome after all, but to the administrative centre of a small town in eastern Finland. I slow my speed and begin my first lap.

The mirror is of no use, as I'm constantly turning. I crane my head out of the window and look behind me. The dark-blue Mondeo is behind me. I'm not driving very fast.

The first lap of the road lasts only about thirty seconds. I continue my circuit. The Mondeo follows me. Halfway through the second lap I look back again and try to see inside the Mondeo.

The driver is stocky. The second lap is complete.

On the third lap we are joined by a red Golf for about three streets. The car clearly has to slow down and soon leaves our little carousel, its tyres screeching angrily against the cobbles. We continue as before – only now I begin to accelerate.

The fourth lap is a repeat of the last, and I increase my speed still further. If a summer bird were to look down from high above us, it might wonder at our strange game of cat and mouse.

On the fifth lap the driver of the Mondeo begins to lose his temper. The voice finally reveals his identity. I look over my shoulder. A bulbous head pushes out of the open window.

'Oi, fatso,' shouts Tomi. 'You hear me, fat boy?'

I haven't thought this scenario through any further. In the cinema and on the TV, scenes in which someone is tailing someone else usually end with the stalker being discovered. It seems Tomi and I haven't been watching the same films. By now he's yelling out of the window, clearly furious. I'm beginning to realise he doesn't plan on leaving our encounter at mere stalking. After all, this is a man who killed his mother over a couple of herrings. What will he do to a man who laughed at his threats of snapped porcini?

'Chubby cheeks! Stop!'

He toots the horn, hurls curses out of the window and continues telling me to pull over.

Fifty kilometres an hour is normally a fairly brisk speed. But going round in a circle – this must be the seventh or eighth lap – it seems slow. I start to feel queasy. The carousel ride, combined with a severe case of poisoning, is quite an overpowering experience.

I accelerate to sixty.

Even Tomi has stopped shouting by now. When the nausea reaches my tolerance threshold, I take a sharp turn to the right.

After straightening the car on Kadettikoulunkatu I put my foot down again and speed up even more. Tomi is still right behind me. After a while I take a left. I don't know the town particularly well, but I have learned that the town centre will soon be behind me no matter what direction I take. And that's what happens.

The only problem – apart from the fact that I'm being pursued by a deranged bodybuilder – is that I'm starting to feel as though I might throw up.

The spinning, the pressure, it's all too much.

On the right of the street there are only a few houses and on the left an abandoned stretch of land, dotted with trees, which appears to slope downhill. The asphalted road comes to an end and turns to gravel. I remember that to the left of the slope there is a small river or stream flowing towards the lake at Kirkkojärvi. On my left I see a section of undergrowth worn away by the tyres of turning cars. I steer the car in that direction, undo my seatbelt, open the door, jump out and vomit on the ground.

My engine dies and I hear the Mondeo approaching. Its bumper scrapes the verge as it pulls up, its engine roars and the car bounces across the terrain like a dry pea. I've managed to throw up, I think to myself; the worst is over.

The Mondeo comes to a halt, and Tomi jumps out. In his hand he's carrying something long and shiny. I'm about to leap back into my car, but the key is no longer in my hand. I can't see it on the ground. I peer into the car; the key isn't in the ignition either.

Tomi is only ten metres away.

He approaches me from the direction of the road, and only now can I see what it is he's carrying.

I would shout for help, but there isn't a single house or passer-by in sight, and anyway, I can't breathe and my throat feels as though it's being clawed from the inside. My eyes focus on Tomi's hand. Some kind of Samurai sword. Perhaps a few centimetres shorter than usual, but the shape, gleam and blade are the same. That's good enough for me. I run in the opposite direction.

The ground is grassy, uneven and slopes downwards. I would shout back at Tomi, ask him what he wants, but I can't. He's coming for me. We dart between the trees. I fumble in my pocket but realise that my phone is still in the car. Before long we arrive at the stream. As far as I can see, I don't have any other option: I lower myself to the edge of the verge. The earth gives way. I slide downwards and find myself up to my knees in mud. For a few seconds I can't see Tomi anywhere, then he appears on the verge above me and takes a wild leap.

The sight of a burly man flying through the air with a sword in his hand is like something straight out of a comic book. Looking behind me all the while, I try to wade through the mud and make it to the other side of the ditch.

There's power in Tomi's jump. The momentum tilts his body forwards slightly, and he moves his arms back to adjust his position. It looks like he's using a stepping machine in the air. Eventually he reaches the ground. His legs sink into the mud, his knees buckle and his right hand lands directly on top of a thick, dried branch. The sword is propped upright, waiting, as Tomi's head follows the rest of his body. The blade enters beneath his jawbone and comes out through the top of his head, the fist gripping the hilt coming to a stop at the base of his chin. Tomi looks like he's sitting down and pondering something – with a sword in his head.

I slump down on the verge and manage to fill my lungs with air for the first time in what feels like an eternity. I clamber to my feet, and when I'm certain my legs will carry me, I trudge through the mud, climb up the verge, locate the end of the path, stagger back to my car and collapse inside. The key has fallen beneath the driver's seat. I pull off my shoes and socks and roll up the legs of my trousers. I clean off the shoes as best I can and slip them onto my bare feet. I walk over to the Mondeo, pull the key from its ignition, lock the doors and throw the key into the thicket.

Then I return to my own car, start the engine, pull the door shut, put on my seatbelt and drive off, peering into the rear-view mirror.

The Mondeo looks as though someone has deliberately left it in the clearing. Tomi will be able to sit by the stream and ponder all by himself, hidden from prying eyes – at least for a while.

Stranger things have happened.

PART TWO
LIFE

1

The water from the potato pot trickles down the drain, and Taina disappears in a cloud. A moment later she reappears, her bare arms tensed, the pot still in her hands. The potatoes are steaming, their sweet scent a mixture of earth and sugar. Taina looks over in my direction but doesn't meet my eyes and doesn't watch me as I walk towards the dining table.

'Hi,' she says. 'I thought you were having a nap. Meatloaf with funnel chanterelles, creamy onion gravy, new potatoes and rye bread with plenty of salted butter. For dessert I thought I'd make pancakes with whipped cream and my own strawberry jam.'

'Sounds good,' I say. 'Delicious; magnificent even.'

She turns her head. I smile at her.

Taina. My wife.

Five foot three and a half inches of woman. Thick, brown, shoulder-length hair, round, greyish blue eyes, a small nose and a big, jocular mouth full of white teeth.

We always eat at six. I've had a shower, thrown my muddy clothes in the washing machine, carried my ruined shoes out to the bin, looked in the medicine cabinet and spent just enough time lying on my bed staring at the ceiling. I lay listening as Taina came home, called out a hello and started getting dinner ready in the kitchen. I don't know where she's been. Hopefully at work.

'Seems like you got a bit more than forty winks,' she says, smiling and carrying the pot of potatoes to the table.

We sit down to eat. I don't know if I'll be able to swallow anything at all. We hand pots and dishes across the table to each other. A moment later the food is steaming on our plates. I raise my glass.

'A toast. To you.'

Taina raises her glass as well, looking at me. We clink and take a sip.

'I haven't seen you wearing that shirt for a while,' she comments.

She's never liked my Snacky Summer Girl T-shirt that I got free with a super-sized meal years ago. The T-shirt isn't stylish in any way, shape or form, and, since I first acquired it, I've gained the equivalent of a small baby in weight; however, the shirt feels oddly appropriate, given the situation. The white, skin-tight T-shirt features a large, garish photograph of an unknown blonde leaning alluringly against a double hamburger dripping with grease.

'A spur-of-the-moment choice,' I say and look down at my plate. I know the meatloaf is melt-in-the-mouth delicious, the gravy so rich that under normal circumstances I could almost drink it. It's a tricky situation. 'How was your day?'

Taina is already tucking in. As always, she has a hearty appetite.

'Pretty average,' she says between mouthfuls.

I look at her. The answer is both understandable and completely outrageous. She swallows.

'Except I heard the boys from the Hamina Mushroom Company visited our office. What was that all about?'

'No idea,' I say.

'What did they want?'

'I suppose they wanted to let us know they're in the same line of business.'

'They visited the office to tell you that?'

'That's the long and the short of it. More or less.'

'More or less,' Taina repeats and looks at my plate. 'Is everything all right?'

'Couldn't be better.' I cut off a piece of meatloaf and slide a chunk of potato on top of it with my knife. 'They're ratcheting up the competition in this business,' I explain. 'Judging by our conversation, they have brand-new equipment and everything else, ready to go. They were asking when the Japanese are arriving.'

Taina's eyes avoid my own, her gaze retreating to her own plate.

'But as far as I know the Japanese aren't coming this summer,' I say, keeping my eyes fixed on Taina. 'At least I haven't heard anything to that effect. Why would they need to come to Finland? Everything here is in order and we have an agreement about shipment times and prices. But that's not what I told those three.'

Taina glances first out into the yard then at me. 'What did you tell them?'

'I said the Japanese were coming in a week and a half.'

'Why?'

'Why did I tell them, or why are the Japanese coming?'

'Why did you say that?' asks Taina, a faint note of irritation in her voice.

'I was playing for time. I don't think those men are who they say they are.'

'And who do they say they are?' she asks.

'The staff of the Hamina Mushroom Company.'

Taina looks at me and eats in silence. All I've eaten today is one ice cream, but I'm not hungry. The plate in from of me has stopped steaming. Taina is eating with conviction; she bites off a hunk of rye bread, scoops up a large slice of meatloaf with the fork in her right hand and pushes them into her mouth one after the other, so quickly that the act of chewing requires considerable concentration.

It seems that a good dose of outdoor hanky panky does wonders for the appetite.

'And while we're on the subject of the Hamina Mushroom Company, or whatever they're called,' I begin, 'what with this heightening of the local competition, I promised Sanni a pay rise.'

Her shiver is miniscule, but I notice it all the same. Taina's fork is about to slip from her hand, but she grips it almost instantly.

'You did what?'

'Sanni is the best picker we've ever had, and during her time as harvest coordinator we've been one-hundred-per-cent certain she'll find the best local pickers to support her. She is skilled and she understands the challenges we face in this business. Think of it as an investment – insurance for the future. We want her to stay on our books and not decide to move to the Hamina Mushroom Company, for instance.'

Taina lowers her fork to her plate and leans back in her chair. The movements aren't big or exaggerated, but they are perceptible nonetheless.

'You've clearly given it a lot of thought,' she says. 'And have you thought about where we're going to find this extra money?'

I too place my fork on my plate; Taina's body language seems to give me permission to do so. The difference, of course, is that her plate is almost empty and mine is still untouched.

'I've got a solution to the problem,' I begin. 'I've done some detailed calculations and had a look at the cars. I've come to the decision that we don't need to get Petri a new delivery van and we don't necessarily have to give him a pay rise this summer. He's still so young, and in some respects so inexperienced, that rewarding him at this stage might give the wrong signal. I think he needs to demonstrate more clearly why he's important to us, show us what he's got to offer. If you ask me, he still needs to … how should I put it … grow up a bit. He's just a boy, a lad, lots of muscle and not much gumption.'

Taina's face seems flushed. The redness runs from her neck all the way up to her cheeks.

'We've already promised him a new van and a raise.'

I shake my head, doing my best to look contemplative. 'I promised him we would think about it. That's something quite different.'

By now Taina's face is red all the way up to her hairline.

'He needs a new van,' she says. She doesn't look me in the eyes but stares over my left shoulder, perhaps into the living room. 'He's unbelievably helpful, he's full of energy, and despite what you think, he has plenty of initiative.'

'Well, I've made my decision,' I say. 'Sanni is the team member we're going to focus on.'

Taina shifts in her chair. She's not squirming, this is subtler, but there's still a restlessness in her movements.

I finally get to the point. 'While we're talking things over, I think we should change to a lighter diet.'

The agitation in Taina's movements disappears, to be replaced by a heaviness I haven't seen before; and a stern expression makes the red in her cheeks look shinier, harder.

'What?'

…we're probably looking at nature's own toxins. As things stand now it looks as though we're dealing with poisons that can be acquired from various plants and mushrooms through a process of…

With the doctor's voice ringing in my head, I place my elbows on the table.

'We eat far too heavily. I've put on quite a bit of weight since we first met – twenty-four kilos to be precise. The same amount I weighed in first grade. Sometimes it feels like I'm dragging that young boy around with me. I thought I'd suggest that for now we leave out the rich sauces and gravies, the heavy stews, bakes, casseroles and meatloaves, as delicious as they are, and switch to a much simpler diet where the ingredients are … how should I put it … easier to identify.'

Taina looks at me. I've never seen her eyes this colour before. Is it because of the setting sun, the painfully faint light from the energy-saving bulb dangling above the dining table, or something else altogether?

'Where has all this suddenly come from? The need to … "identify" the ingredients?'

We stare at each other. The silence is full of humming – radio waves that no machine can reach.

I lean back, raise a hand and tap my stomach. 'I've decided to get rid of this. I'm going to exercise and get back to the shape I was in when we met.'

Taina hesitates for a moment; the delay is infinitesimally short, but I can see into her blind spot.

'Really?' she exclaims as she regains composure, and the blind spot is gone. 'That's quite a challenge.'

'But, with a new diet and a long-term workout regime, it's perfectly achievable. We could start jogging together again. This belly will be gone by Christmas. How about that?'

Taina looks as though she is about to say something, but remains silent. She stares ahead, stands up, picks up her plate then leans over and picks up mine too.

As she turns and heads towards the kitchen sink, I open my mouth. 'One more thing,' I say and watch as she stops in her tracks, the plates in her hand. 'Have you seen Veikko?' I ask.

She doesn't turn to look at me.

2

The morning is golden, the smell of salt in the air. The sea ripples beneath the jetty. I never go swimming in the mornings, but today I decide to do so. I dive in. Near the surface the water is warm, but only half a metre down I can feel an icy fist grip my shins. I kick up to the surface again and blink my eyes.

I perform a gentle breaststroke, my eyes fixed on the horizon. The world is full of new light.

I have survived the night. I have found powers I never knew I had: I lay awake next to Taina without accusing her of murdering me (I'm going to need some evidence first); I managed to down a litre of honey-flavoured acidophilus yoghurt between midnight and six a.m.; and I have pondered my situation, considering my possible next steps.

And you can say what you like about death, but its slimming effect is not to be underestimated. The swimming trunks, which pinched my hips at the beginning of summer and were so tight round my groin that they could have given me a hernia, now sit nicely, thanks to the fasting regime I instituted at dinner last night.

Of course, this is only temporary but, as I now know, so is life. It's strange to think that I've lived this long as if I never imagined I'd die; as if, as one summer came to an end, the next was always a given, and for some reason it always promised to be better than the last. And yet, all we have is a blink of the eye, a glimpse of the sunlight, a brightness we cannot understand, the time we have left getting shorter by the minute.

My nocturnal thoughts are the skeletons of my daytime thoughts – bodies twisted by my dreams. I realised this at four a.m. as I woke from a short, fractured shred of a dream. I was afraid that I'd lived the wrong way, that I'd wasted my life. It was the fear of something irrevocable, as though I'd run off a cliff edge, my feet thrashing above the gaping emptiness below.

But the sun, the sea and the new morning seem to heal everything.

It's hard to say what is the result of shock, what is an effect of the poisoning, and what is caused by the realisation of what my life does and does not include. But what happened yesterday is perhaps the greatest thing that has ever happened to me. It dropped me right into the heart of my own life.

I am so at one with the light and the water, right here, right now, that I only see the man as I flounder to my feet at the shore and find myself standing knee-deep in water.

A pair of badly fitting dark-blue jeans, a T-shirt bearing the logo of the Suonenjoki strawberry-picking festival, black-and-white Pumas for indoor sports. The man is standing in the overgrown grass along the shore. He is about my age but significantly slimmer. Why am I thinking about my weight all the time? Why now, when it shouldn't matter at all? Or does it matter? I can hear Tomi calling me 'fat boy', and I know why the man is here.

'Jaakko Kaunismaa?' the man asks, and when I nod and rub the seawater from my eyes he points to the photographic police ID hanging round his neck. 'Mikko Tikkanen from Hamina police station. I've got a few questions, if it's not too much bother.'

'By all means,' I say.

I wade back to the jetty, pick up my towel and dry my face. For some reason, it feels as though a dry face is my own face, and it's easier to control the expressions of one's own face.

Mikko Tikkanen takes a few summery strides through the grass, gleaming in the sunshine, and steps onto the jetty. It must only be about eight metres long, so a moment later we are standing facing one another halfway along it. There's a dark square round Tikkanen's mouth: a carefully trimmed beard. His eyes are friendly and alert. He takes a piece of paper out of his pocket and looks at it. Given the way he continues – he knows his stuff from memory – I can only conclude that the scrap of paper is a prop.

'A Samurai sword has been reported stolen, and its owner seems to believe you might have taken it when you ... visited ... the premises of the Hamina Mushroom Company at Teollisuuskatu 27 yesterday between the hours of 12:41 p.m. and 12:46 p.m. As proof of this visit the owner of the sword has provided security camera footage and a footprint taken from the floor.'

Tikkanen looks at me. My swimming trunks seem to have shrunk to their early-summer size. I cannot lie.

'I have not stolen any swords,' I reply.

Tikkanen's eyes scrutinise me further. I towel my back dry. The air feels like the warm breath of a small animal against my skin – pleasant and soft.

'But you admit to visiting the premises of the Hamina Mushroom Company between the hours of—'

'If it's on video, it would be hard to claim otherwise.'

Tikkanen is silent. A quick realisation.

'That is, *if* it's on video,' I continue. 'In that case, it would be perfectly clear.'

'What do you mean?'

'Video footage would show that I didn't steal the sword. Or anything else for that matter.'

So far, all true.

'There's only one camera,' he says, 'and the footage I've seen shows you forcing entry into the said premises. I didn't see you leave the premises.'

'I didn't force entry,' I sigh. 'I walked in. The door was open.'

'Did you ring the bell?'

'Yes.'

'Did anyone come and open the door?'

'No.'

'And what do you think that means?'

We stare at one another. Water tickles the inside of my thighs as it drips and trickles from my swimming trunks, but I don't quite feel comfortable enough to start towelling my groin.

'It doesn't necessarily mean anything,' I say. 'The owners might have been busy with work. The noise of the machinery would have drowned out the sound of the doorbell.'

Tikkanen remains silent.

'Very well,' I continue eventually. 'I could have stopped in the porch, but I stepped further inside.'

'Why?' It is as though Tikkanen's question comes at me from a different direction to the others; this question belongs to a down-to-earth guy called Mikko Tikkanen standing in front of me in a strawberry-emblazoned T-shirt.

'I was curious,' is my honest reply.

'Curious about what?' Once again it's Mikko Tikkanen without his detective inspector's persona.

'I'm a mushroom entrepreneur. My wife and I started our business three and a half years ago. We've built our business patiently, always thinking of the long-term plan. All of a sudden the Hamina Mushroom Company appears out of nowhere. I wanted to introduce myself, ask about professional matters.'

'Why specifically yesterday?'

Because yesterday was the day I died. Because yesterday I finally came to life.

'Maybe the upcoming harvest season had something to do with it. We'll be starting the harvest soon; the forecast promises rain and storms towards the end of the week, and the mushrooms will appear almost immediately after that...'

Tikkanen turns his head, looks across the water towards Tervasaari.

'Why mushrooms?'

'Excuse me?'

'What's the fascination with mushrooms? What made you start gathering them in the first place?'

'We don't gather the mushrooms,' I explain. 'I mean, we do, but we don't do the picking ourselves, and picking isn't what we wanted to get involved with. We were both made redundant, and my wife read an article in the paper about Japanese mushroom enthusiasts who fly to Finland looking for the local pine mushrooms. And so we had the idea that we could take the pine mushroom to the Japanese instead.'

'That's what your wife said too.'

'My wife?'

Tikkanen looks at me again. 'Taina Kaunismaa. I've just spoken with her. She told me where I could find you.'

'Of course,' I nod.

By this point I'm almost dry. The towel dangles limply in my hand. I feel the need for clothes, for some form of protection.

'She said she hasn't seen the sword either.'

'Of course she hasn't.'

'So you did not take the sword, and it is not currently in your possession?'

The image of Tomi flashes through my mind, sitting firmly on the embankment by the stream, the sword thrusting through his head like an antenna used to listen to distant radio frequencies.

'No, I did not. I've never even held such a thing in my hand.'

Tikkanen stares at me. I'm not sure what his new expression is trying to tell me. He is serious, but looks as though he is genuinely excited. Perhaps not excited as such, but curious.

'Did you want to take it?'

I want to get off this jetty. I shake the hand holding the towel towards the ground. 'I should be getting to work. The harvest is about to start and…'

Tikkanen looks at me. For a few seconds it seems as though not a single part of his body moves at all. The thought occurs to me that his heart might not be beating either.

'Of course,' he says eventually.

Tikkanen turns and we walk off the jetty and into the grass. The earth beneath my feet feels like the promised land, as though I'd only narrowly escaped something truly terrible. I pass Tikkanen and begin striding back towards the garden. Our house seems to flicker between the leaves of the trees. Tikkanen is like the burr of a burdock. I'm beginning to feel extremely uncomfortable.

'Of course I know you and your wife,' he says behind my back. 'Though we've never met until now. It's a small town, word gets round. There isn't much goes on round here that people don't find out about sooner or later. It's hard to keep secrets. Tell one person and you might as well hold a press conference on the square during market season.'

We arrive at the garden.

'Your wife seems like a nice woman,' Tikkanen continues.

Parked on the drive I see a car I don't recognise. It must belong to Tikkanen. I make a mental note of the make and model.

'I really have to…'

'…the harvest,' Tikkanen completes my sentence. 'I understand.'

I reach the steps and glance behind me. 'So, the matter is done and dusted, then?'

'As far as I'm concerned.'

'And you don't suspect me of stealing the sword?'

Tikkanen doesn't answer immediately.

'No.' He says eventually then turns and is about to open his car door. For a moment I think the interrogation is over, but then he asks a final question. 'Are you all right?'

At first I don't understand the question, but then I feel something beneath my nose. I wipe a finger across my upper lip. Blood.

'Swimming sometimes does this,' I say.

'Right.'

Taina is standing by the window, almost framed by it, and has her back to me as I walk inside. Around her a new day is beginning. When you've lived with someone for years, you can tell by the position of their head and body what kind of mood they are in. Taina does not turn around; doubtless she is keeping her eyes on Tikkanen's car as it pulls out of the drive.

I stop in the doorway between the kitchen and the living room.

There's a draught. By now my thighs are dry. And with that the feeling of contentedness that I'd experienced swimming in the silvery waters is gone. I'm annoyed and cold.

'The police,' says Taina.

'Yes.'

'I don't understand. What was he doing here?'

'Asking about some kind of Samurai sword.'

'I know that, because he asked me the same thing. But why would he be looking for something like that round here, at our house?'

Still she doesn't turn around.

I don't think I've actually seen her eyes since I thanked her for dinner last night and took a bowl of milk out to the garden for Veikko. Perhaps she's trying to keep out of my way, avoiding eye contact. It's understandable. There's a difference between looking at the wife who makes you coffee in the morning and the wife whom only yesterday you saw merrily copulating with the company apprentice. Yesterday; twenty-four hours ago, when everything was different.

'A misunderstanding,' I say. 'They must have the wrong information – they're confusing me with someone else. Of course I haven't stolen anybody's sword. I'm not a thief.'

'What did you say to him?'

'What do you mean?'

'What did you tell the policeman?'

'The very same thing. What was I supposed to tell him?'

Taina doesn't answer immediately. She turns slightly. Despite her diminutive stature she's an imposing woman. She's wearing a tight-fitting pink T-shirt, and from this angle, in this light, her breasts look full and hefty. Again I find myself thinking of *Baywatch*, though I don't really understand why, not after all these years.

'Nothing. Of course,' she says. 'I'm just a bit startled, that's all. It's a small town – you know how it is. Police attention isn't necessarily a good thing, particularly not for the business. Our reputation could suffer.'

As she speaks, Taina turns around to face me. The light is coming in from behind her, casting shadows across her face.

'But if this is only a misunderstanding, then we can draw a line under it and we won't need to see Tikkanen round here again,' she says.

'I'm not about to invite him over.'

'Well, there's no reason to.'

'No reason at all,' I nod.

Taina takes a step closer. Again I pull my stomach in. I'm beginning to understand the mechanics of how this works: when someone approaches me, I try to look somehow better than I am in reality. It's a common enough phenomenon, I realise that, but at this stage in my life – or my death – it requires quite an effort.

'I've been thinking about the suggestion you made yesterday,' says Taina.

'I suggested quite a few things yesterday.'

'About lightening up on the food. You're right. Our diet is too heavy.'

I try to smile. It's as though my face has become salted in the sea, and now I can't move my cheeks.

'You're still prepared to cook?' I ask.

'With pleasure,' Taina replies. 'It'll be an interesting challenge for me. I need something like that. Change is always good. Riding the same bike year after year can get a bit tedious.'

Taina blushes. Perhaps I can guess why, perhaps not. I'm about to say something about maybe changing the saddle, but that would be too much right now. I have a responsibility to my investigation. It's a responsibility to myself.

'What would you like to eat today?' she asks.

I can't say simply a glass of yoghurt. I have to remain my old self, the living me.

'I don't mind,' I say and remember something I've read in one of the women's magazines at the barber. 'As long as it's got plenty of protein in it.'

3

The bonnet of the van is propped open, Petri is hunched inside it, working, shirtless and wearing a pair of red shorts. The sun has only just risen, but already its glare burns the skin. Petri is tanned, toned and excruciatingly young. I am anything but.

Somewhere a moped engine sputters like a lawnmower whose voice is cracking. We are in the backyard of our premises. It's about fifty metres to the edge of the forest. The pine trees look almost orphaned, as though they are in entirely the wrong world, as they stand beneath the baking sun.

I know nothing about cars. If I ever have a problem with the car, I take it to the garage. I've never been remotely interested in what goes on beneath the bonnet. It seems there is plenty going on, because Petri is so focussed, he doesn't hear me approaching. I walk round to the other side of the van, watch his hands as they work with the motor. They are strong, skilled hands; his fingers are fast, his biceps like something straight out of an athletics competition on TV. I watch him for a while. Finally, he gives a start and looks up.

'Don't let me disturb you,' I say.

His eyes only meet mine for a fleeting second, then his dark hair falls once again in front of his face.

'There's a leak somewhere,' he says.

'How's that possible?' I wonder. 'It's a good motor.'

Petri's hands do not stop. 'It's old,' he says. 'We should trade it in for a new one.'

For a moment I remain silent. From his arm muscles I can see that Petri is twisting a wrench or a screwdriver.

'That's the plan,' I say eventually. 'As soon as our finances allow it.'

'The thing is, I spend at least an hour or two fixing this thing every day.'

Perhaps that's a good thing, I think, *otherwise we'd hardly be able to tell you and my wife apart from the local rabbits.*

'Patience,' I say. 'Everything will happen in good time.'

'I suppose.'

'Are you happy?' I ask him.

Petri places both palms on the side of the van and seems to straighten his back by pushing himself up on his forearms. Of course, this is unnecessary. He doesn't need support to stand up straight. He's got a washboard stomach and a swimmer's back. He could stand upright even if he was lying on his back on a sun lounger at the mercy of an overly eager rider. He casts me a quizzical look.

'With your work,' I add. 'Your position.'

Petri continues to look at me. 'What do you mean?'

'How do you feel about your current responsibilities? Are you content with what you're doing? I assume you know our local situation has changed somewhat.'

Petri's eyes move from the motor to the sky, from the sky to the rag in his hand. 'Changed in what way?' he asks.

'We have a competitor now. Three men, there at the end of the road.'

Petri glances around as though he expects the men of the Hamina Mushroom Company to be standing right in front of us, but there is nothing but a white brick wall and a scruff of grass yellowed in the sun. Then he looks down at the van and the motor and says nothing. He looks even younger than he did a moment ago.

'Right,' he nods. 'Them.'

'Have they asked you to work for them?'

Petri hesitates. It shows in his hands. They are suddenly uncertain, they don't seem to know nearly as much about what they are supposed to do as they did before.

'You can be honest with me,' I say. 'There's nothing wrong with someone asking you to work for them. I'd ask you too. A young man like you, with all your skills and boundless energy. A man with initiative who works above and beyond what might reasonably be expected of him.'

Petri gives me an awkward smile. I know from experience how hard it can be to listen to compliments while hiding secrets about the very same topic.

'Well,' he says, 'yes.'

'So they have been in contact with you?'

Petri nods.

'Did they offer you a better wage?' I ask.

Petri looks to the side. He shakes his head. 'A new van.'

'You should have said something. You should have come to me straight away.'

Petri looks me in the eyes. 'But...'

'We could have come up with something. We'll deal with the matter of the van when the time comes. But before that I'm sure there are a few things you and I can reach an agreement on. You and I can really help each other out.'

Petri lowers his eyes, stares fixedly at the insides of the motor.

'I suggest we fix this,' I continue. 'We can start a two-man club, a think tank they call it.'

'I don't know...'

'Petri, let me tell you something in confidence. This is between you and me.'

By now Petri's hands are even less quick and certain. They are trembling. It's subtle, barely noticeable, but I can see it all the same. I hold a long, deliberate pause and lean over the motor so that the bonnet almost forms a den around us.

'I see more passion in you than in anyone else in this business. I've got the feeling you've got what it takes to do anything at all. That's a good thing. Passion, drive, they're good qualities in a man. You want to move forward in life, and so you should. You're doing the right thing by sizing up your options. But I want to give you a piece of advice, as a friend. I can call you a friend, can't I?'

Petri says something, but it is mumbled towards his hand and is so quiet only the rag in his fist could possibly hear it.

'A friendly word of advice,' I continue. 'You need a friend, you see. Someone you can talk to about anything and everything. I don't believe a new van is all you want. You want more. Am I right?'

Petri's hands clench together, he extricates himself from beneath the bonnet, but his eyes remain cast down and he stands staring at his trainers.

'I'm in a bit of a hurry...'

'By all means,' I say. 'But we'll come back to this, my new friend.'

'I don't know...'

'Oh yes. As soon as possible,' I say.

I turn and walk away. Behind me, I can't hear Petri making any movements whatsoever.

4

The biggest problem is, I don't know when I'm going to die. I don't know whether it's going to happen in a minute or a week. On the other hand, isn't this everybody's – I mean, literally everybody's – basic problem? Death: everybody's final stumbling block; the moment when plans end and expectations are dashed.

Nobody can avoid it. I will die, you will die, he / she / it will die. Everybody dies. With a quick look in the encyclopaedia I discover that in the history of humanity approximately fifty billion people have walked the earth in the last hundred thousand years. Every single one of them has died.

All those of us currently alive – and leaving aside those already deceased, that leaves just over seven billion – will all die, and relatively soon too, when you look at it from a wider perspective. Every single person whose hand I've ever shaken, whom I've seen in the morning traffic, whom I know and have ever known or glanced at in passing.

Everyone will pass away, will cease to exist.

When you hold a newly born baby in your arms, the game is already up: death will come as surely as a bottle of milk, and with the same warmth and certainty. Death is the only permanent thing in our lives; in a morbid way it's the only thing we can really trust.

I lean backwards, breathe in and out, and wonder whether, on top of everything else, I really am losing my mind.

The doctor mentioned something about possible brain damage. Is that what this is? I don't know. If we are about to lose our minds, do we even realise it's happening? Doesn't losing your mind mean that your mind disappears and madness takes its place, making it almost impossible to recognise the loss? I sigh and decide to comb my hair, which is still tangled after my morning swim.

Be that as it may, death will be the next room into which I step. It's there, behind my office door. Death is something concrete, a meeting that's been arranged on my behalf and that I can't pull out of. And it won't let me forget about it either.

This morning: nose bleed, sudden headache, stomach and kidney pain, strange flashes at the edge of my field of vision. It's hard to say whether they were there before or whether they've now increased.

Death could come this very minute. I could close my eyes and never open them again; look outside and see nothing more; tie my shoelaces but never take another step.

There's a knock at the door; ergo, I'm still alive.

I place my palms on the table and turn my head towards the door. I can't say how long I've been lost in thought – or caught in mental anguish; it's hard to say which – but judging by the brightness of the room, I'm still living through the same early morning as a moment ago. I know it's Raimo before I catch a glimpse of him. The knock is quick, irregular, robust, and with that the door is abruptly wrenched open.

Raimo always seems to walk into a room as though he doubts the efficacy of the door hinges. Raimo is our purchasing manager, a middle-aged man with a dark beard and someone with whom I've had more arguments in the course of my life than with anyone else. He's dressed in jeans, a light-blue shirt and a burgundy jacket, though the outdoor thermometer showed 25°C when I went swimming.

'Got a minute?' he asks.

I nod, Raimo steps inside, shuts the door behind him. In addition to hinges, it appears he also doubts the functionality of door handles. The door slams shut, and Raimo sits down in the chair on the other side of my desk.

'We have to get our hands on some of those durable plastic

punnets; the deeper model with the holes in the sides. That means the product can breathe properly, and we can guarantee freshness.'

'Why?'

'Because those guys have ordered twenty thousand of them.'

'You mean the Hamina Mushroom Company?'

Raimo nods. He looks at me more closely, as though he's noticed something out of the ordinary. He says nothing.

'How do you know they've ordered so many punnets?'

Raimo clears his throat, though his voice has been clear enough so far. 'I just happen to know.'

This has been Raimo's gift to our business. He hears everything, learns everything and, after much arguing and bickering, always finds us the best prices at the most reliable wholesalers.

'The biodegradable model?'

Raimo nods. 'They're all for this harvest, which means in their first year of operations they're planning to pick double the volume of mushrooms we picked in our third year, which was our best so far.'

Again he nods. It's hard to read anything into his expressions, or rather his expressionlessness. Like me, he is a heavy-set man: a man whom food and the passing years have taken somewhat by surprise. But for him the extra weight has settled more evenly across his body. I carry a beach ball filled with sand round my waist, whereas Raimo's excess energy has spread across his body like butter on a slice of bread.

'And they look better too,' he says. 'People like them. If you put the old punnets next to the new ones, customers will always choose the new one, regardless of the mushrooms inside.'

The story of my life, I think to myself. Raimo strokes his moustache. The whiskers remain stubbornly in place.

'I can see a few small problems with that; in fact they're not very small either,' I say. 'We have enough of the old, non-biodegradable punnets to last another season. Sure, the new, biodegradable ones are great, but they're more expensive too.'

Raimo straightens the hem of his jacket. He wants to say something but is holding back.

'Besides, it can't only be about the punnets,' I say. 'We still have the best product and, I guarantee you, the best pickers.'

'That's right, because we're investing in them,' says Raimo quietly. He won't look me in the eye but stares out of the window, then lowers his gaze to the back of the computer, halfway between us. There can't be anything particularly interesting there.

'We'll invest in the punnets when the time comes,' I assure him. 'But right now…'

'Right now we should be on the attack,' says Raimo and looks at me once again.

'Attack?'

'Show them who's boss. Let them know we're the best mushroom exporter in this town.'

'I was under the impression we were the best mushroom exporter in the *country*.'

'It's the same thing.'

I'd forgotten. Raimo is a Hamina native, born and bred. For him, Kouvola, a town barely thirty minutes away, is every bit as strange and exotic as Venezuela; Kotka is a peculiar, unpleasant place, and might as well be on another planet altogether. I can't tell him I don't believe in the success of the Hamina Mushroom Company. And I certainly can't tell him that one of their number has recently impaled his own head on a sword.

'What do you suggest?' I ask.

'We've got to act quickly,' says Raimo. 'We should order thirty thousand punnets – the new model, that is. We'll fill them and we'll sell them.'

I'm not sure I've heard right. 'And what if we don't find enough mushrooms? We'll be left with tens of thousands of punnets that will be useless by next year's harvest.'

'It's a risk,' says Raimo. 'But we've got to take it. This isn't just about punnets. The punnets are there for the mushrooms, they're there to be filled. Only one of us is going to survive. There isn't room in this town for two mushroom exporters.'

'I agree with you there,' I say, but decide not to add that all we have to do now is wait for the remaining two employees to kill themselves as well. That would be a cheap joke; I don't even necessarily believe it myself.

'But if we topple our own business with unnecessary outgoings, then they will win,' I say, and nod in the direction of our competitors' premises.

Raimo is silent. At first I imagine he is thinking of his next line, but then I see that he's actually staring at me; scrutinising me. He notices it himself and quickly looks outside again.

'It wouldn't be much fun if this was our last season,' he says.

'What do you mean?'

'If the ambulance is going too slowly, the patient will die on the way to hospital.'

I take a deep breath. 'If the ambulance is going too fast, the patient, the driver, the paramedic and the doctors will all die in the crash.'

'You know what I mean.'

We sit in silence. Through the open window I hear the sound of an engine starting in the yard. Petri must have finally got the motor running. I hope that our little conversation has forced him into action and caused him even a modicum of panic. I have a right to that. After all, he has been, to put it mildly, treading on my turf.

I'll have to follow Petri. I stand up quickly. Raimo's expression is quizzical. Petri's van is slowly turning on the forecourt.

'Sit tight,' I say. 'I've got to go.'

'What are we going to do?' he asks.

'About what?'

'The punnets,' he almost shouts.

'Nothing,' I say and take two strides towards the door. 'For the moment.'

Raimo shakes his head. 'It wouldn't surprise me if someone was planning a few bigger changes round this place.'

I don't have time to ask what he means. I have to run; my car is parked out front. I dash out of the door and see Petri's van speeding along the road leading into town. As I turn the car, I think that, in many ways, Raimo might have a point.

Sometimes you have to attack.

5

I knew nothing at all about mushrooms before we decided to start a mushroom exporting business. Of course I'd eaten them like everybody else – button mushrooms on pizza, trumpet chanterelles in soups and sauces, golden chanterelles and ceps in risotto, and so on – but I'd never picked a single mushroom myself.

Then we were made redundant, and Taina hit upon the idea of the pine mushroom.

Suddenly we were up to our ears in mushrooms, both figuratively and literally. I read so much about mushrooms that I started dreaming about them. Sometimes I'd disappear inside a giant cep, into a darkness that smelled of an underground cellar and wild-animal poo. Or I would find myself trapped inside the grey-blue mushroom fungal tissue, like thick drying cement, where I would eventually drown and die in agony.

The initial enthusiasm soon dwindled, as it does with everything people decide to do for a living.

The most important aspect of reading so much was that I gleaned the information, the basic education I needed to convince the powers that be who made decisions about start-up grants in the local area. We prepared them a meal featuring five different kinds of mushrooms. The grant decision came the very next day. An organisation specialising in Finnish–Japanese commerce helped us to make our initial contacts. We flew out to Tokyo and made an offer, and struck our first deal at the airport while waiting for our return flight to Helsinki.

Nothing can beat the feeling we had as we picked our first crop of mushrooms by ourselves. The pine mushroom – or the *matsutake*, as we called it from the outset – starts to appear during the summer, sometimes as early as mid-July.

During the summer months the forest is like an endless series of tall rooms, each more beautiful, more rugged, more plentiful than the next. At first the silence of the forest was unsettling. Then I realised that the forest is never truly silent, that it's constantly full of sounds, everything from the barely audible rustle and murmur of the leaves to the thunder of the boughs and the howling of the branches.

The forest is full of life too – full of other ramblers of all shapes and sizes. It's always busy, if only you take the time to look and listen. I encountered hundreds of birds, thousands upon thousands of insects, snakes, foxes, elks and raccoon dogs. I once caught a glimpse of a wolf, and found bear and lynx tracks in the embankment along the stream.

With time I became attuned to it all. And with that heightened sensitivity, I could sense the presence of another human a long way off.

Encountering another human in the forest is like taking a leap back into the Stone Age: we approach each other peering and mistrustful, taking stock of each other's movements, perhaps with our noses slightly raised, sniffing the air. Eventually, after a combination of a sceptical, cautious greeting, a nod and a movement of the lips, people give each other a wide berth. And we never turn our backs on another person in plain sight. No. We move sideways away from each other, keeping the other mushroom picker in our field of vision so that, should they change their mind and try to encroach on our territory, we are able to raise our baskets against theirs and defend our catch.

Our business grew, and we had to coordinate our operations, make things run more effectively, oversee and maintain things. In a word, we had to *lead*. We needed a managing director. I no longer had time to go out into the woods. I was no longer a mushroom picker. I was now a mushroom entrepreneur.

Perhaps it was at that moment that something happened.

Did something else about me change other than the fact that I swapped my wellingtons for smart, laced shoes?

I think about all this as I watch Petri and the van. It's midday, the sun is about as high in the sky as it ever gets in Finland. This means I can see the town more clearly. I will die here; this will be my place of death. The term doesn't resonate as much as when people mention their place of birth, though perhaps that's hardly surprising. There's so little to say about our place of death, and so few people to say it.

Petri is driving slowly, very slowly. I assume it must either be to do with Petri or the van, and realise it might have something to do with both: Petri is saving the engine because he understands it. For a fraction of a second I feel sorry for him; he won't get a new van, though he clearly needs one. Then I remember – or rather I see (because memories are like a cinema where you can't find the exit door) – the image of Petri and Taina in our garden. Besides, I'm carrying out investigations.

Sitting behind the wheel, my thoughts become clearer. I used to think it was because when our hands have something to do, our brains move into autopilot, but now I understand it is because of what happens beneath us, what drives us. The road ahead is always clear and straight, even when it arcs to the side. The road doesn't meander, doesn't become confused, it cannot shift from the year 2016 back to 1989 with a single leap of flawed thinking. The road is unerring, infallibly chronological and logical. When we look at it, it compels us to straightforwardness and coherence, from point A to point B, though the journey might be painful.

The slower pace suits me fine. It gives me time to organise people and events in my head. I go through everything I know, everything that I know has changed, and compile an exhaustive list of events.

EVERYONE WHO MURDERED ME
(in order of probability)

1. TAINA*

2. PETRI*
(*THESE NAMES SHALL REMAIN ON THE LIST, THOUGH THEIR ORDER MAY CHANGE)

The window is fully open, and I slide my elbow outside. Summer pushes its way inside, dries my left armpit.

We arrive at the Town Hall. We drive almost halfway round the building, and Petri slows until the van is barely crawling along. Then he does something that takes me completely by surprise: he steers the car into a parking space in front of the police station. All I can do is drive past and continue in a circle. I stop the car once I have driven round the Town Hall and reached a spot where I have a clear view of Petri's van.

Petri jumps out, only pulling on a white T-shirt once he is on the pavement. His biceps flex as he gets dressed, his triceps bulge, his abdominal muscles tense. I'm sure he didn't do this deliberately or with a sense of vanity; it simply happens.

And that isn't the only thing I have difficulty watching and believing. After straightening the T-shirt across his chest, tapping the creases smooth and yanking the collar down slightly, he walks up to the door of the police station, opens it and disappears inside. For a moment I cannot understand anything at all.

My wife is screwing the driver.

The driver and my wife have murdered me.

The driver willingly starts talking to the police.

At that moment the Beach Boys' 'Surfin' Safari' fills the car. I look at the screen of my phone before answering. Taina. I pick up and give my full name. Taina is silent for a moment.

'Where are you?' she asks eventually.

'In town.'

'What are you up to?'

I look across the square. 'Getting an ice cream.'

For a moment Taina says nothing. 'Well, while you're getting yourself an ice cream and behaving strangely in all kinds of ways, I've been talking to Raimo.'

'Strangely?'

'Yes. Yesterday and this morning. And now. Getting yourself an ice cream, indeed.'

'And what if I really am getting an ice cream?'

Taina doesn't answer the question. 'We need those new punnets.'

'No.'

'No, what?'

'No, we do not need them. No, we are not getting them.'

'What are we going to do then?'

'We will be pragmatic and disciplined and follow our long-term strategy.'

'Excuse me?'

'I believe in our business,' I say. 'We don't make rash decisions, we don't do whatever pops into our minds. We plan ahead. We have plenty of old punnets and we'll use them for this harvest and save money on a needless expense. The strategy is infallible; only human error can screw it up.'

'Have you come down with sunstroke?'

'Why are you in such a rush?' I ask. 'Are you in a hurry to get somewhere?'

Silence.

'Raimo says that…'

'Raimo says what all purchasing managers say. The job of a purchasing manager is to purchase things. I'd be disappointed if he didn't do that.'

My phone's ring tone starts playing in my head. Beach, sun, surfing. All such a long time ago.

'Taina?'

'Yes.'

'Remember Thailand?'

'What do you mean?'

'Do you remember our honeymoon, the beach in Thailand, our little bungalow?'

For a moment all I can hear is the sound of the summer breeze fluttering through the car.

'Of course I remember it,' she says. 'What makes you ask that? Now, about these punnets…'

'Forget the punnets,' I say almost angrily, then start again, my tone somewhat friendlier. 'Don't forget about the punnets, but let's leave them until later. I was thinking about our honeymoon, how we loved the place and the people. You said we'd have to go back one day, to the same place, visit it all again '

'Did I?' Taina's voice is low and whispery, as though she is in a place with other people around, somewhere she can't discuss personal matters. But who can she possibly be with? Her lover is at the police station, and her husband is in a car park opposite the Town Hall.

'I just thought we could book ourselves a trip for the autumn or winter,' I begin. 'Imagine it: from the November slush straight to a sunny beach. If…'

'November?'

'It's just a possibility,' I suggest, keeping my eyes fixed on the other side of the square. 'It could be the December slush or the January slush if you prefer.'

'That's not what I meant,' she says quickly. 'I meant … it's a long time until then.'

'It's wise to book holidays in advance. I could make a reservation this evening.'

'I don't really—'

'Or, hang on,' I interrupt her. 'I've got a better idea.'

Taina is silent.

'Let's do it together. That would make the most sense. The accommodation, everything. Neither of us will be able to complain if we both look at what's on offer, how much it costs, what kind of location it is. Though I imagine we'll try and get that bungalow again. *Our* bungalow.'

The hot day's faint breeze is warm and stale, the air in the car feels recycled. Taina doesn't say anything for a long time.

'Thailand?' she asks eventually.

'Yes.'

'In November?'

'For instance.'

Again she pauses. 'All right then.'

'Excellent. Let's book something together later this evening. We can make some drinks, take them out to the patio and book the flights and hotel, and make this a nice evening, just the two of us.'

Taina says nothing.

The line goes dead.

A flock of tourists streams into the square, and a familiar piece of theatre begins to play out: an attempt at a group photograph. One holds the digital camera, the others try to stand in a row. Laughter. The camera won't work. The one holding the camera presses its various buttons. The smiles in the row of tourists dwindle. Eventually someone leaves the row and tries to explain how the camera works. Soon everyone is gathered round the camera and the photographer. Eventually the group splits up and explores the square. The camera owner walks dejectedly behind the rest of the group.

The flock managed to block my view of the door to the police station. I don't think I've missed anything, as the van is still parked in the same place. I sit in the car and continue waiting.

I want to know why.

Not just why Petri has come down here, but more generally: why have they done this, why has the situation come to this? Once I know why, I'll know what to do and how to go about it. Perhaps I haven't lost my mind after all. All I have to do is stay alive ... until I die. I mustn't die in the middle of my investigations.

I must not die before...

Petri steps out into the pavement, bathed in the sun. He is followed by a man I met only a few hours ago.

From this distance the red berry on Mikko Tikkanen's strawberry-festival T-shirt looks like a pair of enormous lips right in the middle of his chest. The men come to a halt by the van. They speak for a moment, then shake hands. Tikkanen returns to the police station; Petri jumps into the van and starts reversing out of the parking space.

I haven't got much time.

6

Afternoon in my office: the computer pings as new emails arrive, the desk is covered in paperwork, the sound of work carries in through the open door. Everybody is here; the meeting has been scheduled in the conference room for half past two.

The brightness pushing its way through the window reveals that almost everything visible in the room is covered in a layer of dust a thousandth of a millimetre thick. On closer inspection the dust seems to glimmer, sending millions of small, microscopic beams of stellar light all around, incessantly, as though channelling a boundless source of energy. Maybe I'm imagining it. A dying man has the right to imagine whatever he likes.

Only now do I realise quite how important this business is to me. It is my creation, as they say. I write a short, quick list of the matters I want to discuss, that I *must* discuss.

The minutes pass. If I think about our upcoming meeting, they pass more slowly. If I think about death, they flash by in seconds.

Nobody comes into my office. There's nothing out of the ordinary about that. I've already told Olli that my wife is having an affair. I have strictly forbidden Raimo from buying biodegradable punnets, and I'm beginning to guess he might have half promised the supplier he was going to make a sale. I have frightened Petri, the man screwing my wife, with the offer of friendship. I've recruited Sanni to spy for me. I've perplexed my unfaithful wife on several occasions – notably with talk of Samurai swords and by suggesting we revisit the location of our honeymoon. Everybody wants to keep their distance from a man in whose company you never know quite what to expect.

Suvi, our part-time office assistant, flits along the corridor. She's the only member of our staff with whom I haven't recently had a bizarre conversation, whom I haven't asked to do anything illegal or whom I haven't followed in my car.

Suvi is tall, conscientious, full of initiative, and doesn't talk much. Her attention to detail has saved me on numerous occasions. She is a twenty-seven-year-old mother of two, who went back to college to get a qualification in commerce after her husband died of solvent abuse. The moustachioed Raimo told me the story. It was the same conversation in which he described Suvi as *hot*. Besides biodegradable punnets, I have no desire to know what goes through Raimo's mind when he looks at Suvi.

When the clock reaches twenty-nine minutes past two, I stand up and walk to the conference room at the end of the corridor, glancing neither at the area we call the factory floor on the left nor into the two other offices on the right.

I sit down at the head of the table. People file in and take slightly longer than usual in deciding where to sit. Nobody wants to sit next to me.

Taina sits down at the other end of the table, slightly to the left, almost at the very end of the room. She fiddles with her phone, opens the folder in her hands then turns her attention back to her phone, making sure not to look at me, even accidentally.

And, like every class that was ever held, the seats are filled from the back of the room.

The last two members of staff to appear, Petri and Suvi, end up sitting in front of me. I give Petri a wink. He instantly turns away and stares out of the window. I look at each of the staff members in turn, smile and greet them.

From twenty years of work experience I know just how uncomfortable – how downright terrifying – such work meetings can be, especially those called at such short notice, which almost always heralds unpleasant news: streamlining the business (redundancies); fusion (redundancies); looking into a recent spate of theft of company property (redundancies); or a reassessment of company strategy (going into liquidation).

I begin.

'Great that you could all make it. This is all very last minute, I know. But if needs be, we can all act quickly, isn't that right?'

It isn't really a question and I don't expect an answer.

'As you all know, we have a competitor this summer. We've talked about it before, and I'm sure you've discussed it among yourselves. The big question is: what now? What should we do?'

I look at each of them in turn. I have to observe them carefully while at the same time getting them to trust me and work with me. It's going to be a challenge.

'Do you want me to take minutes?'

Suvi's question is relevant. I nod, and at that she twists a pen in her long fingers, clicks the ballpoint out at the end and, in the same motion of the hand, begins making her first notes on the page.

'To answer my question, we're going to carry on doing things as we have in the past, but now we're going to do everything that bit better. We still have the best workers, the best pickers and the best product. What's more, we have something our competitors do not: experience. I'm aware that some of you – perhaps all of you – have been approached with job offers. It's only natural. And so, I'd like to make you a promise, right here in front of everyone. Whatever they promise you, I promise to offer you something better, one way or another. If they contact you again, please tell me about it.'

A pause, short but effective. For what I am about to say next, I want their undivided attention.

'And another thing: we're going to increase our production, but we're going to keep our expenses and our staffing numbers as they are.'

I glance at Taina. Her face is bright red. She looks like a weight-lifter going for a personal best: her entire body oozes exertion as her back brandishes a hundred-kilo bar in the air. Raimo sits opposite her, stroking his moustache, seemingly unable to make his whiskers stay in place.

I couldn't possibly be more the centre of attention. Even Petri, who is clearly terrified at the thought of meeting my eyes, has turned to look in my direction and sits staring somewhere at the base of my ribcage. This time I don't pull my stomach in. I am what I am.

'At first that means everybody will be involved in the harvesting process, at least for the first few crucial weeks.'

Taina looks at me with the same expression of bewilderment as she had over dinner the previous evening. Raimo gently clears his throat, leans forward in his chair.

'The harvest?' he asks.

'That's right. I'll be there too.'

'In the forest?'

'Wherever Sanni takes us.'

The others turn to look at Sanni. Her ponytail doesn't so much as flinch.

'First I've heard of it,' she says.

Again heads turn in my direction. This is like tennis, I imagine, with one difference: one of the players is about to die.

'What about our other work? Our real work; our own work?' asks Raimo.

'You'll take care of that too.'

'That'll mean a long working day,' says Olli. 'I'm not sure what it says in my contract but…'

I haven't the heart to ask Olli what else he would do with his spare time. Meet his next ex-wife, perhaps? I don't even bother pointing out that my suggestion would increase his income.

'We live in exceptional times,' I say and prop my elbows on the desk, bringing myself closer to all of them at once. I notice the way Petri leans in the opposite direction. He's truly petrified at the thought of my friendship. 'I know that what I'm suggesting is unconventional, but raising our productivity will require input from each and every one of you—'

'I can't go into the forest,' Raimo interrupts.

I look at him. I'm genuinely surprised. 'Why not?'

Raimo hesitates. 'I don't … like the forest.'

'I don't understand,' I say. 'You work for a company whose entire capital comes from the forest…'

'Will this apply to part-time staff too?' asks Suvi.

I haven't thought of that. I have to make a rapid decision. 'Yes.'

'Okay,' she muses and notes the fact in her minutes. If only everybody were as uncomplicated as Suvi.

I turn back to Raimo. 'Nobody has to like the forest. Nobody is asking you to love the woods or start hugging trees. Hard work is all we need. The mushrooms. We go there, we pick them. It's as simple as that.'

'This is all very sudden,' Taina pipes up.

These are the first words she's said in the course of the meeting. All heads turn in her direction. For a moment I'm overshadowed, and that's a good thing. Sparks of lightning again start to flicker at the edge of my field of vision. My abdomen is cramping.

'According to the weather forecast, it's going to rain over the weekend,' Taina continues. 'That means the first mushrooms will be up by the beginning of next week, maybe as early as Monday. Today is Wednesday. That gives us tomorrow and Friday to take care of all our outstanding work. That's not much time.'

She falls silent. As she spoke she looked at everyone present except me.

'Forget Saturday and Sunday,' I say. 'I suggest we work through the weekend.'

An agitated red flushes Raimo's face. It seems Petri wants to look at me, but won't allow himself to. Olli is at sixes and sevens and looks like a tourist standing at the station, timetable in hand, as the train pulls away. Sanni remains calm; she looks at me, her expression neutral. Suvi continues taking notes. Taina looks at me the same way she did early this morning, when Tikkanen came round asking about the sword.

'I don't know…' says Raimo. 'This weekend is a bit difficult. My wife has bought tickets to the opera in Savonlinna.'

'But if we exceed the number of hours stipulated in our contracts…' says Olli, thinking out loud.

'I'm okay with it,' says Sanni. 'As long as we can agree on the terms and conditions, and we're paid overtime.'

Sanni's sentiment takes everyone by surprise, me included. Only yesterday I'd promised her a fifty-per-cent pay rise. Now she wants more. She says she loves mushrooms more than anything else, but I'm starting to have my doubts. Again everybody turns to look at me.

'Of course I don't expect anyone to work for free,' I say quickly. 'I was just about to cut to the chase, to explain why and how we are going to come out of this battle as winners. We will expect more of each other, we have more at stake, so I believe each of us should also have the possibility to earn a bit more.'

I can see their interest awakening. Nothing gets people's attention more than the chance to make a quick buck.

'We still have to iron out the details, and I'll have more detailed conversations with each of you individually, but the basic principle is clear. If we succeed, we will beat our competitor, increase production and succeed in other areas of the business too. All of you will have the opportunity to become shareholders in the company; everyone will have the right to a stake in our business. And shares in a successful mushroom-exporting business – well, it will be like winning the lottery.'

Complete silence. Taina looks instantly at Petri; Petri looks back at her. Both of them are red in the face; that much I can see straight away with my own eyes, though my vision is still shimmering and speckled with flickering light. Eventually they notice they are staring at each other, which only causes them to blush all the more. Taina holds her breath. Petri looks up and stares somewhere where he can see neither me nor Taina.

Raimo strokes his moustache. 'I suppose the opera singers will survive without me,' he says. 'Play is play, business is business.'

Good, I've got Raimo on side. The others still seem to be mulling over what I've just said. It's a radical suggestion, no doubt about it. What's more, it's the best I've been able to put together at such short notice. It's actually not a bad idea. I currently own seventy-five per cent of the business, and I have ultimate authority. Before long I'll only have … Will I be cremated or will they bury me whole? What's most important is that I can see the way my suggestion is affecting Taina and Petri. The confusion – and anger – is written all over their faces, particularly Taina's.

'I think it's a good suggestion,' says Sanni. She turns and looks me in the eye. 'Assuming that everything we've already agreed still stands.'

'Of course it does.'

Taina looks at Sanni. You can't miss the tone of her look. It's full of sudden envy, curiosity and something else I can't quite put my finger on.

'Olli,' I say and turn to him.

Olli grips the edge of the table as though he's worried he might slip backwards.

'If everybody else is—'

'Thank you,' I quickly interrupt him. 'Petri?'

Petri is still staring at the window. He doesn't quite know where to put his hands. In front of him are only his lap or the bare table, not a single tool or bolt, not to mention another man's wife to screw. Taina sits staring at Petri as though they are two suspects being interrogated, each sizing up the other's nerve. It's not far from the truth.

'I don't know…'

'Have you got better things to do than become a shareholder in the company?' asks Raimo, turning to look at him.

'I don't mean that…' Petri is as distressed and red in the face as a man can be without fainting.

'Petri,' I say and lean towards him, 'we're on the verge of something quite new to us. Surely you agree.'

Petri nods. I can't tell whether he's still breathing.

'All of us…' I continue, '…we're all a bit apprehensive; frightened even. Nonetheless, we all want to take this next step. Raimo has taken it, Sanni has taken it, Olli—'

'And me,' says Suvi, as easily as if she's told us she'd like another cup of coffee.

Petri manages to pull his eyes from the window. It seems he has to summon up all his strength and determination not to look over at Taina. He stares at the surface of the table in front of him. I lean a few centimetres closer still.

'Petri, sometimes we've got to take risks, isn't that right? Sometimes we have to step outside our comfort zone and see what the grass looks like on the other side of the fence.'

Petri doesn't look up at me. His lips move, but I doubt anyone present is able to hear what he's saying. He notices it himself. He coughs, clears his throat.

'The van,' he stammers.

'Right,' I nod. At the same time, at the edge of my field of vision I can see Taina doing everything in her power not to throw her head backwards, look up to the ceiling and scream something at the top of her lungs. Something unprintable. Her fingers grip the edge of the table as though it is someone she would like to strangle.

'A new one,' Petri continues. 'A van.'

'I suggest the following,' I begin, improvising. 'As shareholders we will make decisions like that together. That will improve our purchasing protocol in the blink of an eye. And if we succeed in increasing our turnover, the sky is the limit when it comes to buying new equipment.'

I pause for a second, look at each of them in turn. 'Biodegradable punnets, a few extra pickers, a packaging machine, new refrigerated spaces and a van. Anything is possible.'

I return to Petri. His eyes gradually inch towards mine. I've never seen a more conflicted expression.

'Are you in?' I ask in the softest, friendliest voice I can muster.

Three seconds of inner turmoil later, Petri lets out an audible breath. 'Yes.'

I turn to look at Taina, and the others do the same. I don't claim to know my wife, but I know with some degree of certainty that she's doing everything she can to remain in her seat. If the past is anything to go by, she would probably like nothing more than to pick up the nearest frying pan, slam it on the table and scream 'fuckingfuck' at the top of her voice. Instead she smiles and nods her head.

'The majority is probably right. Why not? I'm in.'

The way she says it, the way she abnegates her own emotions, which are all too obvious, sends shivers through my body. I have to look away from her.

'Excellent,' I say. 'We can get things moving quickly. We'll start tomorrow morning. I'll arrange a short shareholder meeting with each of you individually, and after that we'll have another meeting all together. I really appreciate this. You're like family to me.'

I can't hear anyone commenting on this. I walk back to my office, close the door behind me, sit down and lean my forearms on my knees. I feel as though I've just run a marathon, then taken a good beating after crossing the finishing line.

It's easy to conclude that there isn't much time left.

7

I am utterly serious about handing out shares in the business. I can't take them with me. What we have here on earth remains here, to be divided and frittered away by others. But this is all of secondary importance. I want to see what Taina and Petri do next.

In my office I spend only the time it takes me to recover. Once my breathing has steadied, once the strange electrical storms and the blinding episodes have subsided, and I can see what is really in front of me once again, I get up from the floor – where I've been lying awkwardly on my back, half beneath the desk – and concentrate on opening the door and walking out as I would on any other day. Raimo and Taina still appear to be in the building. I wave a goodbye, hear a faint reply and step outside.

The air feels heavy. I can't yet see clouds, but that doesn't mean anything. There's a dampness in the air, the heat seems stickier than earlier this morning. It will rain by the weekend.

I walk to my car, start the engine, roll down the window and slide the gearstick into reverse. As I press down on the accelerator, I glance in the mirror and only avoid a collision at the last second. I slam on the brakes, forgetting all about the other pedals and making the engine stall. I look in the mirror.

The van's bonnet looks so big that it seems to come all the way up to my neck. I hear its door opening. I reach for the keys and am about to try to restart the engine when I hear Asko's voice and see his muscular, copper-brown arm in the window. He crouches down. His eyes are cold and his smile warm.

'Let's go for a pint.'

Tervasaari is one of my favourite spots in Hamina. In general, that is. The area used to be a harbour. In the olden days it was the site of a sawmill, a quay and some small industrial buildings. The train tracks essentially ran all the way to the shore. It's been about sixty years since the last train pulled into the harbour. Nowadays Tervasaari is a conservation area with a large park, a restaurant in the old loading bay and a bar-cum-boat moored at the quayside.

We're sitting on the upper deck of the floating bar, each with a plastic pint glass in front of us. Though not as powerful as this morning, the sun is still glaring and intense, like a lamp that's too bright and hot but that you can't reach to angle it away. Though a breeze tickles me through the slats in the plastic chair beneath me, I'm still sweating profusely.

Following Asko in my car I went through my options. Only yesterday I tried to run away from one of his associates, and was only saved by the strangest accidental suicide. What's more, I've come to the conclusion that there's no way Asko would be asking me to join him for a pint if Tomi's body had been found. He'd be offering me pretty much the same treatment as Tomi had, with or without his Samurai sword. I've also decided that, for the time being, the way to arouse the least suspicion is to behave politely, even if that means having a drink with my arch rival.

The beer tastes weak and stale. In an instant the sun has sucked up its fizz and warmed it to room temperature. I've never understood why people in Finland feel the need to drink alcohol outdoors during the summer – at any cost. For a start it's normally too cold: your fingers freeze round the plastic cup, your teeth chatter against the rim, and it feels like you're fishing through the ice and wearing far too little. Either that or the sun beats down on your head and the beer; your pint turns to piss before it reaches your lips, and your head soon follows suit.

Asko raises his glass. The sea stretches out in front of me; Asko is sitting facing the town and the old Tervasaari bridge. I look at the water – at the waves that could carry me anywhere.

'When I was a boy,' Asko begins, 'jumping off that bridge used to be the kind of thing that gave a man a certain reputation. If you jumped head first, nobody would bother you again. People thought you were a hard man. Of course, jumping off a bridge has its risks. There might be something in the water that you can't see, pieces broken off a ship or washed in from the wharf. After all, it's a good ten, twelve metres down to the surface. You can't see anything. Especially not at night, which was when people jumped the most. Me too. We'd have some liquor in the square, hop on our bikes, take the girls with us, and jump. It was all a show for the girls, of course. One time we went over there, right in the middle of the bridge. It was a warm night and the girls were...'

Asko waves his hand towards a couple cycling along the quayside. A golden retriever is galloping between the bikes. It's like watching a circus act. Asko looks at me, a quizzical expression on his face.

'Where was I?'

'On the bridge,' I reply. 'At night.'

'We were that drunk the bridge wasn't enough for us. We climbed up to the rafters holding the thing up, all the way to the top. That's four metres higher – fifteen in total; high enough that, no matter how warm the night or how much you've had to drink, it's still bloody high. But, of course, by that point it's too late to pull out, when you're up there in nothing but your underwear and the girls are watching. And that's where we were.'

Asko looks over at the bridge.

'Me and the Similä brothers. After all the bravado, none of us knew what to say. We looked at one another. By now nobody was shouting at us to jump head first. But we'd said we'd do it, it was a promise. I looked down to the footpath across the bridge where the girls were standing. They seemed small. The water was like the surface of the moon, and at least as far away. Then all of a sudden Ville dived. Head first. It took an eternity for him to hit the water. Then came the sound.'

Asko takes a sip of beer.

'Like a pair of pincers falling into a tin barrel with only a few centimetres of water at the bottom, or like taking an axe to a branch lying in a puddle. Right beneath the surface was a submerged log. A big one. Ville hit it head first. In the night-time silence, the sound of his skull cracking was like a gunshot.'

Asko looks at me.

'We didn't know it at the time – that he'd split his skull open. All we saw was a human-shaped figure in the water that floated for a moment then slowly sank out of sight. His brains must have spread out across the surface of the water and been washed out to sea. The girls didn't shriek. They jumped on their bikes and cycled off. Me and Kalle climbed down and peddled back to the shore in our underwear. We stood in silence and stared at the black surface of the sea in the moonlight, then we called for an ambulance and the police.'

A pause.

'One of us had gone,' he says eventually.

My armpits are so wet, it feels as though I've just stepped out of the sea myself. I have to squint and rub my eyes. Perhaps it's to do with the sunshine, perhaps the stubborn flickering of light that seems to emanate from somewhere behind my temples. I've only taken a few sips of my pint.

I never know what to say in situations like this. In films people say they are sorry and express their condolences. In real life we so rarely find ourselves in this position that it's impossible to establish a routine. Besides, Asko is well over fifty years old, and if he was a teenager at the time of the bridge-jumping episode, then it must be about forty years since it all happened. I might as well express amazement at the moon landings or my own birth.

'Sad story,' I force myself to say.

Asko wakes from his reverie. 'What?'

'Your story. It's sad. Well, not so much the story itself, but the end. The end was sad.'

Asko leans back in his chair. He is a sinewy hunter.

'That's not the end of it,' he says. 'We've lost Tomi. That's the bigger of the two. You know who I'm talking about.'

'I think I do,' I reply. 'And how exactly have you lost him?'

Asko looks at me.

'We can't get hold of him, can't find him. He's not at home, won't answer the phone.'

'Really?'

'Really,' he says and sizes me up, his eyes blue as icicles. 'It got me thinking, Tomi was pretty upset with you for breaking into our premises and for being cocky with him...'

'I did not break in,' I say firmly. 'And I don't think I've been cocky with anyone. Not deliberately, at any rate.'

Asko sips his beer, then slowly places what is left of his pint back on the table.

'Then there's the matter of the sword.'

'Not really,' I interrupt. 'I haven't touched your sword.'

I realise this statement isn't necessarily true.

'Well, perhaps I did touch it. If I touched it, it was when I was ... visiting your premises. You can see on the security footage that I put the sword back on the wall and did not return.'

'We saw nothing of the sort. When we were looking into your burglary, the system went haywire.' Asko glances out to sea.

'Haywire?'

'It switched itself off,' he explains.

'That's not really my fault though, is it? And if the sword disappeared after I'd left the building, then obviously I couldn't have stolen it.'

'You could have come back again. Perhaps you were so taken with the sword that you had to come back and steal it from us.'

I shake my head. 'I wasn't taken with it. Remotely.'

Asko thinks this over. 'Then Tomi disappears. He was talking about you. He was angry at you. Really angry.'

'I can't understand why,' I say, quite honestly.

'He didn't like you.'

That much I've noticed, I think to myself.

I want to get away. The set-up is too obvious for comfort: I'm being interrogated; I'm a suspect. Nonetheless it's a relief that Asko seems genuinely concerned about Tomi's disappearance.

In all other respects the plot seems to have thickened further: these guys looking for their missing friend have reported me to the police and suspect me of stealing their sword. Their missing friend, a man who for some reason harboured a peculiar grudge against me, is now impaled on said sword. The two people I suspect of murdering me are in contact with the same police officer who is investigating the sword theft. Under normal circumstances I would probably drink my beer and order another one, sunshine or no sunshine.

'It'll all come to light one way or the other,' says Asko. There's something comradely in his voice, something approaching friendliness. 'When Tomi turns up, with or without the sword.'

'Absolutely,' I say, relieved. I can hear in my own voice how keen I am to end this conversation.

Asko gives me an odd, warm smile. 'He easily jumps to conclusions, our Tomi. Who knows, he might have buggered off to St Petersburg. He does that sometimes, comes back in his own time. I suppose we'll just have to wait. He'll turn up again when the time's right.'

'Exactly,' I agree again, this time in a more conciliatory tone, and suddenly realise something.

I'll have to make a short stop on my way home.

8

Petri is hard at work, the large garage doors wide open. This time he seems to be working on some kind of motorbike: a long front fork, a low frame and a seat shaped like a saddle. Hip-hop blares from a set of loudspeakers, its lyrics defiant of the police and the authorities. The music couldn't be less suited to the idyllic Finnish landscape around us, with its open fields, the jagged rows of pine trees serrating the skyline, and the yard at the western edge of which, next to a disused well, stands a bone fide 1950s tractor. It wouldn't surprise me if Petri had renovated that too.

Petri lives with his mother. I know the official reason for this: he has recently divorced; the split was messy and, as far as Petri was concerned, the terms were particularly unfavourable. His former wife managed to secure the couple's house and boat for herself. Knowing the official story doesn't, however, stop me from imagining all sorts of other reasons: the young foal lives with his mother where he can enjoy enough cake and milk to give him the stamina to play the role of the stallion with my wife.

From here it's only six kilometres into Hamina town centre. We could be anywhere at all in Finland. There's an old country house and a large barn, which Petri has commandeered for his motors. I stand in the doorway and watch Petri as he works. He could be in a trance. His hands fiddle with the motorbike's engine and his left leg appears to be living a rhythmical, hip-hop life of its own.

I've spent the drive out here gathering my strength. I've eaten both chocolate bars I picked up at the kiosk and drunk almost a litre of Coca-Cola – the full-sugar version. I feel noticeably better than an hour ago sitting on the deck of the pub boat. I can feel the sugar in my blood; after all I have the equivalent of a hundred spoonfuls of the stuff rushing through my system.

I move in the doorway, and my shadow passes into Petri's field of vision. He turns as though he's had an electric shock. And he looks like it too.

'Jaakko,' he says.

'Sorry if I startled you. Great place you've got here.'

I step inside the barn and look around. The space is full of engines and car parts; cluttered yet tidy at the same time. Tools hang in neat rows on the walls. I come to a stop in front of him.

'Thanks,' says Petri. 'Cars and bikes like this and…'

To describe Petri's expression as confused would be an understatement.

'Petri, I need your help. And a few tools. It's a delicate matter. I need someone I can trust.'

Petri sits silently as we drive back towards Hamina. The summer's evening hums mild and soft through the open windows. We pass only a few isolated houses on the way. It's like driving through an exhibition of works by the great nineteenth-century landscape artists: forests, fields, the glint of water. No people, no traffic. The radio is switched off, and I drive calmly.

Petri stares straight ahead, trying to find a suitable place to put his hands. Secrecy and shame are a powerful combination. He hasn't even asked where we're going yet.

'It's about a friend of mine,' I begin. 'We're going to help him, do him a favour. He's had a little accident. Do you want some Coke?'

Petri shakes his head as I offer him the bottle. I take a long sip. The black, sugary liquid is like an elixir.

'It's the kind of accident my friend doesn't want to talk about. You'll understand when you see him. I'm sure of it. Sometimes things happen; things that we can only tell our closest and most trusted friends about.'

Petri says nothing. The dirt track comes to an end, and I steer the car onto the main road. The asphalt is like a pillow beneath us.

'As soon as I heard about his accident, I thought of you.'

Petri turns his head a centimetre or two towards me.

'You're young, you're strong,' I say, 'and you can keep his accident between us.'

I glance at Petri. I can see his Adam's apple rising and falling. I gulp down the rest of my Coke.

'Have you got a friend like that?' I ask.

'What?'

'Have you got a good friend? Someone you trust?'

His Adam's apple bobs again. 'I … don't know.'

'Let's look at this from a different perspective. Do you have any secrets? Maybe only one secret? One is enough.'

'I don't know … Maybe.'

'And who knows about it?'

'I really don't…'

I wave my hand, swipe the issue out into the summer's evening. We're almost there. I want Petri to be functional when we arrive.

'You understand the principle,' I say. 'My friend and I had a secret. Our friendship was the secret. I don't think anybody else knew about it. Maybe you have or used to have a friend that nobody else knows about.'

Petri says nothing.

'I'm telling you all this so you're not surprised when you meet him. You'll recognise him. Even though, since his accident, he looks a bit … different.'

'What kind of accident?' asks Petri.

I tell him the truth. 'The Japanese kind.'

We arrive at Hovimäki. I drive to the end of Simonkatu and am relieved to realise I've remembered the place correctly. The road comes to an end. In front of us is a narrow, sandy path that seems to lead in the right direction. I think for a moment, turn the car and reverse it as far into the trees as I can, then switch off the motor. I pull the keys from the ignition, take two pairs of rubber gloves from the dashboard and tell Petri we'll walk the rest of the way. We step out of the car, and I gesture to him to walk in front of me. I quickly glance behind me. The car is hidden from view.

The sandy path leads us right into the heart of the green, darkening evening. Between the thick, verdant trees are scraps of meadow and tangles of undergrowth, confirmation, as if any were needed among the surrounding green, that nothing can hold life back; even amid all this beauty, life is erratic, powerful, chaotic and utterly uncontrollable. There is no order to it whatsoever.

Petri glances over his shoulder every twenty metres or so. We carry on until I can see the trees thinning on my right, and the ground disappearing then rising up again further ahead. That's where the stream runs. We descend almost to the water's edge, then turn and follow the course of the stream. It's important that nobody can see us from the path above.

The summer's evening is full of insects. The air is thick with mosquitoes pushing their way into my mouth. I can feel them stinging my neck and arms. For the first time in my life I'm not worried about ticks either. Our pace is slow, as the grass is tall and the ground soft. Our shoes are already ruined. I stop and listen. We've almost reached our destination. I want to make sure we're the only people around. All I can hear is the buzz of mosquitoes and the sound of Petri walking.

'Petri,' I call out before the final bend in the stream.

He stops and turns around.

'I don't want you to be frightened,' I explain. 'My friend's accident was both strange and serious. I need you to remain strong.'

We trudge round the final corner and catch sight of Tomi.

Petri vomits.

A moment later we're wrestling in the mud.

You could say Petri isn't quite at full capacity; he's been caught off-guard. My weight is to my advantage, as is the fact that being further up the embankment gives me a better position to wrestle with him. I quickly straddle him, my knees on both sides of his chest, and press his hands into the earth. He thrashes and struggles, sputtering a series of incomprehensible gurgling sounds. Thankfully he doesn't shout out. It seems panic is the same, whether we're awake or asleep: our legs won't carry us, our voice is suddenly mute. I talk to him, try to calm him.

'Petri, you can see for yourself that Tomi's not in trouble anymore. He's sitting over there as peacefully as can be. I'm going to let you go now. Do you promise to behave, to keep calm?'

Petri is staring up at the sky, his eyes wide. He stops wriggling. I clamber off him and take a deep breath; I'm at the limits of my physical capabilities. Petri's eyes are still gazing up at the great beyond.

'Why?' he asks and swallows. 'Why?'

'Tomi is – was – very temperamental. Even I was surprised to find out quite how temperamental he could be. It all happened very quickly.'

Petri shakes his head in the mud.

'Why? Me? Why me?'

Now I understand what he means.

'He's a big man, probably sixteen stone. I'd never be able to lift him by myself. You're going to help me.'

Petri opens and closes his eyes. He sits up in the mud and cautiously looks over towards Tomi, slowly inching his head round a little at a time, as if steeling himself to take in the sight again. Perhaps this is the only way to do it. Looking at Tomi is hard for me too, though at least I wasn't surprised by what I saw.

The pensive bodybuilder in yellow shorts with a Samurai sword sticking out of his head like an antenna is certainly an imposing sight. His skin is entirely marble-white, except for the fist holding the sword, and the arm and knee beneath it, which are covered in blood that by now has dried and turned pitch black. Tomi's posture is sturdy and poised; he hasn't moved an inch since the last time I saw him. The surrounding terrain – the branches beneath his armpit and elbow, the tree trunks behind his back, the mud into which the soles of his feet have sunk – everything seems to hold him firmly in its embrace. He looks like a grotesque work of art.

I can smell something putrid in the air.

'An accident?'

Petri's question is understandable.

'This probably isn't quite how Tomi thought it would end,' I explain, telling him the truth. 'But he had some bad luck.'

'You two are friends?'

'We were,' I say, stressing the past-tense nature of the matter. 'For a brief while, but we were friends all the same.'

Petri says nothing. He looks like he's thinking this over. Perhaps he's not thinking any more than usual. In the last few weeks it seems to me as though Petri would rather fit in with other people's plans than make decisions by himself. I give him as much time as I can. But we have to get to work. I take Petri by the arm and lead him towards Tomi.

Yes, the rotten stench is coming from the body. I look at Tomi and try to think of the best way to do this.

First we have to lift him from the bottom of the stream and onto the verge. Then we'll have to move him from his sitting position into a shape that's easier to carry.

'What are we going to do?' asks Petri, again with good reason. His voice is hoarse, anxious.

'I'm sure you appreciate we can't let anyone find Tomi like this. He was so particular about his image and appearance, he wouldn't want anybody to find him looking like this.'

'But isn't it a crime if…?'

'Petri. He's dead.'

'But isn't messing around with the dead a…?'

'We're not defiling the body. We're here to help him.'

We stand facing each other in the Finnish summer's evening, with

Tomi sitting next to us. The scene is surprisingly natural given all that it entails. Petri is covered in mud from head to toe. I guess I must look fairly similar. And I know what's keeping Petri here: his conscience. Unless they are utter psychopaths, people are like that.

Petri has wronged me but he is unable to tell me about it, so he's trying to make up for his acts in another way. There's a dialogue going on inside him, one that he's probably unaware of. On one side of the scales are his previous deeds (sleeping with Taina, murdering me); and on the other side is the current situation (helping me dispose of Tomi). He can't make the decision by himself, so I make it for him.

'Lift him beneath the arms,' I say and hand him a set of gloves. 'Be careful of the sword, it's sharp.'

Petri looks at me. 'Where are we taking it? Him?'

'To the car.'

'Jesus Christ.'

'He'd walk by himself, but this is Tomi we're talking about.'

Petri shakes his head. 'It's … a long way back to the car.'

'That's why you're here,' I say patiently. 'Come on, under the arms.'

Petri shakes his head a few more times, then pulls on the gloves. He takes a few wary steps round the bodybuilder and gets into position behind him. Slowly he slips his hands beneath Tomi's arms and I grab hold of his ankles. Petri looks at me.

'On the count of three,' I say. 'One, two, three.'

Tomi comes free of the mud. He has stiffened into his current position. Petri has to avoid the sword sticking out of Tomi's head; it's as if a stubborn unicorn is attacking him. Petri has to do most of the lifting. We manage to get Tomi onto the verge and lay him down on his back. With his legs hunched against his chest he looks like a giant beetle turned upside down, only with a Samurai sword jutting out of its head. We stop for a moment to catch our breath.

'What now?' asks Petri.

I think about this for a moment. I take off my shirt. It's a good shirt, made of quality material. The sleeves are long and should hold.

'Lift him a little.'

I turn the shirt into a sled: the strengthened section at the shoulders is beneath Tomi's backside; the back of the shirt is beneath his back; I tie the sleeves firmly across his thighs.

'Here,' I say and point to his left ankle.

I grab the right ankle, and together we pull Tomi like dogs pulling a sleigh. Tomi slides across the grass. Neither of us utters a word; pulling him along is hard work. The mosquitoes eat at my bare flesh. Moving is slow, but we eventually reach the path. We stop, both of us soaked in sweat.

'What now?' Petri asks again.

'We pretend we're skiing, that's what.'

I snap off some branches from a nearby pine tree and use the needles to create extra padding beneath Tomi. Petri sees what I'm doing and helps me. He's making amends for his deeds, I can see it. He doesn't know that what we're doing involves him every bit as much as it does Tomi. For me this isn't just about buying myself some time; I'm conducting an investigation. As long as Tomi and his sword remain missing, I'll have nothing to worry about from either Asko or the police, and I can use what little time I have left for more important matters.

We gather a thick, soft layer of branches and pine needles beneath Tomi and secure the bundle with the shirt sleeves. And we're off again. Tomi glides across the rough sandy path far more easily than the undulating meadow. Petri keeps an eye behind us, I watch ahead.

We reach the car. I open the boot, and with considerable exertion we manage to haul Tomi into the car. Almost all of him. Tomi is so big and the sword so long that the boot won't shut properly. I ask Petri to give me his T-shirt. Initially he's reluctant – apparently it's his favourite T-shirt – and it's then that I tell the first out-and-out lie, claiming that the smell of the body won't come out in the wash. He sniffs his shirt and hesitates for a moment. I tell him the stench seeps in first and starts to smell the next day.

Petri looks at me and pulls off his shirt. I wrap the shirt around

Tomi's left foot and make it look like we're transporting a large piece of furniture or something similar. Now for something to attach the boot lid. I find a short bungee cord. The result is crude, but it'll have to do.

I glance around. At least nobody has seen us.

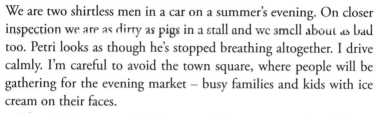

We are two shirtless men in a car on a summer's evening. On closer inspection we are as dirty as pigs in a stall and we smell about as bad too. Petri looks as though he's stopped breathing altogether. I drive calmly. I'm careful to avoid the town square, where people will be gathering for the evening market – busy families and kids with ice cream on their faces.

The windows are rolled down, and the sweat, mud and dirt is caked to our skin. In places the layers of grime are as thick as a shirt. When I run my tongue over my dried lips, the taste resembles a rancid pork pie. My throat is dry, and I start coughing. The fit is so powerful it makes my eyes water and blurs my vision. Suddenly it's night, dark and impenetrable. Something heaves within me.

'Watch out,' Petri shouts.

I swerve to avoid the cab of the oncoming lorry and struggle to pull the car back to our side of the road. The fright wakes me up, brightening my eyes. I clench my fingers tightly round the steering wheel and glance to the side. Petri is clearly breathing now; his mouth is wide open and his chest is moving up and down.

'It's all right,' I say. 'Just a spot of dizziness.'

Petri says nothing. I turn onto the main highway leading to Neuvoton, a small village ten kilometres outside Hamina. With a name meaning 'Clueless' the place seems appropriate enough for what we're about to do, but I've actually chosen it because of its stretches of uninhabited coastline rather than its name. I remember there's a small marina in the village. We pass the neighbouring village of Summa. I increase our speed to ninety kilometres an hour, and the sun ahead of us slowly begins to set, lighting the sky in soft shades of red.

It is a summer's evening.

I locate the marina easily enough and park as close to the shore as I can. We step out of the car. It's just the two of us – three, if you count Tomi. And we have to count Tomi: he still weighs as much as he did a moment ago. We borrow a rowing boat that is moored at the quayside; Petri opens the locked chains with a set of bolt cutters and we pinch a couple of anchors from the nearby boats. I leave a few fifty-euro notes on the thwarts of each boat as payment and place a stone on top of the money. I'm not a thief.

Then we row out to sea. Or rather, Petri rows, and I attach the anchors to Tomi.

It looks as though the entire world is arching its way towards evening. Out at sea there's a gentle breeze, with ripples shimmering across the surface. The intense crimson of the sky reflected in the water plays tricks on your senses. It is at once gleaming and metallic, yet soft as velvet. The thump as the oars plunge in; the splash as they are pulled out again; the quiet rippling of the water against the sides of the boat. Like zooming out of a photograph, the shore disappears behind us.

For a while I simply sit there and let Petri row us out to sea.

Then we roll Tomi overboard.

He sinks like a boulder.

As I drive Petri home I try to read his expression. He knows something I don't, and I know many things that he doesn't know. Our secrets bind us together, and now we have a shared secret too. I need them both.

We cross the bridge at Tervasalmi, and I look down to the deck of the pub boat. Only a few short hours ago I was sitting there having a pint. It feels as though I'm working and moving at precisely the pace you would expect of a dying man. Events that in the past would have taken a year, now fit into a single day.

We arrive at Petri's barn. I turn the car while he's still sitting in the passenger seat.

'Petri,' I begin, 'I imagine this goes without saying, but I'll say it anyway. We don't talk about this to anyone.'

Petri doesn't look at me. His eyes are gazing out towards the edge of the woods. The point where the fields meet the trees is already dark, like a black hole in the landscape.

'Petri?'

He gives a start.

'Nobody,' I say firmly.

He nods.

'Say it.'

'We talk to nobody.'

'Good.'

He doesn't move.

'You can get out now,' I say and tap him on the knee.

He opens the door, gets out and paces round the car. I put the car in gear and release the clutch. In the mirror I can see him walking towards the barn. I wonder how long he'll be able to keep our secret. A day perhaps, maybe two or three. I try to guess who he'll tell about it. I hope I've guessed right.

Taina's car is parked outside; I pull up behind it. As I step out into the yard, I fill my lungs with fresh air, stuff my shoes and socks straight into the rubbish bin and steel myself to step inside. I have a good idea what I must look like, and I've decided how to explain it. I walk barefoot up the steps, feeling the cold of the concrete on the soles of my feet, and open the door.

The smell is mouth-watering: chicken in red-curry sauce, naan bread, basmati rice. My favourite food. I hear Taina's footsteps, and she appears in the doorway. For the first time in all the years we've been together, I can't read her expression. She seems unfazed as she looks at me, doesn't so much as bat an eyelid.

She steps closer and smiles.

'There's a leech on your neck.'

9

A hot shower has never felt this good before. The water caresses me, lightens my burden, makes my skin feel like it's my own again. The leech came off with a quick tug. I wonder why Taina still hasn't asked why I looked like I'd been crawling through a ditch just a moment before. After all, it's the truth. I doubt Petri has broken under the pressures of all his secrets. Not yet. There must be another explanation for Taina's friendliness.

I let the hot water soften my face. When I look in the mirror after the shower, my cheeks are glowing and red, and I see that the leech has left a hickey on my neck. Otherwise I look like my old self, or thereabouts. I get dressed and go downstairs, and only now do I understand the evening's theme.

Thailand. Of course.

I'd asked for this myself, suggesting we go on holiday and return to our bungalow. Or should I say 'our' bungalow? How much of our lives do we put in inverted commas, I wonder? Imaginations, assumptions, things we've made up, memories that remain so beautiful in our minds though the truth is something else. I realise that again I'm thinking the wrong things in the wrong place. I must remain alert, both figuratively and literally. The latter may be easier said than done. Today has been one long, uneven judo match.

Taina is busying herself, her hip against the countertop. Her fingers sprinkle something here, something there. Like a rerun of the previous evening, I walk to my place and sit down. My wife has clearly put a lot of effort into our shared evening meal. Presentation is everything, and she's put a great deal of thought into it, right down to the oriental-themed napkins. An array of Eastern and Southeast Asian delicacies are laid out before me, and it seems there are more on the way. Taina is utterly focussed as she scoops something from the frying pan into a deep, black serving bowl. A cloud of thick, hot steam puffs up in front of her. There's enough food here to feed an army.

'I thought we were supposed to be lightening up,' I say.

Taina looks over at me, and the sight appears to please her. That's a first.

'Exactly. Only parboiled vegetables today. The chicken is marinated in herbs and roasted in the oven. Fat-free yoghurt for the sauce. Wholegrain rice instead of basmati. Baby-leaf salad with seeds. The only thing old about it is that this is still your favourite food. What's new is that everything is low fat.'

She smiles, and now I can read her expression more clearly. She's looking at me like a child. It doesn't feel flattering. I try not to show that I think she's looking at me like an eight-year-old. I'm a middle-aged man, I'm wearing a pink Tommy Hilfiger shirt and beneath that a T-shirt, awkwardly stretched across my bulging baby bump, which I can't seem to get rid of even by dying.

'And after dinner,' she continues as she hands me a dish of vegetables, 'we can look at some holidays and talk about our plans.'

'Great. Let's do that.'

To be honest I'm not really in the mood for a lengthy conversation. My body is crying out for rest. I've just thrown a heavy-set muscleman into the sea and before that I wrestled in the mud with my wife's lover. Yet this might be the most important encounter of the day, more important than my meetings with anyone else, living or dead.

Taina is still staring at me, her gaze warm. 'I must admit, I was surprised,' she says.

'At what?' I ask, honestly. Any number of recent events would take most people by surprise.

'The speech you gave this afternoon. About the shareholders and … everything else.'

I think I'm beginning to understand what is behind all this Asian hospitality.

'We have a competitor, and they mean business,' I explain. 'I want us to come out of this battle on top.'

'You seem very determined.'

She says this almost in passing, but her words are charged – and she's still smiling. She's not eating. This in itself is so out of the ordinary that it alone would catch my attention.

'I suppose I've – how should I put it – woken up. What do you think? About making people shareholders, doing the harvest ourselves and, of course, doubling our production?'

Taina manages to keep a straight face, but I can see it's difficult.

'Well,' she begins. 'It would have been nice if you'd talked to me about it first.'

'Everything happened so quickly. Everything seems to be happening quickly right now.'

Neither of us has eaten anything yet, though the table is laden with tasty morsels. What have I actually eaten today? A few chocolate bars, some fizzy drinks, half a pint of beer and maybe something else.

'Life certainly is full of surprises,' she muses, and I can see her forcing her eyes back to the table. 'Let's eat before it gets cold.'

I do exactly the same as I did last night. I ladle onto my plate everything I know I would normally enjoy, though this time I leave out the chilli sauce, just to be on the safe side. If Taina asks any questions, I'll just tell her a pork pie played havoc with my stomach earlier this afternoon. I'll leave out the fact that the pie's name was Tomi.

'Where did it all come from?' she asks eventually. 'All these changes?'

I shrug my shoulders, as if I make sweeping structural changes to the company every day. 'The business has reached the point where we either have to grow or we'll be forced to shrink. We can't just tread water. It's not an option.'

'You sound terribly businesslike.'

Again the abruptness of her reply takes me by surprise. Now I understand where it's coming from: she feels she doesn't really know me, and that bothers her.

'And you sound surprised,' I reply.

I cautiously scoop some chicken and rice onto my fork and pop it into my mouth. Taina doesn't look at me; she seems to be thinking about something. Outside the evening has darkened; the soft duskiness wafts inside. The light glowing dimly above the dining table creates a shelter around us.

'The day-to-day running of the business has become quite ... routine.'

'I've always liked routines,' I say.

Still Taina can't bring herself to look at me as she skilfully uses her knife to place just the right amount of each element on her fork. I manage to swallow a tiny amount and feel the food sliding down my gullet.

'I agree,' she says. 'Routines are good. But sometimes you've just got to strike, to make a move—'

Taina interrupts herself. She's becoming agitated, agitating herself. She's also starting to blush. I can see it.

'You've got to take risks,' she continues, now more subdued. 'You showed us a good example today.'

I'm truly shocked: my own wife is flirting with me. I think of my hot, sweaty, rotund face, my pink stomach, the leech's bloody kiss on my neck. I'm hardly Brad Pitt. The reason for her flirting is something other than my appearance. Taina is after something, but what? I'm going to die soon – isn't that enough?

'Thank you,' I stammer and decide to play my part in the flirtation fest. 'Thank you for taking all this on board in such a positive way. If I'm honest, I thought you might have some objections to these changes.'

Again Taina does her best to keep her expression friendly, her voice calm.

'Why's that?'

I recall Raimo's comment as I ran out after Petri: *It wouldn't surprise me if someone was planning a few bigger changes around this place.*

'I just thought – or, I used to think – that you might have your own ideas about how to develop the business and that they might be slightly different from mine.' My voice is full of warmth. I look her in the eyes. I am her husband, her friend.

'Well—' she begins.

I interrupt her: 'Of course, that's perfectly understandable. I've been deaf, stubborn, indifferent. Stuck in my ways, as they say. I've only done the bare minimum and never tried to broaden my horizons.'

I listen carefully to what I'm saying. It sounds about right.

'That's exactly it,' I continue. 'I haven't been bold enough, haven't seen how much I can give. I've been holding back, not living at … full capacity. Perhaps you've noticed it.'

The last sentence was deliberately marked.

Taina looks at me. 'Perhaps…' she hesitates.

'You might have lost faith in me,' I ask and aim my words directly at her.

Taina continues to hesitate. Filling her fork with food takes longer than before.

'No,' she says at last. 'I … Of course not.'

She's lying. My wife is lying to me.

'Good to hear,' I say. 'Mutual trust and respect are everything.'

Taina stares at her food. A tiny, almost imperceptible tremble might just have appeared in the hand holding her fork. She says nothing.

'It's essential,' I continue, 'when you're about to make big structural changes—'

'You can't make them shareholders,' Taina cuts me short. The words gush out of her like water from a broken pipe, exploding under pressure.

We look one another in the eye.

'Could you pass the naan bread?' I ask.

'At least, not before we know … more.'

'And the butter, please.'

Taina looks at me, then hands over a slice of bread and the butter dish. She pulls herself together right before my eyes, forces herself to remain calm.

'You can't hand out shares like caramels,' she continues. 'The employees have to earn them. And for that we have to watch them over time, let them demonstrate what they're capable of.'

I lean back in my chair. 'What kind of timeframe are you thinking of? When would be a good time to reassess the situation?'

Taina's expression lightens visibly. 'We'll know more in the autumn.'

No doubt about that, I think. When you and Petri are standing at my grave – if you can tear yourselves away from the comfort of your sun lounger, that is – you'll know a lot more indeed.

'Why the autumn?'

'The harvest will be over, the mushrooms picked, and we'll know how well we've done this year.'

I look down at my plate and take another mouthful. The act of eating doesn't feel that bad now.

'So, Thailand?' I say, keeping my eyes firmly fixed on the coconut milk, the chicken and rice. 'You'd like that?'

'If you want,' says Taina. I can hear that she's trying to force a modicum of enthusiasm into her voice, but the result sounds taut and fake. It looks decidedly as though Taina has a lot at stake here. I don't know how far she's prepared to go, but I'm curious to find out.

'My neck has been sore all day, my shoulders are really tense,' I say and try to catch my wife's eyes.

'I can give you a back massage after dessert,' she says with a warm smile.

I am convinced my wife has murdered me.

10

What was it about Hamina that I eventually fell in love with? The calm slowness of summer mornings, with a gentle breeze the smell of the sea and the morning market with all its sugared doughnuts and delicacies, which, over the past three and half years I've enjoyed enough to cause at least one diabetes scare?

The window is open, the air is motionless and stagnant, though I put my foot down on the accelerator. It's as though pressure is building beneath a lid somewhere high up in the sky, preparing for an eruption. The sky is still cloudless; it looks as though it's been freshly painted: it shines and glows a deep, strong blue. It must be a mirage; surely there are dark clouds hidden behind it, a bracing wind, the rumble of rain. That means a storm. And that means mushrooms.

'Let's talk. Come round before work.' Sanni's text message was waiting for me when I woke up on the sofa at half past six.

I don't remember much of what happened after watching and commenting on the competitors on *The Biggest Loser* and snacking on crisps and sweets while receiving my neck massage that evening. I must have drifted off to sleep.

I remember our evening meal and how surprised I was at being able to eat, at how my hunger literally seemed to grow the more I ate, how delicious the chicken and rice were, how perfectly sugary the strawberries and cream tasted and how I picked them from the bowl one at a time thinking, *This is the last one. This is the last one. This is...*

I remember the feel of Taina's hands on my bare shoulders, at once so familiar and now so ... not strange, but as though their warmest, most intimate touch – the millisecond when the fingers relax and get ready for another press – was absent.

My senses have sharpened, that much I must admit. Now I sense things that before I would barely have registered. At least that's what my damaged brain seems to be telling me.

Death feels at its most unreal in the mornings. My experience of death is only a few days in length, but already I can say that the nearer the day gets to evening, the closer the end always feels. Perhaps this is only natural.

The sun rises, the sun sets. Life is a single day.

In the mornings life seems like a foregone conclusion, but by evening the certainty slowly crumbles away. Even in normal times, the day's events are by their nature so ephemeral, so fragile and forgettable, that it's a wonder I haven't thought about my own death every evening of my life.

The familiar hubbub of the market place: bread vans, the coffee tent, old men on bicycles. I take an unnecessary drive round the square just to let everything sink in. For a brief moment I think that, if I were allowed to live longer, I'd stop and enjoy a pot of coffee and a sumptuous, fatty doughnut, its sugar crust crunching between my teeth. Nonetheless I'm forced to admit to myself that my situation is by no means a given. If life is capricious and unpredictable, there's no trusting death either.

Saviniemi is still in its place. The yard outside the house on Kalastajankatu, where I'd seen Keith Richards with his log cutter, is empty. The pile of logs is now as tall as the house. For some reason I'm convinced the man must be out somewhere, fetching more wood, probably straight from the forest.

As I park the car on Kipparinkatu, I instinctively check the mirror. I realise I'm doing it because of Tomi. But he's not following me; the only things he'll be following right now are the occasional pike or the lowering of fishing nets – from beneath.

Upon seeing it again, the yard looks greener than I remember: ferns like volcanic eruptions, rows of flowers standing like fruit stalls. Smells, the earth, green caves and boughs leading into the shelter of the trees at the end of the garden.

The door is unlocked. I open it and listen for a moment. I step inside, leave my shoes in the hallway and walk into the kitchen.

Sanni is naked apart from her underwear. She is standing with her back to me and using a food blender, doubtless preparing a high-protein runner's shake. Her long crimson hair hangs halfway down her back. One side of her light-blue satin underpants has become lost between her buttocks. Her buttock is white and round, half of an athlete's taut bum. Sanni has already turned around by the time I realise my eyes are still fixed on the spot where the buttock was only a moment ago.

'Good morning to you too,' she says.

I do three things at once: I remove my gaze from Sanni's buttocks, apologise, then pull my stomach in, puff out my chest and position my arms so as to show off my biceps. I don't know which of these is the most embarrassing. Sanni has raised her hands to cover her breasts.

'You said in your text to pop round,' I say. 'I thought it was an invitation…'

'It was,' she says. 'Have some coffee while I get dressed.'

I try to pull myself together, pour some coffee and sit down at the kitchen table. I look around. The kitchen is pretty, cosy. It's a twist on an old country kitchen, probably furnished with items from the catalogue of a Swedish interior design retailer. All the bits and pieces of food on the table are labelled with at least one of the words 'organic' / 'diet' / 'light' / 'natural' / 'protein'. *Everybody eats so healthily these days*, I think; *even me, a man who could live on butter alone.* I'm not feeling that bad today, if you don't count the slight dizziness, the tinnitus in my ears (a new symptom) and the pain radiating from my kidneys. These feel like merely small inconveniences, particularly as yesterday's hearty meal is still inside me.

'I paid Asko and Sami a little visit yesterday,' says Sanni as she returns, wearing a baggy red T-shirt and a pair of ripped jeans. 'I learned one or two interesting things. We talked about work, their plans for the summer and autumn, and how they are planning to dominate the local mushroom market.'

'They told you that?' I ask incredulously.

'Of course,' says Sanni and lifts the lid of the blender. 'I said I'd start working for them, said I could start straight away.'

I nearly spit a mouthful of coffee across the table. Sanni pours a beetroot-red drink from the blender into a tall glass.

'Holymotherofjesus!' I exclaim and carefully place my coffee cup on the table.

'Music?'

Sanni doesn't wait for a response. She flicks her phone and music begins to sound from the speakers above the table. I know that song. Bob Marley: 'Is This Love'.

'You said you were going to start working for them?' I ask, bewildered. 'Yet only yesterday you signed a new contract with me.'

'How else am I going to get information on what they're up to?' she says. 'I've checked it out; everything is above board. I could sign a hundred simultaneous contracts if I wanted to, unless one of them specifically precludes me from working elsewhere. Sometimes they do, when there's a non-compete clause or something like that...'

'I know,' I say. 'It seems there's no non-compete clause in their contract. It seems *we* don't have one either. But that's not my point. I mean in practice. Of course, an employee can accept fifty jobs on the same day if they wanted to, but taking care of them all might prove a bit challenging.'

'It's a probationary contract,' she says and takes a sip from her glass. For a moment she has a bright-red moustache. A quick lick of the tongue across her lips and it's gone. 'I can hand in my notice anytime I want.'

'Well, yes, but right now – and in the next few weeks – we're going to need you more than ever before. You can't be in two places at once.'

Sanni says nothing. The deep, smooth pulse of the bass, the jangling guitar and the soft morning sunshine transport the fragrant kitchen in the wooden house somewhere far away, somewhere where I can easily imagine us in a cottage, on an island, me and Sanni, those divine panties and her beautiful left buttock...

'How content are you?' she asks me. 'With your life?'

I look at her, puzzled at the thoughts hurtling through my mind.

'I don't know,' I reply honestly, and think about this for a moment. 'For a long time I haven't … Let's just say looking at the larger picture isn't all that easy at the moment.'

Sanni has already drunk half of her shake.

'I realised something the first time you visited me here,' she says. 'It was exactly what I needed: a new opportunity. I'd been treading water for far too long. I was in a rut. That's what they call it. "You're in a rut." It didn't feel bad, but it was the truth. You could say I've had an awakening, but without any of the religious overtones. Still, the feeling must be quite similar. Your eyes open, and you can see things right in front of you that you haven't seen before, though they've been there all the time. And suddenly you see the whole world, your own life and the truth about your life. The scales fall from your eyes, and you see what's really going on, what's happening right now.'

'I know what you mean,' I say, partly because I agree with her but also because I enjoy Sanni's voice, enjoy listening to her.

'Do you know what I want to do?' she asks and looks at me across her glass. The drink has been drunk.

I shake my head, take a sip of my coffee.

'I want to conquer the world,' she says.

Drinking coffee with Sanni is turning out to be an impossibility. First the palpitations caused by her near nakedness, then the news about her job, and now this. There's a hint of green in the blue of her eyes, making her gaze positively glow.

'I'm talking about mushrooms, of course,' she says.

'Right,' I say.

'Everything is in our hands. We have the best product, the best pickers, the best fresh storage and preserving facilities. We have good contacts. And now … now we've got the best management too: a man who is interested in developing our operations.'

I stare at her. 'Really?'

She gets up from the table. Her jeans are so torn that I can see her groin, and I realise that my eyes have yet again alighted in the most entirely inappropriate place. Sanni leans her back against the counter, places a hand on the edge. She's not wearing a bra, and her flimsy red T-shirt lets the rays of sunlight through.

'Why only Japan? Why only one customer over there? Why not the rest of Asia too? Why not Central Europe? Why not London, New York?'

I'm about to say something, but Sanni raises a hand.

'It's not your fault, Jaakko. We're all at fault. Me too, it's as though I've been asleep. I was looking at the woods when I should have been looking in the other direction. Don't get me wrong, I love the forest; I love mushrooms and everything about them. But ... the mushrooms have to serve a greater purpose.'

Everything Sanni has just said is true, sensible. To be honest I'd go as far as to say it's invigorating and exciting. And yet there are many reasons why I can't think about New York right now. I don't know if I'll ever see Tervasaari again. Not to mention what I'm doing with the time I've got left: investigating my own murder and trying to save my business. I need Sanni, need her help going undercover, her role in this jigsaw. I count the cheerful yellow tassels of the rag rug on the floor; sunlight spreads across the rug like a spilled egg yolk.

'Jaakko,' says Sanni.

I look up.

'Did I go too far?' she asks.

'It's not that…'

'Is it about Taina?'

The shade of green in Sanni's eyes seems to have deepened. Her position, the way she is leaning against the kitchen counter … She is alert, serious, genuine. And I've been honest with her too – about everything except my death, that is.

'I think so,' I stammer.

'You think?'

'I'm not sure.'

'Who would know a thing like that if not you?'

'I'm looking into it as we speak.'

Sanni looks at me as though I were a bit slow. More Bob Marley:

'Don't worry about a thing,
'Cause every little thing gonna be all right.
Singin' don't worry about a thing,
'Cause every little thing gonna be all right.'

'Who are you going to ask about it?' Sanni asks

I look at her, slide my coffee cup further across the table.

'You're right,' I say eventually. 'About the mushrooms. And about Taina too, unfortunately. I get the impression she and I see things very differently at the moment.'

'How differently?'

'About a hundred per cent differently.'

'And what about you?' she asks in a voice that now sounds softer than before. 'How does she see you?'

'If I say I don't think she sees me at all, at least not in the long term, I think I'd be pretty close to the truth.'

Sanni looks at me in silence.

'Maybe Taina is just looking in the wrong direction,' she says eventually.

11

I decide not to glance in the mirror but hang my left arm out of the car window the way I haven't done since I was a child. It's a warm morning; my arm is like a wing gathering air beneath it. I steer the car with my right hand, taking wide curves around corners, pressing the accelerator gently but decisively.

I am alive.

Everybody should die at least once, if only to see how beautiful the morning can be.

Everything sparkles, glistens. The great blue lid of the sea carries small white boats, and beneath the sky the earth is like a soft, green blanket.

Dangling my arm out of the car window has an unexpected side effect too: people think it's a greeting and they respond to me, often pleasantly surprised. I smile at them, mouth the word *morning*. Together, we are this shared morning, every last one of us.

I blow a kiss to an old lady, who looks startled and almost drives off the road and into a hedgerow in front of a terraced house on Mannerheimintie.

The sun warms me, my arm is flying, my mind is…

Petri's car, with Petri behind the wheel, crosses the intersection ahead of me and continues on its way into town. The car is coming from the direction of our office, but of course that doesn't necessarily mean anything. Hamina is a small town with a limited number of roads: if you drive a lot, you'll probably drive up and down most of them several times a day. But it's not even eight o'clock yet. Petri doesn't seem to be looking to the side. I'm approaching the intersection from behind a warning triangle; he has right of way so he doesn't need to look in my direction. And neither does he – at least not as far as I can see. By the time I've turned left at the intersection, straightened up the car and looked in the mirror, he has disappeared.

My arm is no longer dangling out of the window. It's gripping the wheel instead.

Inside the office it is dim and quiet. I think I must be the first to arrive, but then I hear the low hum of the drying machines and see that the back door is open. I walk through the hall, arrive at the door and recognise the feet propped on the chair. I step out onto the patio and see the rest of their owner.

Olli is having his morning coffee and tucking into a long, sticky Danish pastry.

'You're early,' he comments.

With his brown eyes, his angular jaw and the greying hair round his temples he really would look unmistakably like George Clooney, if only he wouldn't talk with his mouth full of sugary pastry. And if there wasn't a large globule of raspberry jam stuck in the corner of his mouth. And if he didn't look like he enjoyed jam so much, raspberry or any other flavour. Still, he doesn't have a paunch like me. I don't know why I've suddenly started feeling so uneasy about the life buoy around my waist. I imagine the answer to the question would be hard to bear.

'The machines are up and running,' I say, stating the obvious.

'I know,' Olli nods, his mouth still full.

'Well, I don't doubt that,' I say. 'I just wondered why they're switched on. To my knowledge we haven't got any mushrooms yet. We're still waiting for the rain to come, hopefully by the weekend, and after that we'll have mushrooms to dry. We follow nature's own cycles, or we try to at least.'

'I know that.'

I say nothing and look at Olli. He notices this, takes a sheet of kitchen paper from the roll on the patio table and wipes the corner of his mouth. He swallows so loudly I can hear it.

'I'm trying out a new technique,' he says. 'A method of drying them more quickly. I don't know if it's possible yet, but I think I've come up with something.'

'A new drying method,' I say and hear how surprised I sound.

'That's right. You were talking about doubling our production, and that means we'll have twice as much to dry, which means that…' He's talking as if he's apologising, his delivery hesitant and cautious.

'Olli,' I interrupt him, 'it sounds good. Great, actually.'

I can see the relief in his eyes, and the hand holding the half-eaten Danish pastry returns to its resting position.

'I just thought … you looked so…'

I take a few steps forward, from the shade into the sunshine, stand in the middle of the patio and feel the sun on the top of my head. There are a few irritating quirks to Olli's personality, but he always makes up for them with these positive little surprises. I want him to know that.

'I'm sorry. Maybe I'm a bit tense at the moment. I'm glad you're using your initiative like this. That's exactly the kind of positive spirit we need round here. Have you been here by yourself all morning?'

Olli looks at me and seems to be wondering how to answer the question.

'Of course,' he says. 'That's why I got here so early. So I could check things out in peace and…'

I give a short nod of the head, take a step closer.

'Do you remember what I told you before? About my wife? And you told me how you've had similar experiences yourself – with women in general, if I understood you right?'

The raspberry pastry in Olli's hand is like an object he has just discovered and that he now wants to present to me. It doesn't move at all, and he has stopped eating it.

'I remember it well,' he says, and now there's something more self-assured in his voice, something assertive. 'And I've been giving the matter some thought.'

'Really?' I say, surprised.

Olli nods.

'You can't take it lying down, mate.'

'That's what I was going to ask you about,' I say and quickly glance up at the sky. The sun is climbing rapidly. Now it's whiter and has lost the yellow hue it had this morning. 'I was talking about my wife. Now I think I might be infatuated.'

'With your wife?' Olli asks, clearly bewildered.

'No,' I say with a shake of the head. 'Not with my wife.'

Olli gives a more decisive nod, a gesture that says more than a simple 'yes', something more along the lines of, *Aha, well indeed, I think I get the picture.*

'That's the spirit; chin up,' he says. 'Always on hand when the pipes need a good seeing to.'

I look at Olli. I recall our previous conversation with all its metaphors about ponds and turf and other such things. This plumber's romanticism is…

'Look, my wife isn't dying,' I say. I decide not to mention that she's made certain I'm the one who's dying.

'Of course not,' he replies quickly.

'Have you ever had another woman on the go?' I ask.

'Have *you* got another woman on the go?'

Olli's question comes out of the blue. I think about it. There's only one answer.

'No.'

'I don't understand.'

'There's no … other woman. I mean theoretically. At the moment the most we're talking about is an infatuation.'

'In that case,' Olli begins and seems to remember the remnants of the pastry in his hand. He bites off a large chunk and washes it down with a glug of coffee. I can only imagine what two decilitres of pastry-and-coffee dough must feel like in his cheeks. I wait for him to continue, but he doesn't. He notices me looking at him.

'What?'

'"In that case", you said. People generally follow that with some sort of clarification.'

'Right,' he concedes. 'Infatuation. That's the right direction. But I wouldn't pay it too much attention if I were you.'

'Why not?'

Olli places his coffee mug on the table. The mug's rim is smeared with pink and light-brown smudges.

'When I go to the shops, I feel a bit of a thrill. When I drive a car, I get a thrill. When I watch TV, I get a thrill. When I walk across the square, I get a thrill. I feel infatuated about a thousand times a day, but by evening I couldn't tell you any of the reasons why.'

'People are different,' I say.

'Maybe, but the important thing is you're getting over the bloke who's drilling your wife.'

'I prefer not to think of it as drilling.'

'That's what it is though. Drilling, banging, pummelling…'

'Yes, all right,' I say, stopping him in his tracks.

I stand on the patio, the sun beats down on my skin. I'm about to say something that I suddenly remember; the thought is already in my mind, the question forming, it's of the utmost importance – but I don't have time to say it out loud, because Suvi appears in the doorway. She's so tall that the glasses propped on her head almost touch the top of the doorframe, and she has to hunch her shoulders.

In her right hand Suvi is holding a bunch of papers that she lifts up to show me. The quick movement of her head, the stretch of her long arm, the graceful sideways movement of her thin, slender figure, look like a very short stage performance.

'Could you take a look at these right now?' she asks.

I show Suvi to the chair on the other side of my desk, close the office door behind me and wonder how normal it is for everybody to arrive at work so early. It can't be very normal, not at all. Suvi sits down in the chair and crosses her left leg over her right. Her thigh is long and shiny, and about halfway up it there's a bruise, blue and violet around the edges and almost black in the middle.

The papers are still in her hand.

Suvi's brown hair is tied in a bun, her face is serious and narrow, as it so often is, and as usual her blue eyes are at once neutral and alert. She's wearing a green-and-blue summer dress and a pair of white sandals, and for the first time she looks every bit as young as she really is: twenty-seven years old. In terms of the quality-price ratio, Suvi is probably the best recruitment I've ever made: last year, using only her own initiative and common sense, she'd already saved us more than her entire annual salary by the early spring – the time when we tally up the wages for the pickers in our last-minute scramble to gather the false-morel harvest.

If anyone has earned a pay rise, it is Suvi, and besides, if what I know about her past is true, Suvi might have much more to offer the business than her attention to detail. She already has the kind of experience some people never achieve in their lives – or deaths, however you wish to look at it. The two concepts are increasingly mingling and overlapping in my mind: I'm inhabiting two worlds at once, and, oddly enough, it all seems perfectly natural.

Suvi brings me back to earth as she hands me the papers. I hold out a hand to stop her. She lays the papers in her lap and continues to look at me fixedly.

'Just a moment,' I say. 'Before we get to that, there's something I want to talk to you about. If that's okay with you.'

Suvi says nothing.

'I'll take that as a yes. Just say if I go too far. This is a personal matter. And I want to stress this is entirely voluntary. You can leave whenever you wish.'

'Do you want the long or the short version?' She shifts position in her chair, uncrosses her legs and crosses them again the other way. There's no bruise on her other thigh.

'I'm sorry,' I stammer. 'If I'm being—'

'My past.' Suvi interrupts me. 'It always comes out. Sooner or later.'

'Would you like to talk about it?' I ask, and even I can hear how unnatural and downright stupid it sounds.

'No,' she replies. 'But I can.'

Suvi places the bunch of papers between her thigh and the arm of the chair, frees up her arms and folds them across her chest.

'Esa was a promising rally driver; in the junior league he was one of the best in the country. Always conscientious and enthusiastic. We started dating when I was fifteen and Esa was sixteen. He liked to drive fast. Every evening we would career up and down the local dust tracks. It made a real stir, especially as neither of us was legally old enough to have a driver's licence. At the same time he was taking part in more and more competitions. And that's when he got a taste for the booze. It was then that I realised there was one thing he loved more than me: lager. Lager and rally driving is a tough combination. Naturally, at first nobody noticed anything. Esa would drive with a hangover, throw up between the stages of the race, jump back behind the wheel and drive like there's no tomorrow. Then, every evening he would drink himself under the table, drink himself to oblivion. He loved that lager. One crate a day was nothing – that was just to quench his thirst. I became pregnant. Sometimes we joked that our stomachs were growing at the same rate. But I didn't find it particularly funny. Esa drove his rally cars, his face ruddy and bloated, and we had our first child. He celebrated by wrapping his car round a tree for the first time. We got married once he'd remained sober for three days. It felt like an eternity. He was always on the road. Each time he came home his face was chubbier and redder, his driver's jump suit was so tight round the waist that I had to yank the zip up as he held the sides together. Then he started drinking while he was behind the wheel. His map reader was a substance abuser too – popping

Diapam like throat sweets – so he was unlikely to tell anyone what Esa was getting up to. God knows how they managed to win any races. Cheap lager and Diapam, the breakfast of champions, they joked. By this time I was pregnant again. They kitted out the car with a ten-litre tank for Esa's lager and fitted it with some kind of cooling system. For the map reader they drilled a hole into the door big enough to fit a tube, and at the bottom of the hole was a spring that pushed out a new tablet each time he finished sucking the last one. They even showed me the drawings they'd put together. On a long, hot, sunny day of competition, Esa would easily empty the entire tank. He would barely be able to stand up and someone would have to lift him out of the car and carry him to the hotel. Then the next morning he'd be back behind the wheel. His face was so red and swollen that he looked like a traffic light. I don't know how he could see anything, as I certainly couldn't see his eyes. He found himself driving for a small-league European championship title. Winning would have meant a transfer to the world championships and a substantial contract, and finally our family would have been able to afford a home of our own. It was the day of the final race. Esa and his map reader decided to leave nothing to chance: they doubled the size of the beer tank and the pill popper. The first four stages went brilliantly, and they were leading the race. And it was then that they were overcome with hubris: they decided to try one another's provisions. During the fifth stage Esa munched his way through the rest of the sedatives and the map reader gulped down what little Esa had left in the beer tank. The result was that, during the sixth stage, the car stalled on a long, straight road in the middle of the plains. A technical car drove out there and found the two of them. Esa was snoring like a languid walrus and the map reader was sitting next to him, his trousers soaked. Needless to say, there was no contract and Esa was sent home. His rally-car days were over. He tried all kinds of things, but ended up in a garage painting car bodywork. It's a job that involves a lot of solvents. He never sniffed anything, but he was always so drunk – and because of that so short-sighted – that he had to paint the cars with his nose right up against the body. One day he keeled over and died. People said he must have been sniffing something, but he never did. He just died.'

The story has come to an end, I realise that, but something is missing. I feel certain of it. I don't know what. What's more I'm unable to show as much empathy or interest as I would have hoped, as a wave of faintness washes over me.

This time I don't see any of the familiar bolts of lightning, but it's as though there's a problem with the signals in my brain: the screen goes blank, flickers on and off, remains out of focus for a moment, colours flashing, whirling on top of one another, bright and garish. My stomach muscles start to cramp, my chest heaves, I bend over double and hit my head against the desk. First my heart misses a beat, then shudders painfully, emptying itself as though it is full to the brim. I don't know how much longer I can take it. When I can see again and manage to sit up straight, Suvi is still sitting in front of me.

'Not to worry,' I stammer. 'It's not to do with you or your story.'

'Are you ill?' she asks.

'No,' I reply, because I feel perfectly healthy.

As contradictory as it seems, it hasn't for one moment occurred to me that I might be ill. I'm merely dying, that's all. There's a difference.

'I'm just … Let's look at these papers, shall we?'

Suvi hands over the bunch of papers. Receipts, bills, order forms. I skim through them and hurriedly sign them.

Then I stop in my tracks.

A non-refundable booking, to be paid in advance. Six rooms at the Seurahuone Hotel in Hamina.

I stare at the booking dates. I look up to check the date – first in the upper right-hand corner of my computer screen then with Suvi, who gives the same answer as the computer. I ask her what day of the week it is too, just to be certain.

'Thursday,' she says. 'It's 2016, in case you're wondering.'

'Thank you, Suvi.'

The two-page booking confirmation doesn't tell me who made the reservation. It simply lists our business and gives my mobile phone as the primary contact number. And that's not the only thing that chills me about this reservation. The booking is for this coming weekend. Tomorrow is Friday. Six rooms, check-in tomorrow. The confirmation slip doesn't give the names of the occupants. I show Suvi the document.

'Did you make this booking?'

Suvi shakes her head. 'I found it this morning.'

'Where did it come from?'

Suvi looks at me. 'The Seurahuone Hotel.'

'I know that. I meant how did it come to be on your desk?'

'It didn't, that's what I'm trying to say. I found it in the company's email account, the general one that nobody checks anymore. Someone must have given it as the contact email. It's there on the reservation form, on the second page. Do you want me to check—?'

I stop her with my hand while I look at the second page.

Stranger still.

The reservation isn't just for the six hotel rooms. There are tables reserved at the restaurant too: dinner for a total of eight people on Saturday and Sunday. All at once I can see the connections I've been looking for. Now that I seem to have found them, I feel a mixture of fear and disappointment. In the blink of an eye the two combine, blend together, then erupt in a burst of rage.

'There's no need. You can forget this now. I'll take care of it myself.'

I leaf through the rest of the papers. Routine stuff. I hand the bunch back to Suvi and thank her. She stands up. She's a serious young woman, which is hardly surprising. Her story is an extraordinary tale of survival. I firmly believe I understand that better today than I would have only a week ago. I also firmly believe that I can appreciate at least some of what Suvi has had to go through.

'Suvi,' I say as she's almost at the door.

'Yes?' she asks and turns.

'The things you told me...'

'That was the short version.'

'I didn't mean that, but thank you for confiding in me. About the other thing – don't mention this reservation to anyone.'

Suvi's face is open, her blue eyes too. 'You're the first person to hear that story who hasn't asked me how it made me feel or what I feel about it now. Thank you. As for the reservation, I've never seen it.'

The Seurahuone Hotel has recently been renovated. Not a moment too soon, some might say. The hotel dates from the late nineteenth century – a handsome stone building with wide, grandiose staircases and hallways. The hotel's reception is on the first floor, the same floor as the restaurant. Light streams in through the tall, churchlike windows. The silence reminds me of church too, that and the stone floor that oddly seems to count my steps.

I'm out of breath after walking up the stairs. Only this morning I'd been as fit as a young foal, or at the very least a good workhorse. I hope this worsening in my condition is only temporary, as these spells have been until now.

The hotel reception looks empty. The breakfast rush is over, the dining room cleared and tidied. I look on the reception desk for a bell or some other way of getting the staff's attention. There is nothing. As I can't think of anything better, I call a 'hello' into the air. The word has an unexpected effect. A man jumps up from behind the desk. His oval face is dark red and desperate.

'Hello,' he says. 'Printer. Playing up. Good afternoon. How can I help?'

I unfold the booking confirmation and turn it to face the man. He looks at the form, first one page then the other, then replaces them meticulously one upon the other and returns them to me across the counter.

He is about my age and my height, and as we look at each other our eyes are at almost exactly the same level. His brow shows the deep furrows of a stressed man, and there's a pained look in his grey eyes. The top button of his pink shirt is done up, and the shirt is so tight that it seems only a matter of time until one of them gives way: the shirt or the man. The name tag pinned to his shirt sits firmly above one of his pectoral muscles; I wouldn't be surprised if the safety pin was travelling beneath the top layer of skin. Ilari certainly doesn't look the slapdash type.

'The booking appears to be in order,' he says warily.

'I have no reason to believe otherwise,' I say.

The printer starts to whirr and creak and rattle. Ilari casts his eyes down somewhere behind the counter. His expression betrays a sense of despair; either that or barely checked rage. I can hear papers belching out of the machine and rustling onto the floor.

'It won't stop. It just won't stop.'

'Printers are like that,' I say. 'It's in their nature. They print when you don't need anything. And when you really need something printed out, the ink cartridge is empty or there's a sheet of paper jammed inside, the printer tells you it's lost its internet connection or that it doesn't recognise the computer you're trying to print from. If you ask me, the whole idea of a digital, paperless future is down to the fact that printers have driven so many people to despair and insanity. Paper is a good thing; it's beautiful. There's nothing wrong with paper: it feels pleasant in your hand and it's the best way to read something. The only problem is getting those little black marks onto the surface of the paper in the first place. Even with all the modern technology at our disposal it's all but impossible. I suspect – no, I'm absolutely convinced – that the printer companies and the anti-depressant manufacturers of this world are in cahoots.'

'All morning,' says Ilari, now almost with tears in his eyes. 'It just won't…'

'I know,' I say, and we share a brief moment of silence. We look each other in the eye.

When I'm sure I've gained another friend, I return to the reason for my visit.

'I'd just like to check a few details of my booking.'

'Of course,' says Ilari as he wipes the corner of his eye.

'The confirmation only shows our company name, but it doesn't give the names of the guests or the person who made the booking.'

'The reservation was made in person, right here. I remember it well.'

'I'm the CEO of our company.' I open my wallet and give the man my card. 'I still have to confirm the booking.'

Ilari taps at his keyboard, his eyes still moist. The printer is still spilling out sheets of paper, but now Ilari has shared his burden, the printer no longer controls him.

'The names of the guests are in our system, though they're not on the booking confirmation.'

I lean on the counter, stretch out my neck slightly. White block lettering on a blue background.

NORIYUKI KAKUTAMA, MR
KUSUO YUHARA, MR
DAISUKE OKIMASA, MR
MORIAKI TAKETOMO, MR
SHIGEYUKI TSUKEHARA, MR
AKIHIRO HASHIMOTO, MR

Only the penultimate name is unfamiliar. The others I know very well, personally and otherwise.

'And the booking is for two nights?'

'Four,' says Ilari.

I do some quick arithmetic. Arrival on Friday, departure on Tuesday.

'Why does it only say two nights on the confirmation slip?'

'Because that one was made first. This one was made later; it amends the first one.'

'And that booking was made here too?'

'I remember that one too,' he says. 'Quite vividly. The situation has changed significantly, apparently – for the better. Those were the very words, with the same emphasis. And with a smile too. A beautiful smile.'

Ilari smiles. His eyes are still glistening with tears. The overall impression he gives is of a man slightly off kilter.

'Now, I'm going to do something quite unusual and unofficial,' I say. 'But you and I have an understanding…'

I take a photograph from my wallet and show it to Ilari. 'Did this person make the booking?'

Again Ilari smiles. A tear rolls down his tense cheek. He nods.

'Said she'd use her own mushrooms too.'

12

There's a quiet lull in the daily cycle of life on the market square: the morning rush has quietened down and there's plenty of time before the evening customers start to appear. The sun is unrelenting, white and large. Its light almost stings the skin. The thermometer on the supermarket wall shows 28°C in the shade.

I'm sitting at one of the coffee stalls, at the furthest table. At a table on the other side of the cordoned seating area sit two old men in baseball caps – one bright red, the other a faded blue – chatting in a thick Hamina accent.

I haven't picked up the local dialect. It feels more complicated and slower in my mouth than normal spoken Finnish. Which raises a few questions. Isn't the point of slang or dialect to make communication faster and less complicated? I don't know why I suddenly think of such things. Maybe because thinking of anything else inevitably makes me agitated – or worse, which for the moment I'm trying to rein in.

The coffee tastes off, like trying to drink a glass of tepid juice while in the sauna. The sugar crust on the doughnut gleams as though the pastry is sweating.

I've been murdered. The Japanese are arriving tomorrow. Taina has reserved their hotel rooms herself. In all probability she has also taken care of their invitations, and there's no doubt whatsoever that she will be hosting them all weekend. I'm taken aback as I ponder the fact that hurts the most, that touches the rawest, most sensitive nerve of all.

Nobody has consulted me. I have been overlooked, completely sidelined.

So what if someone poisons my food, tries to impale me with a

Samurai sword or dips his wick in my wife? This is something far more serious; moreover, this is personal. Of course, I realise this is the same vanity that makes me pull my stomach in in the company of women. You'd think a dying man would have other things to worry about. My imperfections will die along with me, but until then I can revel in them as before. Until my dying breath, as the saying goes.

Only through an act of concerted will power do I finally manage to look at the broader picture. There must be a reason for the imminent arrival of the Japanese. The obvious reason is the mushrooms. Is there another reason too?

I might imagine that this other reason lies in all the insinuations and half-sentences here and there, the content of which boils down to the idea that I'm not dynamic, curious, modern or bold enough. I've heard this both directly and indirectly from almost everyone I've bumped into recently. For a moment I wonder as to the timing of the visit, as to why the Japanese are arriving right now. Then it hits me.

I'm alive.

By someone else's calculations, I was supposed to be dead by now.

In thinking like this – by imagining I'd died, say, last week – I see the situation in a new light. I have already died and the business has been transferred into my wife's name. The Japanese arrive. Taina negotiates new contracts, of course. Still, a group of six businessmen would hardly travel all the way from Tokyo to Hamina just to talk about the minutiae of a contract. They're coming here because they expect to see something new.

In light of this I go through all the conversations I've had in recent days: what people want and what they are planning. What new concept can they have to offer – to the Japanese of all people? I can't think of anything particularly revolutionary. There are small things here and there, such as Raimo's biodegradable punnets or Petri's van, but nothing cataclysmic. But does it have to be something big at all?

The business and a young lover. Isn't that actually quite a lot already?

Twenty-thousand punnets made of recycled plastic in colours of your own choosing?

A van with a decent sound system?

No.

No.

No.

These aren't the sort of things that Noriyuki Kakutama or Kusuo Yuhara would travel here to see or hear, to experience or … to taste.

I glance down at my doughnut. It seems like it's laughing at me. As though it has just whispered a secret in my ear and is enjoying the fact that I've finally cottoned on. I laugh out loud and look around me. The two old men look back.

'Doughnut's got a wicked sense of humour,' I say and smile at them.

The men hesitate, then give me a friendly nod and return to their conversation. One of them peers over at me again, as if to make sure I'm not dangerous. I take a bite of my doughnut. It is hot and crisp, straight from the oven.

Then I see Raimo.

I find it very difficult to understand Raimo's dress sense. I don't mean his style but the number of layers, the long sleeves, the thick fabrics. In the direct sunshine the temperature must be close to forty degrees, but Raimo is dressed the same way he would in November. My short-sleeved shirt is wet with sweat, both on the back and under the arms, and beneath the booking reservation from the Seurahuone Hotel, which I've folded and put in my breast pocket, the fabric is glued to my chest. Raimo is quite a sight in his suit jacket, his dark trousers and moustache. He walks towards me briskly, the flaps of his jacket fluttering at his sides like an ice-hockey coach who has escaped from the stands. In the open square there's no opportunity for him to slam doors or test the durability of the hinges, but on a general level his movements uphold the same old principles. If the cobbled stones of the market square could speak, they would surely wince with his every step.

'I spoke to Suvi,' Raimo begins. 'She told me you were heading into town. I somehow guessed you'd be here having a doughnut, thought I'd stop off on the way ... Can I join you?'

The metallic chair creaks as he sits down, its legs screeching against the cobbles.

'Would you like something?' I ask and nod towards the coffee stall.

'Those are from Reitkalli.'

'So?'

'I only buy local produce.'

'Reitkalli is three kilometres down the road.'

'Eight and a half.'

'Besides, it's part of Hamina nowadays.'

'I'll never accept those boundary changes.'

'Would it help if I bought it for you?'

Raimo gives a sigh. He genuinely looks as though this is an enormous concession.

'Just some Jaffa, thanks.'

I fetch a bottle of orange lemonade from the counter. Raimo gulps down half the bottle before I've even sat in my chair.

'Damn, it's hot today,' he says.

I look at his attire and say nothing. I'm not going to get drawn into a discussion about summer clothes. Knowing Raimo, we'd end up having an argument that he would feel compelled to win. And I have to conserve my strength in any way possible. I have to choose my battles carefully. That much I have finally come to realise.

'This hits the spot.' Raimo nods, pushes out his cheeks as he belches, blows from beneath his moustache a mouthful of air that smells of old oranges and wipes the sweat from his brow.

'We've got to talk,' he says. 'I was going to bring it up now, but I got a phone call on the way down here and now I've got to drive

... It's such a long story there's no way I'll be able to explain it now. I have a suggestion. Come over to our place in Pitäjänsaari this evening. Let's say seven o'clock? We can have a sauna conference.'

'A what?'

Raimo looks at me. 'Where else do people talk about the important stuff?'

There's no way I can tell him I don't think I'm up to a sauna. I already feel like I could faint at any minute without sitting in his wood-burning sauna in ninety-degree heat and possibly thrashing myself with a birch whisk. On the other hand, this could be the opportunity for something else, something far more important.

'Seven, you say?'

'We can have a sauna in peace and quiet. Hanna-Mari has gone to Kotka with the kids.'

Raimo downs what's left in his bottle. I find myself wondering how much of his dehydration is caused by that jacket. He must sweat a bucketful in this weather. He stands up.

'See you in the steam,' he says.

Raimo marches back to his car, managing not to trample on anyone. I watch as he reverses out of his parking space and turns. I wipe the corner of my mouth and notice that the two old men have disappeared. I walk off back to my own car, which is still parked outside the Seurahuone Hotel. I arrive at the busy southeastern corner of the square.

The bustle of people is primarily down near the Alko off-licence. In the summer months Finland drinks with serious conviction. On a hot July day, the automatic doors open and close as much as they do throughout the whole of January.

At the pedestrian crossing I follow the rules of the road to the letter: look first left, then right, then left again. On the second look to the left my heart starts to race and my legs feel weak. I catch a glimpse of Sami, and I realise instantly that he's moving in the same direction as me – and at the same pace.

There's no mistaking Sami's identity. The man is quite literally a whiter shade of pale: his skin is unnaturally pasty, an effect heightened all the more by the black sheen of his long, straggly hair. He's wearing a pair of white trainers, black drainpipe jeans and a white T-shirt. He could be mistaken for a British rock star of yesteryear, but I imagine that's where the similarities end. I recall what Sanni said about her former boyfriend: *Like every time he tried to hit the ball he hit himself round the head instead.*

I still haven't forgotten my encounter with his sword-wielding business partner. I turn at the corner and head towards the Town Hall. A moment later Sami appears behind me. Thankfully he's moving more cautiously than before and seems to be keeping his distance, and at least for the moment his body language isn't threatening. But he's following me, make no mistake. I count the number of streets and blocks, and calculate the distance to my car. I grip the keys in my hand and wonder whether I could make it if I started running, but I know the answer. I'm already walking as quickly as my legs and breathing will allow.

Sami catches up with me. In my defence this wasn't a foregone conclusion, as I don't seem to be the only one suffering from some form of physiological impediment. Sami is limping on his right leg. I do my best to increase my speed. My shirt is soaked through, and I have to gasp for breath. Moving in this heat is hard work. I glance over my shoulder.

Sami is so close that I can see his expression. It's more anguished than bloodthirsty. I turn at the final corner. The car's lights flicker to life in front of me.

Sami is right on my heels, his white face gleaming. It seems the sweltering heat is as excruciating for him as it is for me. I reach my car; it is parked right in front of the restaurant at the Seurahuone Hotel.

People are sitting out on the terrace drinking beer, taking it easy; some are in the shade, some in the sunshine.

For them it's summer; they are not dying.

I open the door and manage to get inside. Two cars have boxed me into the space in the time I've been parked there – first on my investigative mission to the Seurahuone Hotel, then thinking things through over my doughnut on the square.

Sami raps on the window, crouches down and peers inside. I can't move anywhere, at least not very quickly. His face is pallid and agonised. It strikes me that above all his expression is one of uncertainty. I look once more in the mirror.

The hub of a Subaru is almost right up against my back seat. The back of the red van parked in front is touching my front bumper. In the three and a half years I've lived in Hamina, I can't remember once being sandwiched in like this. Trying to steer myself out of this will take all afternoon. I give in. I press the keys into the ignition and the car roars to life. I don't turn on the motor. I roll down the window and whisper a quiet prayer.

Sami's eyes follow the window as it scrolls down. They rest momentarily on the edge of the door, the space where the window has disappeared. Then Sami raises his head, licks his lips. His eyes are blue, the left one is lazy and seems to be staring at the terrace behind me.

'I'm looking for Tomi,' he says.

His voice is thin and trembling, either from exertion or general rage. I hope it's the former.

'He's not here,' I reply. 'As you can see.'

Sami's eyes scan the interior of the car. I don't know whether he thinks I might actually be hiding his violent bodybuilder friend in the back of my Škoda. He places a hand on the doorframe. The mere fact that his fingers are on the inside of the car feels unpleasant, like a territorial violation.

'He said he was going to pay you a visit.'

'Me? Why would he do that?'

'It was something you said when we were at your office, and something to do with the sword.'

'Is that all?'

Sami appears not to hear my question. He continues to lean on my car door, his white arms are scrawny but sinewy, as I've noticed before. I quickly run through everything that's happened with Tomi. All that, just because I offended him? Then I realise that the sword must have been the straw that broke the camel's back. The sword I touched at their premises. The sword that was meant to cleave me in half. I hope Tomi is happy now: nobody will ever touch his sword again. It is his and his alone.

'He's my best mate,' says Sami.

At first I say nothing. Then I remember what Asko said on the deck of the pub boat.

'Asko said Tomi might have gone to St Petersburg.'

'Asko?'

Sami's blue eyes are glued to my own. He couldn't possibly look at me any more closely. And still his left eye is looking off somewhere towards the terrace.

'I met your boss,' I say. 'At least I assume he's your boss. He came to see me.'

Again Sami licks his lips; they look dry and anaemic. 'Asko doesn't know Tomi like I do. He would have told me if he'd been going to St Petersburg. Tomi told me he was going to pay you a visit.'

I don't want Sami to continue. He's dangerously close to asking logical follow-up questions.

'I'm in quite a hurry,' I say. 'If it's all the same—'

'Why did you run off when you saw me just now?'

Perhaps Sami hasn't suffered as much brain damage as I'd thought. Even so, flattery might still be the best defence in this situation.

'You cut an intimidating figure,' I say, and I mean it. 'You've got a certain … charisma.'

Sami seems to think about this. Then, for the first time that I've ever seen, he smiles. His smile is as skew-whiff as his eyes. It curves upwards on the right-hand side of his face, which only serves to highlight the tautness of his overall expression.

'Keep that in mind,' he says with an air of satisfaction.

I don't plan on asking quite what he's referring to. I nod all the same.

'If I find out that you know something about Tomi and you're not telling me, I'll…'

'I don't doubt it,' I say and flick the switch to start closing the window. The rising window seems to startle Sami and he nervously pulls his hands away from the doorframe.

'We've got our eyes on you, remember that.'

'I won't forget it for a second,' I say.

Sami is still bending over towards me. The window rises and the glass appears between us. Instantly I can breathe more easily. I turn the key in the ignition, reverse an inch and wrench the steering wheel. This is the driving school from hell, I imagine: a three-point turn in front of an instructor hankering for revenge. Eventually I manage to get the front of the car out into the road; Sami is standing so close that I'm worried I might crush his toes. It doesn't happen. Sami remains standing in the middle of the road as I pull away and turn left.

It's lunchtime, but the people of Hamina don't go out for lunch; they drive home or eat a packed lunch at work. The lunch hour in downtown Helsinki looks like a wild carnival compared to what I now see before me.

A leisurely cyclist, a few cars, someone crossing the street with a walking frame. The local pizzeria is open, but there are no customers inside. The large elms in the park stand motionless like enormous, deep-green heads of broccoli. There's no queue at the ice-cream kiosk; the vendor is sitting in a chair on the side nearest the park, her eyes closed, her face angled up towards the sky. The price list has yellowed in the sunlight, the images of the different ice creams fading; what was once banana could now be mistaken for vanilla.

I recall a song in which the protagonist, a young housewife, realises one sunny morning that she'll never drive through Paris in a sports car with the warm wind fluttering her hair. I think I know what she must have felt like. I don't mean that I feel the desire for the big city or to ride in a sports car. And I don't have enough hair – be it in volume or style – for it to flutter in the wind. If we got up enough speed, my hair might just about shift position. I don't believe even the protagonist of the song necessarily wanted all those things – Europe, a fast car, a dashing hairstyle – but what she realises is essentially that life is gone, dreams are only dreams, they never come true, there is only the here and now, and even that is only temporary.

I recall another thought, from one of the great philosophers. The basic idea is that it makes about as much sense to grieve for your own death as it does to grieve for the time before your birth. Of course, this theory isn't entirely watertight. One particular weakness is that before I was born I couldn't conceivably have had any experience of what it means to be alive, whereas when another cycle of infinity begins I will already have had that experience, and this in turn makes relinquishing that experience difficult. It's such a challenge to find any point of comparison for life as we know it, it's painful.

Another weakness in the theory is to do with the time before my birth: I simply cannot remember anything about it. I imagine a similar situation awaits me down the line, an endless cycle of unconsciousness and oblivion. Same old, same old, as they say. It doesn't feel very attractive. It might very well be that this short life is the only one in which I will be able to walk around with my eyes open, to breathe the scent of the summer's day wafting in through the window I've opened again.

My thoughts are confused, but I'll allow myself that much.

How sensible can anyone expect me to be?

Millions of years of nothingness stretch out ahead of me, billions of years are behind me. There's no way of knowing when the next period of oblivion will end: does it end when our earthly life ends, soon or slightly further down the road, or is our collective coma cut short only when the universe begins to turn in on itself, compresses and shrinks to the size of a pinhead? And if that event is the catalyst for the birth of the next universe, does my oblivion start all over again and do I have to wait billions of years until I'm finally woken up … and so on *ad infinitum*?

If and when I'm honest with myself, I have to admit that, with or without eternal life, this universe starts to feel like an unbearably stressful and exhausting place, especially when you think about it more closely. It's like a workplace that you really want to leave, but you don't have the courage because finding a new job might prove too difficult.

I'm distressed, disappointed and agitated. I've never thought about matters like this before. But who wouldn't rather spend their time pondering the nature of infinity and the universe than thinking about the fact that his wife and business partner has invited a group of Japanese associates to a meeting without telling her husband and principal shareholder in the company? And all this after murdering him first?

13

Things in the warehouse are in good shape.

Olli has been meticulous: the machines are gleaming, clean and ready, the refrigerators are humming at exactly the right temperature. Everything is ready for the switch to be flicked; only the mushrooms are missing. Raimo's concerns about the punnets are needless. We have more than enough different boxes and packages. I have a sneaking suspicion Raimo's worries might have more to do with his image of himself, what people think about him as a purchasing manager, how punnet merchandisers see him, how he views his status within the business.

Like everything, this too is only human.

Most things we do have little if nothing to do with anything concrete or necessary but are motivated by what we want other people to think of us. I'm a perfect example of this. I'm caught in a struggle between life and death, and I'm worried what I look like in the process. I remember Sanni and remind myself that I need something from her at the first possible opportunity.

The thought of Sanni causes a sensation that hurtles from my head to the bottom of my stomach and back again, leaving a painful, stinging void in my body. I can see her auburn hair. The sensation is dizzying, almost frightening. Either that or this is another symptom of the poisoning. Or infatuation and poisoning are so similar to one another that it's impossible to tell them apart.

Did I say infatuation? Is that really how I think of Sanni?

The thought couldn't possibly be worse. It's catastrophic. To put such thoughts behind me I try to take comfort in concrete sensory observations. I run my hand along the cool steel surfaces in the dryer, I look at the equipment, the implements, naming and registering them in turn. This takes my thoughts away from her locks of red hair and focusses them in the warehouse with its concrete floor, its metal, stone and brick.

This is my creation. Not only mine, of course, but this is what I have spent years building. And with things as they are at the moment, this is my life, my purpose. I have no heirs and I don't have much time. What I have now is all that will be left of me.

The mushrooms.

At first it sounds small and nondescript, but it's true. And for that reason it's a powerful image. My purpose in this world is to find good mushrooms, to make sure they reach people's tables and mouths, and to build up this little business. I won't go down in history, but still, I have a purpose – one that will last the rest of my days.

My thoughts about the time after my death give me unexpected energy. Looking at things in perspective always helps, even now. Full of newfound energy I march into my office, say hello to Suvi, who is sitting with her back to the corridor and either does or doesn't answer my greeting, and close the door behind me as I sit down to make a phone call. I've barely managed to lift up the phone when there's a knock at the door. But the door doesn't open, as it usually does in this firm the second after a knock. There is another knock.

'Come in,' I call out towards the door, though it feels idiotic.

Taina has never once knocked before walking into my office. And now she's done it twice in the space of ten seconds. Her sleeveless summer blouse suits her and her broad-shouldered frame. Her tanned javelin-thrower's arms are strong and feminine, and well worth showing off. Her thick, brown hair is tied at her neck as though she is about to perform an athletic feat. Her grey-blue eyes quickly fix on my own, and there's a friendly smile on her lips.

I gesture towards the chair on the other side of the desk. The situation feels odd: I'm behaving as though Taina were just another member of my staff. Technically, of course, she is, if you think of the hierarchy of the business. But neither of us has behaved like this in the past.

Taina sits down, looks at me.

'I've been thinking about what we've discussed,' she begins.

'What bit exactly?'

'Everything,' she says. 'Absolutely everything, darling. I don't even know where to start, what order to put things in. But I've been watching you these last few days and … thinking. About you. A lot. And I'm sure, given a little time, you'll see things the same way as I do.'

'If you mean the things I said about the business…'

Taina shakes her head. Not the way you shake your head when you disagree with someone, but the way you shake your head when you want to stop the conversation running off at a tangent. The movement is gentle but firm, full of a sense of adult certainty. I don't know if I have any better options than to wait and listen. And so I wait and listen.

'When I rubbed your shoulders last night I realised what this is all about. I saw it, understood it, and to be honest I felt it in your body – something I've suspected for a while now. You fell asleep, by the way. I sat and watched the rest of *The Biggest Loser*. It was Harri, the blond guy, who won. He'd lost thirty-eight kilos after his divorce. And when the presenter comforted him, he explained he lost another six and a half while he and his wife divided up their belongings. Then I put a blanket over you and decided I'd do it in the morning.'

There's a sense of warmth and concern in Taina's voice – as if she cares and wants to help. It's more marked than I've heard from her for years. Maybe more than I've ever heard before.

'And what is it you decided you're going to do?' I ask.

Taina turns to look at me. Her round, watchful eyes are attentive, full of a sense of genuine concern.

'You're exhausted, darling. You need a holiday. Right now. And I've organised one for you.'

Apparently I can't even die quickly enough. That's my first thought. My wife wants to send me away because I haven't died in the timeframe she'd imagined. I keep my eyes fixed on hers, which now look like they could belong to a nurse with the gentlest bedside manner.

'Really?' is all I can manage.

It's not the cleverest of questions, not even the most challenging, but it buys me some time.

Taina nods. 'Starting today,' she says. 'I insist.'

'That's impossible. We've already agreed…'

'Jaakko, honey bunny, listen to me.'

I look at Taina and do as she asks: I listen. Again, I have a few seconds to think.

'You've been acting very oddly recently. At first I thought you were having some kind of midlife crisis…'

'I'm thirty-seven years old.'

'Exactly. But now you come home at all hours, you talk about the strangest things, the police visit our house because they suspect you of theft, and then there's your erratic behaviour at work. For a while I was worried that you'd gone mad – totally lost the plot. But then I read an article about burnout and I realised what was wrong with you. And last night you fell asleep mid-sentence, while I was rubbing your shoulders.'

'What sentence was that?'

'Excuse me?'

'What was I saying when I fell asleep?'

'That doesn't matter. Something about some heavy lifting you'd been doing, and that's why your back was so stiff.'

'Then what happened?'

'I went to bed upstairs, but I couldn't get to sleep. Because I was thinking of you. You, Jaakko.'

'You lay awake because of me?'

'Yes. But then I found the answer. We're going to give you a little time off.'

'How much time off?'

'A long weekend to start with.'

I look at Taina. I understand my wife. She's in a tricky situation.

It seems I simply won't die quickly enough. The Japanese are on their way, and I'm supposed to be dead and buried by now.

'Where would I go?' I ask her.

'To a spa. I've booked a suite at a hotel in Tallinn. The ferry leaves Helsinki tomorrow morning. If you like, I can book you a hotel in Helsinki for the night too. That way you can enjoy a spot of nightlife.'

'Nightlife?'

'Visit the old bars and restaurants.'

'They're all gone now.'

'You know what I mean,' says Taina. 'Have some fun, take it easy, rest and recover.'

'I'm not burnt out.'

Taina gives me a warm smile, raises her hand and stretches out her forefinger. 'The article I read specifically says that a person suffering from burnout is the last to recognise the problem. You're showing all the symptoms. I can see it, poppet.'

Poppet? Seriously?

'I've told the staff to cancel their plans and be prepared to work all weekend. What will they think if I swan off to a spa in Tallinn at the last minute?'

'Of course, we won't tell anyone about the burnout. You're the main shareholder in this company. You have better things to do than crawl around in the forest. We'll just say you're on a business trip.'

'That doesn't answer my question,' I say. 'How will we get all our work done?'

Taina's eyes are still friendly, emanating warmth, but she's nervous too. I can tell because I know her. To some degree, at least.

'So that's settled then,' she continues. 'Shall I confirm the booking?'

'Why this weekend, specifically?'

Taina does her best to conceal her frustration, but a hint of tension appears in her body language nonetheless.

'Because this weekend, specifically, you're so exhausted, darling. Not last weekend. Now. You need rest *this* weekend.'

'It sounds like you're really worried about all this.'

Taina nods as though I've finally hit the nail on the head and we are now both about to win a fantastic prize.

'I am,' she says, stressing both words. 'Very worried.'

'Perhaps I…'

'That's right, darling.'

'But who…?'

'The rest of us, that's who. All of us. Together. You know that I know how to run this business. You won't have to worry about anything at all.'

Taina stands up and walks round the table before I have a chance to hide my email account from the computer screen. She stops behind me, places her hands on my shoulders and rubs gently, stroking and pressing; it's almost a caress. The last time this happened was during the first four months after we started dating, and even then possibly only once.

'And when you come back,' I hear from behind me, 'we can reassess the situation in a fresh light. You've been carrying so much responsibility that the stress has seeped into your body. These shoulders are rock-solid with tension.'

They're rock-solid because there's a cheating murderess standing right behind me.

'You're so funny, my little cuddlekins,' she continues. 'The rest of us know a thing or two too, you know.'

'I don't doubt it for a second.'

'Shall I book some treatments for you too?'

'Treatments?'

'At the health spa. Massages, baths, saunas, thermacare, facials, foot rubs, the barber?'

Taina sounds like a walking advert for the place. I hold back my answer.

'Perhaps you're right,' I say once I think I've kept her waiting long enough. 'Maybe I'm a bit stressed. What say I think about your offer?'

Taina's hands stop mid-stroke, then start again, rubbing gently.

'You're always so resistant to things, Jaakko, darling. Even things that are good for you. Particularly things that are good for you.'

'I'm not being resistant,' I say. 'It's just I don't want to burden you with all these things. You're in your element when you're thinking about new tastes and recipes. But running the business – I'm not sure you really want to take on so much work, so much responsibility and worry. There are many things you might not have given any thought.'

Taina's hands are no longer moving. I can feel their warmth, the tips of her fingers like hot needles. Then the sensation of her warm breath caressing the top of my head, the place with only a few wisps of hair, and her soft, moist lips as they press against my scalp.

'Silly-billy,' she says, her lips tight against my head. 'I've thought of everything. This is for your own good. A few days' rest and everything will look different.'

The only way to get Taina out of my office is to promise – multiple times – that I'll think about it and tell her soon.

How soon?

Very soon.

Taina steps towards the door, her hips swinging, letting her bottom wiggle as she goes. I've never seen anything like this before. As she reaches the doorway she looks back and smiles. As well as a sense of compassion, there's a clear sexual undertone to that smile, a promise. It's a perplexing combination. I'm not used to seeing such things from Taina. I've never had promises like that from other women either. Not in all my life.

I don't know how to respond, so I turn back to my computer and wait for the door to shut. When I hear the latch click into the keep I breathe out the pent-up air inside me, lean back in my chair and release my grip on the armrests as though I've just survived an emergency landing.

Was this all about sex? I don't think so. Surely not. Of course not.

I realise I'm probably not the most skilful or passionate lover in the world, but I'm sure I can't be the worst. To my knowledge my strategic measurements are average. I haven't literally got out the measuring tape, but I've spent enough time in saunas and changing rooms to know that, though I've nothing necessarily to brag about, I've nothing to be ashamed of either. My stamina is about as good as it can be without chemical enhancement: I might not be a cross-country endurance skier, but let's say I can last longer than a commercial break. I might not have the body of a Chippendale, but I've got a good sense of rhythm. Or at least so I've heard – and not from Taina. When was the last time we made love? Last weekend perhaps. That's right. If you ask me it all went very nicely, everything from the foreplay to the final round, and I think we both got something out of it. Maybe this isn't just about sex after all. That makes Petri's part in all this rather more interesting than I've imagined until now. What if he's not a brainless penis after all, who runs on a single protein shake from Midsummer to Christmas?

I don't have time to give the matter much thought before the phone rings.

Detective Inspector Mikko Tikkanen's voice sounds every bit as pleasant on the phone as it does in person: he talks in a friendly way as he cunningly fishes for information. No, I'm not too busy, I tell him, though I doubt anything I have to say – or whether I'm busy or not – would have any bearing on what he proposes next.

'I'd like you to pop down to the station. Straight away, if that's okay.'

'What's this all about? Can't we talk over the phone?'

'I prefer talking face to face.'

I don't suppose it matters what I prefer, I think to myself. This is a matter of finding the right balance: I don't want to arouse suspicion, but I don't want to sound too keen either.

'If you tell me what this is about, I can think about it on the way over.'

'Just a little routine chat. Great that you can make it at such short notice.'

Tikkanen hangs up. I look at my watch and think about my state of health.

Though my doctor is on summer leave, he answers the phone almost instantly. In the background I can hear a rabble of small children, high-pitched yells, screams of joy, perhaps the sounds of a day at the beach, the whoosh of wind in an open space, waves even, the crashing of water against the shore, the movement of the sea. I wonder whether these are the doctor's children or grandchildren. It's hard to guess his age. But that's not why I called.

I introduce myself, and the doctor says he recognised my number.

'I'm glad you called,' he says straight off. 'I've just received some new information. How are you feeling?'

I tell him I feel surprisingly well. Physically, that is, though mentally…

The doctor seems less interested in my mental wellbeing as he all but interrupts me: 'That conforms with what we already know. Your most recent samples have all been tested now, and to our surprise what we now see is a hiatus of some sort. We can't say whether this is the body's own defence mechanism or a decrease in the levels of toxins and the elements causing the poisoning, though ultimately it doesn't matter either way. What does matter, judging by what you've just told me, is that the poisoning has stabilised somewhat.'

Before I can ask a follow-up question, a child squeals, a wave breaks against the sand and the doctor continues.

'This is very similar to what we often see with cancer patients. Through a course of treatment, and sometimes for an undefined period of time, certain toxins reach a stage when they are simply dormant.'

The doctor pauses for a second.

'Of course, this doesn't mean they are worsening or that they have disappeared,' he adds. 'It's simply a matter of the timetable and the speed at which things will eventually take their course.'

That is the answer to my follow-up question.

'But for the time being…?' I ask.

'You could say that right now you are as healthy as you can possibly be. Until one day you are not.'

The police station is a child of its time. The 1990s will not be remembered as one of the golden ages of Finnish architecture: the prefabricated sections of the building are in such bad condition that even looking at it is excruciating. On the inside the station is dark and claustrophobic, and the smell of poor construction instantly catches you in the nostrils. I stand in the foyer for a moment, breathing in microbes that must surely be a health hazard, and listen.

A door opens along a short corridor and Mikko Tikkanen cranes his head into view.

'You got here quickly. Come on in.'

With this he disappears back into his office. I walk up to the door and step inside.

The room is small and reminds me distinctly of the doctor's surgery: a light-coloured desk, on the desk a computer, Tikkanen in a chair behind the desk and an empty chair opposite him. He gestures me towards the empty chair. I sit down and glance to my left. On the wall are two shelves lined with folders alternating between red and blue but with no indication as to their contents. On the right-hand wall is a free calendar from the local supermarket, opened at the wrong month. This office could belong to any number of businesses or organisations.

Tikkanen himself doesn't look much like a detective inspector. He is wearing a black AC/DC T-shirt bearing the dates and venues of a tour, and his sunglasses are casually propped on his forehead. The police badge dangling from his neck is the only sign of what this meeting is about.

That and the way he looks at me.

'Do you mind if I take notes as we go?' he asks, tapping at his computer keyboard.

The situation is a repeat of our recent phone call: Tikkanen appears to ask me questions, but will still do whatever he wants and what he has already decided. Nice to be here, I might have said if the situation and the atmosphere were different. I still haven't forgotten the little piece of theatre that took place outside the station only yesterday: the conversation between Tikkanen and Petri, which I watched from the other side of the square, behind a herd of tourists. The knowledge of their little rendezvous lends the situation a paranoid nuance all of its own.

'Let me just write down your name, the date and time, and the fact that you've come here today voluntarily,' Tikkanen says. 'Then we can get down to business.'

Other than the sound of Tikkanen's fingers on his keyboard, I can't hear anything else in the building. There's a good chance we might be the only two people here. Tikkanen stops typing, looks at the screen for a moment, clicks the mouse, leans his head to one side as if to align himself with an image on the screen, purses his lips and gives the mouse a few more assertive clicks. When he is happy with what he sees, he turns to look at me.

'Did you know Tomi Alatalo?' he asks.

Straight out, just like that. I note his use of the past tense.

'I don't think I know the surname,' I begin. 'I'm not sure I've ever heard it.'

'Tomi Alatalo: used to work for the Hamina Mushroom Company. A big guy, blond, the bodybuilder type.'

'I've met him. I can't say I know him in any way.'

'Are you aware that he's been reported missing?'

'Yes. His boss told me.'

'Asko Mäkitupa?'

'Correct.'

Tikkanen types something into his computer. Now I see that he is touch-typing. So much for all the jokes about policemen. Again he turns to me.

'What kind of conversation did you have?'

'What do you mean?'

'Asko Mäkitupa is a competitor of yours. Now, I don't know anything about the mushroom business, but I assume there's an element of competition just as with any other line of business. I'd imagine – if you'll allow me to speculate – that, if a competitor pays you a visit and wants to talk about one of his employees, it must be a matter of some importance and will have an impact on what kind of conversation ensues.'

'Asko invited me for a pint.'

'Where did you go?'

'The pub boat in Tervasaari. The top deck. The furthest table from the shore. I was sitting facing the harbour and the open sea.'

'When was this?'

'Yesterday, around this time in the afternoon.'

I'm taken aback at how quickly everything is happening. It's simply not true that before you die your life plays out in front of your eyes like a sped-up film reel. This is all happening so quickly that following the film would be impossible.

'And?'

'Asko told me exactly the same things. He hasn't seen Tomi either. He thought he might have gone to St Petersburg. Apparently he does that from time to time – disappears suddenly and eventually lets you know he's in St Petersburg. Or he only lets you know once he gets back. I can't remember which.'

'Didn't this puzzle you?'

'That someone should travel to St Petersburg? Not really.'

'That your competitor Asko Mäkitupa should visit you and ask you where one of his employees is.'

'I misunderstood.'

'Why do you think he imagined you might know something about it? How would Asko Mäkitupa get it into his head that you know something about his employee?'

Despite my initial reservations, I'm starting to like Mikko

Tikkanen. He is doing his job, trying to find out what's going on while most people he meets tell him anything but the truth. I can relate to that. I don't want to lie to him. All I have to do is leave out a couple of things. I wonder whether he was sitting here in this office, the windows behind the Venetian blinds looking out into the courtyard, while right outside Tomi and I were doing laps round the Town Hall.

'I'd touched his sword,' I explain. 'Tomi's Samurai sword. I believe this annoyed him. And as far as I know he — Tomi, that is — had spoken about his feelings to Asko, his boss.'

Tikkanen was about to turn to his computer. His hands stop in the air, his fingertips hovering a fraction above the keyboard.

'So you admit you stole the sword? Yesterday you denied it.'

'I still deny it. I've never stolen anything in my life. I lifted the sword from its display case on the wall and held it in my hand. Then I put it back. That's all.'

Tikkanen's fingers are still hovering in the air.

'Is there anything else you've told me in the past that you'd now like to amend?'

I shake my head. 'No.'

'Nothing at all?'

Tikkanen looks at me, his fingers almost touching the keyboard. For some reason it makes me think of a finger tensing round a trigger.

'No,' I repeat.

Tikkanen continues to scrutinise me for a moment, then his fingers move across the keyboard, fast and practised. He stops, reads what he has written and turns to me.

'When you met, did Asko tell you the story of his friend who jumped off a bridge?'

I nod.

'In truth, the story didn't quite go the way Asko might have told you.'

'Didn't his friend jump and die after all?'

'The friend died all right,' says Tikkanen. 'But whether he jumped by himself is another question. The Similä brothers weren't both at the top of the structure at the same time either. Kalle only climbed up there once Ville had already jumped. Or fallen. Or was on his way down. Kalle didn't see how the jump or fall took place, though he later claimed he heard Ville say something – something like, "Don't, for Christ's sake, there's a log down there", or something to that effect. Later on it transpired that Ville had pinched Asko's girlfriend some time before the incident. Of course, this might just be a chain of unfortunate coincidences. Ville might have jumped by himself. Kalle might have heard him wrong. Kalle might have heard right too, that Ville saw the submerged log and Asko pushed him off the bridge in revenge for stealing his girlfriend. Who knows? At the end of the day we only have Asko's account, so that's that. Just so you know.'

Someone has lowered the temperature in the room. I feel cold. Tikkanen has shifted in his chair to face me fully. He is sitting slightly askew, propped on his left elbow.

'What do you mean, just so I know?' I ask.

'Exactly that,' Tikkanen replies. 'Just so you know. In case you're planning on getting involved with Asko.'

'And why would I do that?'

Tikkanen looks at me, his eyes clearly trying to read me.

'We found Tomi Alatalo this morning just off the coast. Caught up in a pikeperch net. A few amateur fishermen were out there early this morning. At first they thought their luck was in, they managed to haul in the net just enough to see the shape of a man and something shiny, then reported it to us. Because this is an ongoing investigation I can't tell you any more at present.'

I say nothing. Tikkanen moves his fingers slightly, silently tapping the arm of his chair. On the surface he looks slightly bored with our perfectly amiable conversation. Of course, it's quite the opposite. And I have to say something. I can't simply walk out of his office in silence; at this juncture that would arouse more suspicion than anything else.

'I don't plan on having anything to do with Asko,' I say eventually. 'I have no reason to do so.'

Tikkanen slowly shrugs his shoulders. 'Let's hope Asko doesn't decide otherwise.'

'Why would he do that?'

'Tomi has disappeared, Asko pays you a visit and asks his whereabouts. What do you think Asko is going to do now that Tomi has been found?'

I've got to give Tikkanen credit; he's spun this web very cleverly indeed. He hasn't said he suspects me of anything, he hasn't even suggested that he's interrogating me or that this is in any way an official interview. But here I am, caught between Scylla and Charybdis. I don't answer immediately, and Tikkanen doesn't appear to be in any hurry.

'Was there anything else?' I ask.

Tikkanen holds out his hands.

'Unless there's something else on you mind,' he says.

We look at each other. I shake my head. 'I can't think of anything.'

'Very well.'

I'm about to stand up.

'One more thing,' says Tikkanen. 'I'd like you to stick around town.'

I stand up and find myself looking down at him. 'Of course. Why would anyone leave Hamina at this time of year?'

Tikkanen leans back in his chair. 'My thoughts exactly.'

The back of my shirt is wet and cold, and it's glued to my skin. I pull it down, turn, and I've almost reached the door when I remember something that's been on my mind.

'About Asko's story: it sounded important to you, important enough for you to correct his version.'

Tikkanen looks at me from his chair at the other side of the room. Thin strips of light filter into the room through the blinds behind him. He is about to say something but hesitates. It's a brief moment, barely perceptible at all, and the first of its kind – that I've seen, at least. He quickly regains his composure and says:

'It's good to know who you're dealing with, don't you think?'

14

At first the tub of ice cream feels like a lump of winter in my hand, but it quickly warms. The ice cream melts at the edges and eventually comes apart in the centre too, soft and milky. I read the text on the side of the tub: free, happy cows, merrily milked milk and joyfully churned butter, Grandma's old biscuit recipe and bananas from the family farm. Of course, none of this is remotely truthful.

Afternoon arches towards evening. The sea seems bluer the longer I watch it. I try to see the end of the earth but it hurts my eyes, the horizon becoming first uneven then blurred. You can't see all the way to the end of the world.

As I left the police station I imagined I knew what paranoid people must feel like. At first I couldn't even count the number of people I thought were openly hunting me down or otherwise plotting my downfall and ultimately my death. For a moment I sat in the car, frustrated, and waited for the end, either to be arrested or to be struck down by an assassin. When nothing happened, and the end didn't come, and the car started to feel unbearably hot, I stopped off at a kiosk and drove down to the shore.

There are plenty of things I count obsessively, but not calories. I need energy, and ice cream is the only food I can think of that doesn't make me feel nauseous. Maybe my internal organs are so traumatised that only sweetened dairy products are gentle enough for them. I open another tub of ice cream: chocolate made with cocoa beans grown on a mountainside in the southern hemisphere, English toffee made with a secret recipe handed down through the generations. The world isn't built of steel and concrete after all; it's made of sugar and candyfloss.

About halfway through the tub I manage to get my thoughts back on track.

I go through my conversation with Tikkanen, his tone of voice, his cunning, leading questions and his fleeting moment of hesitation. I think of my meeting with Raimo, his sudden invitation for a sauna conference, the fact that Taina is preparing to host the Japanese and wants to send me out of town in the name of care and compassion. I think of Asko's story, the possibility that he's a coldblooded killer and experienced at extracting his revenge. Tikkanen appears to realise that I know more than I'm letting on about Tomi's fate, but he seems to have decided to hide his time. For what, I don't know. And I don't even want to think about how Sami will react to the news that his best friend has been dredged up from the sea, impaled on his own Samurai sword.

I'm well aware that whatever I plan, I'll probably end up having to improvise; there are simply more variables in play here than anybody could hope to control. On the other hand, if we have the strength and desire to think about the situation from a wider perspective – like a blue, open sky and the sea stretching out before our eyes – life has never been more exciting and eventful. I've flicked through women's magazines and watched Taina's favourite chat shows long enough to know that people have an innate desire to *feel* things, to gain *experiences*.

Am I out for revenge?

The thought has crossed my mind. Sometimes it's swirled through my mind like a blood-red flag in a brisk wind, at others it churns like a black bog hole sucking up everything in its path. Naturally I want some form of justice, I want to get even. But then again, what I want most of all, and what I hope I will have enough time to see through, is to rescue my business. I cannot let it fall into the wrong hands. I will not sit back and watch from the sidelines as it is destroyed – even after my death.

Today Sanni has started working for our competitor. I try to call her, but she doesn't answer. I take the booking confirmation slip from my shirt pocket and read once again through the names of the guests I've written out. I have an idea and note it down.

The second ice-cream tub is empty. I place it on the ground next to the first one and adjust my position between the rocks. The terrain near the shore is a mixture of uneven grass and rough sand. It takes a while before I am lying comfortably. My aim is not to doze off but to think, but as so often in life, thinking proves too much and I find myself in a dream in which I'm fighting off a horde of faceless men with ice-cream tubs as weapons.

The reason for the men's lack of faces becomes clear: their heads are ice-cream tubs. I try to run away, but it's futile. My stomach aches, my legs won't carry me, my shoes sink into a mire of ice cream. All of a sudden I pick up a sword, long and gleaming. I slice, snap and lance the ice-cream men, and I'm no longer standing in ice cream but on a jetty, my very own jetty, and the ice-cream men are nowhere to be seen. It's a beautiful, calm summer's evening. The sword is still in my hand, but now it feels heavy. I lift the sword and see Taina's head cleft in two.

I bellow and fumble at the air as I snap wide awake.

The shade of the sky has changed; it is now one degree, two degrees darker. The wind has gathered pace; I can feel it as soon as I raise my head from between the rocks. There's a sickly taste in my mouth, a milky sock knitted to the top of my palate. I lean against the boulder for a moment and pull my phone out of my pocket. It seems I needed that rest: I've been out cold for several hours.

Raimo Lavinto, our acquisitions officer, lives in the Pitäjänsaari neighbourhood. The district is located on an island on the other side of the Tervasalmi bridge. At its narrowest point the distance between the island and the mainland is only twenty or so metres, but nonetheless the atmosphere and surroundings change dramatically.

I've heard people call Pitäjänsaari a fantasy island, and I can understand why. The houses are mostly old, some built over a hundred years ago, and some of the original wooden buildings are quaintly slanted with picturesque low ceilings – so low that anyone of average height has to stoop as they step inside. The houses with their red and yellow walls, gardens and jetties, renovated and completed over the years, are like something straight out of a history book.

Raimo lives in a house just like this, right at the end of a peninsula on the northern side of Pitäjänsaari. Though the houses on the island are relatively close together, Raimo's property has plenty of privacy: the attractive red-painted log house with its gleaming-white window frames cuts off the view from the road, while an oblong sauna-cum-barn, erected long before the advent of modern building regulations, means nobody can see in from the bay either.

I drive round to the yard behind the house, turn the car on the gravel and reverse it in front of the garage. The garage door is locked; Raimo's car is doubtless inside. I step out of the car and wait for Raimo to appear from somewhere or to hear his deep, resonant voice coming closer. All I hear is the sound of a motorboat passing.

Smoke putters from the sauna chimney. Perhaps it's not smoke, just a wave of warmth that refracts the air and softens it, doing to the blue sky what crazy mirrors at the fairground do to people's faces. Raimo is warming the sauna; after all, he's invited me for a sauna conference, and the stove needs wood. The luscious, tended garden rolls down towards the shore, and to the left of the sauna a jetty strides a long way into the blue waters. Halfway down the garden an unimpeded view of the bay opens up before me.

A wooden boat is heading out towards the open waters. It is about ten metres long and looks like it might have once been a fishing boat, before being adapted for recreational purposes with an extended cabin up top. I wonder what it would feel like to ride in one of those, on my way to beautiful, rugged islands, free of my present concerns, many of which are of a distinctly and painfully permanent nature. The thought is so attractive – the low rumble of the diesel motor and the rush of water against the prow so enticing – that I very nearly set off swimming after the boat. Instead I walk across to the sauna and am about to call out Raimo's name when I hear a text message beep in my pocket:

'Jaakko, had to fetch the wife. She's ill, can't get the bus. The sauna is heated. Use it. Key is under the porch rug. Let's talk tomorrow. Raimo.'

The garden is empty and silent. The trees and buildings protect me not only from prying eyes but from the wind too. The evening sunlight takes me in its arms. The flowers are fragrant, the sea too. Now I can only hear the sound of the boat if I concentrate hard or imagine even harder. I won't use the sauna, heated or not.

All the same, I stoop to lift the key from beneath the porch rug, unlock the sauna door and step inside. The dressing room is immediately in front of me, the door into the sauna to the right. I peer inside.

It's an old-school sauna: no shower, no separate washing facilities. Fresh water is brought directly to the building via a hose, and the barrels of water look to be filled and ready. The stove is in the middle of the far wall. It is large, and so is the hatch in the front of the stove. I guess the temperature is just about right to bathe, and the thermometer on the wall confirms my estimate, showing around 84°C. Raimo can't have left long ago. I step towards the stove, crouch down and use a ladle to prise open the hatch; I don't dare touch the metallic handle with my bare hands.

The heat that surges out of the stove almost knocks me on my back. The live coals glow bright red. Raimo clearly takes the task of heating the sauna very seriously indeed. I adjust the position of my legs, transfer most of my weight to the balls of my feet and begin to stand up. At the same time I turn and feel a wave of dizziness. The combination of the heat and the exertion is too much after all. I stumble and stagger to the left, towards the window. The water ladle is still in my hand, and as I lurch forwards it pulls the stove's hatch wide open.

What occurs next happens with such extraordinary speed and such inexplicable force that it's almost as if every movement, from the start of the sequence of events to the very end, was optimised and attuned to perfection.

The axe is perhaps the heaviest and most expensive wood-chopping implement in mass production. It weighs four and a half kilos, and in addition to the razor-sharp blade, the pole widens at the ends. This is the king of all axes, the Bentley of the wood-chopping world. I know this because I've considered buying one for myself. I've held one in my hands at the hardware store and swung it a few times to find out what it feels like. The difference between this and a standard axe from the supermarket is about the same as the difference between an aircraft carrier and a rowing boat, and moving the thing is similarly deadly: once the speed and direction of the swing has reached a certain point, stopping or turning it is out of the question. The axe will stop only once it comes into contact with its target, and when that target is reached, it will be annihilated.

It's a good thing I stumbled and staggered to my left for support.

The axe comes to a halt against the footstool right next to me. The wooden slats explode in splinters, the axe goes straight through them and smashes against the concrete floor, which cracks too under the force of the blow. The axe grinds against the ground as I fall on my side, the sauna ladle still in my hand.

Next the blade of the axe approaches me from the side.

I've underestimated Sami.

His scrawny frame and his music-student's pallor notwithstanding, he packs a lot of force behind the axe. Only then do I understand the reason why: the former baseball player is using the axe like a bat. He understands the laws of physics, probably without being able to name a single theory. The blow from the side whooshes towards me as I try to regain my balance. Stumbling randomly is in fact the best way of avoiding the blade: from the hitter's perspective my movements are unpredictable and don't follow a predetermined trajectory, such as that of a ball thrown by a pitcher or a log placed firmly on the spot.

The axe slices the hairs from the top of my head, I feel the brush of the blade at the point where my hair is thinnest. On its way it leaves a painful graze on my scalp. Which, of course, is preferable to life without my forehead.

The axe comes crashing into the wall of the sauna.

The wooden panelling – the beautiful, darkly varnished boards – smashes apart like a jam jar. Again I manage to clamber to my feet. I'm still stooping, and there are two reasons for this: I feel very faint indeed and guess this is a more advantageous position for me at the moment than standing up with my back straight.

Sami's movements are erratic. In addition to his limp and his lazy eye, he appears to be suffering from a profound, immutable rage. But he certainly knows how to hit. He handles the axe as though he is getting ready for a force play and spins the weapon so deftly into position, ready for another blow, that the mere sight of this would have most people fleeing for their lives. Except I can't go anywhere. Sami has positioned himself right in front of the door.

Again the axe slices through air. This one is clearly a switch hit.

Sami tries to plunge the axe through my head: the blade comes down from above and will rebound upwards again, and the contact with the ball – in this case, my skull – will be as low to the ground as possible. The aim is to strike the ball very powerfully so that it bounces up as high as possible and travels a long way, so that the player waiting on third base has enough time to run home before the ball can be returned.

I doubt, however, that my head will bounce anywhere at all if the axe makes contact, at least not in one piece. I grip the sauna ladle in my hand as I lunge forwards and upwards at an angle. I only have enough energy for one leap; my vision is blurred, the electric shocks have returned, and I'm short of breath.

Sami's movement is so loaded that it carries him with it in the same way it carries the axe. The blade cuts through the air; his hands move in an arc, and Sami moves with them. The axe misses me. I stand up, see Sami in front of me, and charge towards him. I raise the ladle in an attempt to hit the axe from his hands. I hit hard and miss both the axe and his hands. I strike Sami somewhere around the head. He dives forwards. The doorway stands like a dusky gate ahead of me.

Head for the door.

I concentrate on making my legs follow my instructions. My body moves.

Sami passes me as he falls forwards. The ladle must have given his motion plenty of added momentum. I hear crashing, clattering, a bang, and knock into something I assume must be the wall. I collapse and hope I am already in the garden.

The shorn grass scratches my cheeks. Ants tickle my neck. The evening sun is filtered through the thick birch trees, casting long, languorous fingers of light into the garden and along the walls of the house. The air is heavy with the smell of barbecued sausages. My mouth is so dry that it feels like it belongs to someone else. My senses awaken one by one, my limbs too. I move my arms and legs. They're all intact.

My first attempt to stand up is too quick, too abrupt. The second is more cautious. It is successful, though I have to prop myself against my knees. Eventually I straighten my back. It seems I am halfway there; the house and the sauna are equidistant, and I am probably in the very centre of the property. I listen for a moment, try to look for movement in the garden or the sauna building. I cannot see or hear anything. Not a breeze in the trees, not a boat in the bay or cars on the street. Nothing.

The day is reaching an end, and the sea looks darker now. The door to the sauna is open. At first I think I should dash back to the car and escape, but then it dawns on me that if Sami were still hunting me down, small pieces of me would already be smeared across the lawn. I walk gingerly, my sense of balance has still not entirely returned. On the veranda outside the sauna I look over my shoulder; nothing about the view has changed.

In the sauna the temperature has dropped. The door has been left wide open – for how long, I can't say. The axe appears to have flown high into the upper boards. Sami is resting on the floor, his body stretched out. All except for his head. His head and shoulders are lodged inside the sauna stove.

Back in the garden again, at first I think of calling for an ambulance, but I don't make the call. Sami's head is nothing but a charred lump: a gnarled, rounded ember which only seems to be attached to the rest of his pallid, glowing body by a trick of Frankensteinian ingenuity. A defibrillator will not revive Sami now, and I'm not convinced the kiss of life would do much good either. I think of calling Raimo, but that's an even worse idea: either Raimo is somehow involved in planning all this or he knows nothing about it whatsoever. In either case, I have nothing to say to him. At least not right now. I even consider calling Tikkanen, but getting the police messed up in this would mean getting the police messed up in everything else too, and I have no more desire for that than I have time on my hands.

And now for Sami.

15

I bury Sami behind the sauna.

He lies beside me as I sink the spade I found in the garage into the soft earth in the strip of land between the sauna and the sea. I am hidden from the bay by a thick tangle of bushes, and by the tall reeds and birches standing along the shore. From the garden I am completely hidden behind the sauna building. The strip of land is about five metres wide, and Sami's final resting place will be much nearer the sea than the sauna. This is simply to maximise my cover from prying eyes. I cannot afford another unfortunate slip like there was with Tomi. I work fuelled by a bottle of orange Jaffa I found in the sauna.

Digging a grave is slow, hard work. Every spadeful of earth – first a skimming of black topsoil, then a denser, moister layer of dark-brown sand and gravel – must be individually removed from the ground and lifted to the side. I've kept the turf in a separate pile; I'll try and landscape the grave as best I can once I'm finished. I don't believe Sami will remain in his grave forever, but I'm going to do everything I can to make sure he stays there for as long as possible.

I'm sweating, the palms of my hands are chafed, my arm muscles ache and my back is stiff. At times I have to lean against the wall of the sauna and hope I remain conscious. At first I consider trying to conserve energy and burying Sami bent over double like an Olympic diver, but the idea soon feels inappropriate. And so I dig a tradi-tional-shaped plot, though it takes much longer.

Eventually the hole in the ground is a metre deep and about Sami's length. I'm standing up to my waist in another man's grave when a text message beeps on my phone. I wipe my hands on my shirttails and pull the phone out of my pocket:

'Best sauna in the world, don't you think? Bet you've never felt steam like it. Swing the ladle for me too! Raimo.'

I clamber out of the pit. I had to pull Sami here by the ankles. He's left a trail of soot across the sauna floor, the patio and over parts of the lawn, as though someone has drawn across the landscape with a thick black crayon. There's plenty for me to clear up once I'm done with the burial. I take hold of his ankles again and pull him a little further, stopping at the edge of the pit to gather my strength. I count to three, then haul the body up and drop it into the grave. Sami falls a metre and thumps down on his back. In both length and width, the measurement is perfect.

Filling the grave is a much quicker affair than digging it. I don't glance downwards until Sami is covered in at least half a metre of mud. When I finally look down, all I can see is a dip in the ground that could have been caused by all kinds of gardening work. I fill the rest of the hole, stopping several times to stamp the earth more firmly into the ground.

I seem to have forgotten that, like all of us, there's a certain volume to Sami's body – whether we're above ground or below it – and that volume is considerable. There's so much excess soil that I have press it down many times. Finally I arrange the clods of grass on top.

In the early-evening dusk everything looks passable. I hope Raimo doesn't have any business behind the sauna in the next few days. If the weather forecast and my own instincts are correct and it rains at the weekend, this should soon look like a perfectly average strip of waste-land – the kind that you'd find in almost every garden in this town.

Back in the sauna I use the hose to clear up. The hose is long enough that it reaches out to the patio and the garden. I turn the water on full blast, and soon Sami's charcoal smudges follow the rest of his body down into the earth. I put things back in their place, pick up the bottles of soap and shampoo, the sponges and sauna cloths that have flown here and there, return the ladle to the water pail, close the sauna hatch, clear up the splinters of wood and tidy the hole in the wall. Despite my best efforts, the wall still looks like it's been struck with an axe, and there's little I can do about it. And as for the axe, I'll have to decide whether it belongs in the house or whether it was brought from outside. I decide to take it with me.

Not perfect, I surmise as I look around, *but good enough*.

I close the door, replace the key beneath the rug and walk back to my car. My legs are trembling with the exertion. I drop the axe into the boot. In the boot's light I notice my own hands and realise that I must look a miner. I'm covered from head to toe in mud, sweat and grime. I peer at my face in the side mirror: I look like I've been crawling through the mud rather than digging it up. I wash my face, my hands and arms in the barrel of rainwater at the corner of the house. I pull off my shoes, my socks, my shirt and trousers. They could belong to a three-year-old who has spent a few hours playing in a mud pit. I stuff the bundle of clothes into the boot next to the axe. I'm holding my phone and standing in nothing but my underpants.

The situation isn't ideal, but when was the last time things were ideal? I wonder.

Again I cross the Tervasalmi bridge. Once I reach the mainland I turn back towards Tervasaari and drive all the way to the end of the peninsula. The parkland area is empty and darkened, so I take my dirty clothes and the axe from the boot of the car and stuff them into a large rubbish bin used by hikers and visitors whose boats are moored in the marina. My things will blend in naturally with the general waste. The heavy axe hits the bottom of the bin with a dull thud. I walk back to the car, drive off and call Taina. She has never sounded so thrilled to receive a phone call from me. I explain that I want to take her up on her offer.

'You're right,' I say. 'I'm stressed out. I need some rest.'

'Oh, Jaakko, yes you do,' Taina sighs, her voice heavy with relief. 'That's exactly what I've been trying to tell you.'

'I'll leave this evening. I won't be coming home.'

A short silence.

'Are you already on your way?' she asks. 'Where are you?'

The next time you try to murder your husband but fail to time his death right, I feel the urge to tell her, *the next time you drive your dying husband out of town so that you can steal his business associates while trying to play the caring, compassionate wife, try and make your little performance sound at least remotely credible. Now I can hear your barely restrained glee in every syllable.*

'Just setting off,' I say. 'But I think I'm heading in the right direction. I wanted to confirm a few things about the weekend's schedule, because it looks like it's going to rain.'

'You're on holiday now, darling.'

'It feels bad not to be out there picking the harvest with everyone else. Especially as I was so determined to get everybody to work overtime in the first place.'

The seat belt chafes the skin between my chest and shoulders, my back is stuck to the chair, the pedals feel hard and stiff beneath my bare feet. Driving around in your underpants is far more uncomfortable that you might think.

'What kind of silly-billy wants to talk about work when he's about to enjoy a night out in Helsinki followed by a relaxing weekend at the spa?'

'You're probably right.'

'I know I am.'

'I'm sure I'm worrying about nothing.'

'As always.'

'Have you heard anything from Raimo?'

This time she doesn't hesitate. 'Raimo? Why's that?'

'Just wondered. I think he said his wife was out of town, that she'd come down ill and he had to go and fetch her.'

'And what about it?' Taina sounds genuine. Or rather, she genuinely sounds as if she couldn't care less about Raimo.

'I guess it's nothing,' I say. 'How were you thinking of dividing up the picking sectors?'

'Who's almost on holiday?'

'I am.'

'That's right, sweet pea.'

Sweet pea?

'But if someone asks me where you are, then I might be able to give them an idea of where to find you.'

Another short silence.

'I can't imagine anyone will ask you things like that,' Taina replies eventually. There's a distinct note of impatience in her voice. She notices it herself, corrects it immediately and returns to sounding like she's coaxing a child to eat his greens.

'Don't worry, darling. I'll email you everything important. How about you concentrate on enjoying yourself and thinking about all the wonderful things in store for you this weekend?'

The evening is warm and still, the shadows deep and black. The air is soft and brooding, as always before heavy rain. I focus my eyes on the house, look first in the mirror then straight ahead. I can't see movement anywhere. I listen, but cannot hear a sound.

The gravel hurts my soles. This path wasn't designed for bare feet. I proceed with difficulty, swaying from one side to the other and lifting my feet unnecessarily high off the ground, though I realise this is pointless. I can only imagine what I must look like in my underpants, which only this morning were clean and white.

I make it into the garden and onto the lawn. The grass feels heavenly. After the rough gravel of the path this feels like walking on a mattress covered with downy blankets. I can see the illuminated windows, the empty rooms. I climb up the stairs, ring the doorbell, and I'm about to pull my stomach in again, but even to me it now feels like such an absurd thing to do that I give up on the idea. I don't believe for a second that a puffed-out chest will replace the need for an explanation. And indeed it does not.

Her expression isn't quite as perplexed as I might have expected.

Sanni folds her arms across her chest and leans a shoulder against the doorframe. A warm glow surrounds her. Her hair is loose and falls at both sides of her face, casting a shadow across her eyes. I note that she doesn't ask me inside.

'Maybe I should have called first,' I suggest.

'Or put some clothes on.'

I nod. 'Are you alone?'

'Would it be reckless of me to say yes?'

I wave my hands by way of an explanation. The gesture comes naturally, but I realise immediately that it must look like I'm showing her what's on offer. I don't know whether she can see the redness in my cheeks in the soft glow of the dusky evening and the electric light shining from inside.

'I'm in a bit of a jam, if I'm honest. I need some help. I could really use a shower and, if it's okay, I'd love to borrow some clothes. Until tomorrow. Then we have to talk about Asko and the Hamina Mushroom Company. And a few other things. I have a suggestion.'

Sanni is wearing the same thin, baggy red T-shirt as this morning. The grey jogging shorts fit the general aesthetic. I can't stop thinking about the underwear episode earlier this morning. Then I realise it's my turn to speak.

'And that suggestion would be…?' Sanni asks.

'Not here,' I say and show myself off again. 'It's the suggestion of a boss to his employee.'

Even worse, I think to myself, and I'm about to correct the situation when Sanni interrupts.

'Taina has thrown you out, hasn't she?'

I wasn't expecting this. The sudden change of direction has an almost physical impact, one that I only appreciate after it's happened: I experience a similar Neanderthal moment to the one earlier this morning and instinctively straighten my posture, suck in my stomach and reposition myself in a more manly fashion at the foot of the porch.

'In a way,' I say. After all, it's almost true: Taina has driven me out of town; that if anything is surely tantamount to throwing me out. 'All in all it's been quite a puzzling evening.'

For a moment we stand in the balmy summer air. Then Sanni turns away.

'The bathroom is the first door on the right.'

Even the shampoo has added protein. That's what it says on the bottle. I can't begin to imagine how the protein travels from your hair to your biceps, but I use plenty of it just in case. My legs won't stop trembling, so I sit on the floor of the shower. First I aim the showerhead at my mouth and guzzle down the water. Then I rinse off.

At first a puddle of grime forms around me, soil and sand rinsing from every part of me: my hair, my ears, even my nose. At the ends of my fingers are ten black waning crescents; each of my cuticles has to be scrubbed. Finally I am clean. I haul myself upright and dry myself on a thick, citrus-scented towel.

Sanni has left a T-shirt and a pair of jogging bottoms on the washing machine for me. I pull them on. The jogging bottoms are the right size, but so tight around the backside that I daren't look in the mirror to see what I look like. The pastel-green T-shirt is the right fit, but there's no denying the low-cut neckline feels somewhat awkward.

Sanni is sitting on the living-room sofa and watches as I walk into the room. There's a floor lamp directly behind her. The warm, low lighting catches her red hair and bare legs.

'Tea?' she asks and nods towards a wide-rimmed mug set on the small coffee table. 'I'll bring you a cup too if you want.'

I shake my head, say no thank you, and sit down in an armchair.

The living room is small, almost like a den, and pleasantly dim. A brown, comfy-looking sofa, a dark-wooden bookcase, full of books and framed photographs, on the floor a long, wide rug. From among its patterns I can make out a tree, birds with colourful tails perched on its branches. On top of the rug and right in the middle of the room is a table with sturdy legs. Old-fashioned, Taina would call it. Cosy, I'd say.

'Do you need a pair of socks?' Sanni asks once we've stared at one another for a few quiet seconds.

'I don't think so,' I say and glance self-consciously down at my feet. 'Seeing as I don't have any shoes either.'

'Seems you left in quite a hurry.'

'You could say it came quite out of the blue,' I admit. 'Did you meet Asko today?'

Sanni nods. 'I showed him my harvest schedule. And apparently tomorrow I'm going to meet one of his Japanese contacts. Asko wants to show him everything we can offer: we'll take him to a few spots and show him how we harvest, where the mushrooms come from, and reassure him that our produce is organic and top quality.'

'Him? There's only one? Not more? He didn't say *them*?'

'We were both speaking Finnish. I'm quite sure he said we'd take *him*, not *them*.'

'Did Asko tell you the name of his contact?'

Sanni shakes her head, drinks some tea. The rim of the mug is as wide as her face; her chin disappears behind the china.

'What else did Asko tell you?'

Sanni places her mug on the table. 'He said you're up to something,' she says nonchalantly, as if she were talking about the weather.

Sanni pulls her feet up onto the sofa. Her legs are pointing towards me. Her eyes have been fixed on me all the while, but now it's as though her gaze suddenly sharpens. I keep my hands on the arms of the chair, move my toes across the soft, pleasant surface of the rug.

'Anything else?' I ask.

'*Are* you up to something, Jaakko?'

We look at each other. Then it hits me: a fatigue that stretches through my bones like an ache without a specific location. I'm utterly exhausted, I've used up every last vestige of energy. I've been at the police station, in the sauna, in a grave. No matter how stable my organs might be right now, they are still far from normal. I can feel the darkness approaching. I have to act fast.

'I am up to something,' I say. 'Of course. I've asked you to spy for me. I've also visited Asko and his friends' premises. Asko thinks I've stolen one of their swords. You probably noticed the swords on the wall.'

'It would be hard not to notice them. Asko seems passionate about them. It seems they have something to do with the arrival of the Japanese contact. Did you steal his sword?'

'Of course not.'

'Asko thinks you did.'

That means Asko still hasn't heard about Tomi, and when he does find out, will he demand to get his sword back, and will it be released to him, and if it is released to him will I once again have to worry about being imminently dismembered?

'What else does Asko suspect?' I ask.

'He doesn't think you'd give me up, not that easily.'

'Did he say that?'

'It was more a case of reading between the lines.'

I remember what Sanni said about waking up and seeing things differently.

'I'm not surprised,' I say. 'He probably sees a lot of potential in you.'

'What about you, Jaakko? What do you see?'

A beautiful and ambitious red-haired woman with gleaming legs; a woman I have to decide whether I can trust.

'Where did you suggest starting the harvest?' I ask.

Sanni stares at me. It's hard to isolate the foremost emotion in her eyes: a cold disappointment that I've brushed her question aside or a quiet consideration of everything that our collaboration might entail.

'At Onkamaa,' she says. 'There's a good mix of pine forest, fields, meadows, undergrowth, a few decent hillsides and a logging zone. It's the best place – the best combination of factors, and the best if we assume we'll be going there right after the rain, perhaps even while it's raining…'

'While it's raining?'

Sanni nods. 'Asko said that we're playing with the big boys now.'

'He really said that?'

'I took it in a gender-neutral way. I guess all he meant was whinging snobs shouldn't bother.'

'Exactly,' I say and try to muster some strength. Even sitting down requires strength. I lean my back more firmly against the chair. The effect is twofold: it gives me more support but it makes me sleepy too. The armchair is soft, it sucks me in. The room seems dimmer than a moment ago. 'That's probably what he means. What's the latest weather forecast?'

'It could rain quite heavily starting tomorrow afternoon.'

'And it's tomorrow you're taking the guest into the forest?'

'Weather permitting, if the guest shows up and if Asko says so.'

'Hang on,' I say. 'You, Asko and the Japanese guy? Nobody else?'

Sanni looks as though she has just remembered something. 'Now that you mention it, I wondered about that too. Why hire a minibus when there are only three of us and we'd all fit perfectly well into my car? I guess Asko was counting on Sami and Tomi being there too. That would make five.'

I think about this for a moment. Sami and Tomi are clearly not going mushroom picking any time soon. But perhaps Asko wasn't counting them after all. That means he must have other passengers in mind.

'Send me a text message as soon as you know anything. This is important. I mean, it might be important.'

Sanni says nothing. There's a faint shadow across her eyes, but still I can see a glint in them, a burgeoning question in the angle of her head. I'm so tired that I release my stomach into freedom, one centimetre at a time. Despite all my notions to the contrary,

I've been sucking the beach ball in, trying to puff out my chest and broaden my shoulders, but right now it feels too much like hard work. The green mound above my tummy swells and gleams in the soft light.

There are moments when, in all its sheer wretchedness, the unfettered embarrassment of middle age can surpass even death. This is one of those moments, and I should know what I'm talking about. I don't imagine Sanni expects me to say anything in my defence, though. And what would I say if she did? *I'm always home in time for dinner. I enjoy my food. I have a soft spot for sugary doughnuts. I'm dying a fat death.*

'What happens next?'

Sanni's question wakes me from my slumber, from my pitiful self-flagellation.

'Then we'll have a clearer idea of what Asko is actually planning,' I say. 'We'll have a better overall picture of things. And we'll save this business.'

Sanni's hair is now covering her face almost entirely. Light falls from above and behind her. Her hair hangs either side of her face like a set of curtains.

'And are you going to answer my question?'

I look up at the spot where I guess her eyes must be.

'Asko is right,' I say, and I mean it. 'I'm not going to give you up that easily.'

Sanni explains to me how we will conquer whole cities one at a time. We'll charm the leading restaurateurs, start delivering to specialist outlets, provide tasting expeditions to exotic locations across Finland. And if someone doesn't want to come to Finland, we will take the Finnish forest to them. One influential figure at a time, one *matsutake* at a time, one tasting at a time…

'We need to work through some of the details,' she continues.

'Especially if Taina, who has been in charge of all the tastings, has just thrown you out.'

It's only temporary, I tell her. I leave out the fact that I'm referring to my entire marriage and, indeed, my life, the transitory nature of which is highlighted all the more now that the poisoning has entered some kind of stasis. I add that organising tastings is only a secondary concern. First we have to take care of what's most important.

'Sanni,' I say once I truly fathom my current situation. 'I really need to rest.'

'You mean you need to sleep?'

Sanni jumps up from the sofa before I have the chance to ask what else the word rest might mean. I hear a cupboard door opening and closing, then Sanni's steps as she returns to the living room and places a pile of bed linen on the table. I look at the sofa. It's too short. It's soft and doubtless very comfortable, but it's far too short. At the same time I compare it to the place I might have been resting if I wasn't so lucky in the sauna. The sofa looks good. I gather my strength and stand up.

'Will you be all right with these sheets?'

'I'm sure I'll cope.'

We look at each other. Sanni's eyes are blue-green and beguilingly gleaming in the dim of the room, the kind of eyes that I find myself instinctively latching onto and only notice I'm doing it once my eyes are there. At first I think I haven't been like this with anyone but Taina for years; but then I ask myself, *Like* what *exactly? I'm only going to sleep, right?* Sanni makes me say and do and think things that confuse me. And she probably knows it.

'You know where the bathroom is, and the kitchen. If you need anything.'

'Thank you, Sanni. Good night.'

'Good night.'

And again we find ourselves looking at one another and again a few, silent seconds pass between us.

Then I ask her the question that's been plaguing me all evening.

'How do I know you don't have these exact same conversations with Asko?'

'I do,' she says. 'But for the time being you pay me better.'

Exhausted or not, I'm a bit startled. I see a smile on Sanni's face.

'I'm teasing you, Jaakko,' she says and turns away. And when she has almost disappeared from view, I hear her in the doorway. 'And I see a lot of potential in you too.'

16

PEOPLE I KNOW:
– NORIYUKI KAKUTAMA
– KUSUO YUHARA
– DAISUKE OKIMASA
– MORIAKI TAKETOMO
– AKIHIRO HASHIMOTO

PEOPLE I DON'T KNOW:
– SHIGEYUKI TSUKEHARA

The morning light makes the trees, the lawn and the bushes shimmer green, it shades and colours every leaf, every stem and petal individually and in its own unique tone. From right to left, from east to west, second by second, minute by minute, the garden flickers into flame as the morning sunlight touches the flowers, the fire spreading until the whole garden glows, flares and rises into the heights as though engulfed in flames.

I leave the window, return to the kitchen table and stare at my list.

I've woken early, as the sun was rising. It doesn't feel bad at all. I'm not tired. My mind seems oddly light. I'm happy that I'm not dead. I don't know what happiness is, but I imagine it must be intrinsically linked to being alive. I take a sip of tea. I'm not in the habit of drinking tea, but then again neither am I in the habit of being murdered or waking up on Sanni's sofa.

I feel my stomach and ribs, look at my tongue and throat in the mirror. My insides aren't exactly painful, and I don't feel nauseous, but I think I notice a small change, a certain slowness, like driving a car that still works but that is losing horse power little by little, slowly but surely.

After the names, I write down their respective jobs.

- Kakutama, director.
- Yuhara, quality control.
- Okimasa, marketing.
- Taketomo, logistics, preserving, storage.
- Hashimoto, retail.
- Tsukehara … No idea.

As I search for information on Tsukehara I notice that the battery on my phone is down to two per cent. I need to recharge; I need my phone. There's a charger next to the toaster but it's a different model and doesn't fit my phone.

The wall clock says it's thirteen minutes past six.

If I leave now I'll be at the office in a few minutes, there won't be anyone else there at this time and I can pick up the spare charger before the shops open at nine. I'd be well advised to avoid the centre of town. Moving around in public, there's always the danger I'll bump into somebody I don't want to see right now, as I'm officially at a spa in Estonia.

I creep silently into the hallway and look at the selection of shoes. Sanni's feet are like those of a small animal: her shoes are so narrow and short that as far as I can see the only things that would fit into them are small paws. I'm a large-footed man. I go through the shoe rack, the hallway shelves. Eventually, in the closet by the front door, I find a pair of men's rubber boots, black, size forty-eight. Next to the other shoes on display they look like items of furniture. I estimate they've been used once at most. The stains are distinct because the boots are otherwise so pristine and black. I don't quite know what to think. I pull on the boots; they come up to my knees. I examine myself in the mirror: long, shiny boots, a tighter than tight pair of jogging bottoms and a flimsy T-shirt with an open collar. I'd rather not contemplate what I look like.

At the front door I realise something else too. I can't drive my own car, as I mustn't be seen in it. The keys to Sanni's car are on the hall table. I slip off the boots, return to the kitchen and leave a note. I wish her good morning and explain I'll have to borrow her car. I return to the hall and leave.

Sanni's car smells better than mine. Having said that, it's perfectly possible that my memory is still tainted by the deathly reek of yesterday's journey. I take the roundabout route to Teollisuuskatu, turn right just before the bridge at the end of Mannerheimintie, and in a matter of minutes I'm outside our offices. There are no other cars in sight.

The warehouse is quiet and empty. This morning it feels like a church, and I know why: because it's my church. I'm just about to head off towards my office when I see that an orange light is on above the door of one of the drying machines. I can't hear the hum of the machinery, so the drying process must be in its final phase, probably with only a few minutes left. I am about to step into the drying area, but on my way I catch a glance of the wall clock. I turn on my heels; I'll have to be quick.

The charger is on the shelf. I wrap the cable round the plug and am about to leave when I hear the sound of footsteps. There's something familiar about them, their gentle, breezy gait. I relax. I can explain this. I walk towards the steps, appear from the side and give a cheery hello.

Olli was in full stride across the warehouse, like a man on a mission, but now he stops and turns. The light shines in through the windows behind him. He says nothing. Whenever he manages to remain quiet for a moment the uncanny resemblance to George Clooney becomes all the more pronounced. The spell is broken as soon as he opens his mouth. I begin to understand his numerous divorces: I can see the beginnings of relationships, the middles and the ends: grand dreams, perfect misunderstandings, eventual shipwrecks.

'Morning,' I begin.

'Is something wrong?' Olli asks me.

'No,' I reply instinctively. 'Of course not.'

'You're here early.' There is an implicit question in Olli's statement. I realise that.

'I had to pick this up,' I say and raise my hand. I don't know whether Olli can see what I'm holding, but perhaps that's not so important. There are far more pressing matters at hand… 'Olli, you and I need to have a little talk.'

Olli says nothing.

'All right,' I say eventually, once the silence has run to more than just a few seconds. We are standing about four metres away from each other, almost in the centre of the warehouse. 'I shouldn't be here at all.'

Silence.

'Taina thinks I'm in Tallinn. I must ask you not to tell anyone you saw me here this morning. Not today, not ever.'

Olli visibly relaxes; a heavy burden lifts from his body. He gives a few nods. 'Women,' he scoffs.

'No—' I begin but cut myself short as I realise that this is my chance, this is the better option. Keep this. 'Tell me about it. Women.'

'Taina threw you out.'

It's not a question. Olli is the second person to assume that Taina has thrown me out. Why couldn't I be the one that threw her out?

'Planning on shacking up with her young lover boy, is she?' he asks without a pause.

'Hard to say,' I begin, and I'm about to correct his first misunderstanding when Olli provides a third.

'Then you'll have nothing to worry about in Tallinn,' he says. 'That's the way it goes. While the cat's away, the mice will play, eh? I could give you a few addresses if you like.'

'Thanks, but actually…' I stammer before realising that if I just agree with everything Olli has said I can both stall the conversation and steer it in the direction of my choice. 'A few addresses might do me a world of good.'

'What goes around comes around, mate,' he says. 'And vice versa. Will Taina be continuing at the firm?'

The question genuinely catches me off-guard.

'What?'

'If your bird's banging the delivery boy, you can't very well keep her on at the company.'

I look at Olli.

'The delivery boy?'

Olli clasps his hands together, rubs the thumb of his right hand between the thumb and forefinger of his left hand. At first he looks me in the eyes, then looks to the side, and finally lowers his gaze altogether.

'Since you told me about the situation, I've been keeping my eyes open,' he says.

'Keeping your eyes open?'

'Over there,' says Olli with a nod towards the office. 'Up against the filing cabinet. Petri was holding her up in the air … He's a young lad, strong as a stallion, probably does it fifteen times a night…'

'Olli,' I interrupt him. 'Did they notice that you were … keeping an eye on them?'

Olli shakes his head. 'All that moaning and groaning, the slapping and flapping and…'

'You haven't told anyone else about this, have you?'

Again Olli looks me right in the eyes. He seems determined, assertive, like a man who knows what he's doing and what he stands for.

'In this matter I'm on your side one hundred per cent.'

I make Olli swear to discretion regarding every aspect of our encounter: he hasn't seen me, hasn't heard from me; Taina and Petri are colleagues, nothing more, nothing less, people about whose private life Olli knows nothing whatsoever. Besides, Olli doesn't know anything about what's been going on here. I'm about to leave the building when Olli remembers the list he promised me.

I let him compile it, though the clock on the wall is ticking away, the movement of its hands growing quicker and more blasé with each passing moment, the minutes becoming shorter before my very eyes. Olli is reminiscing, I can see that he's trying to taste the memory of his experiences. He nibbles the end of his pen, taps it against his lips, drifts to a place far away. I'm worried that if I try to hurry him this will only slow down the process; worse still, it might cause tension in our newly found brotherly friendship.

Olli finally straightens his back and surveys what he's written. It takes several full minutes to read through the few lines of text, and it takes all my will power not to wrench the piece of paper from his hand and run out of the door. Eventually my patience is rewarded and Olli hands me the paper. As he does so, he looks me up and down.

'I'd change your clothes before setting off, though.'

Sanni mixes muesli and yoghurt in a bowl, then dribbles some honey over it straight from a large pot. Outside the wind has picked up. A rain front is approaching. The only remnants of the morning sunshine are occasional glimmers behind the thickening clouds. The weather is turning quickly now. Sanni closes the honeypot and presses the lid down with both hands.

'You stole my car,' she says. 'And now you want me to give you free clothes.'

'I borrowed your car. And I'll pay for the clothes. As soon as I find my wallet.'

My wallet is either buried along with Sami or in the rubbish bin at Tervasaari. I've made a few mistakes, I'm aware of that. But I can't really blame myself. I'm a first-timer: I'm not accustomed to hiding bodies or destroying evidence. The situation is new and surprising. The same applies to my entire life, as I've now learned from bitter experience. Everything is happening for the first and last time.

'I'm pulling your leg again, in case you hadn't noticed.'

'I hoped you were.'

'But I have to ask: Why can't you pick up your own clothes at home while Taina is at work?' Sanni's blue-green eyes are sharp and alert from the word go. 'Wouldn't that be easier and cheaper than buying a whole new wardrobe?'

It's impossible to keep anything secret in this town, I think to myself. Here even the dead are brought back to life, and there has to be a suitable explanation for everything. Sanni looks at me, I hear the movement of her dainty jaw, the crunch as her white teeth grind through the nuts, raisins, flakes and dried fruit. I look her in the eyes and tell her about Tallinn, impress on her that I am actually there though in fact I'm sitting in her kitchen, that I mustn't be seen anywhere or by anyone. I can't quite read Sanni's expression, though now I can see the whole of her face. Her red hair is tied in a ponytail.

'Your shirt is an L,' she says as she prepares another spoonful of muesli. 'Your shoe size about a forty-five. Your jeans are a thirty-eight waist and a thirty-two length. Taina must really want you out of the picture.'

'Maybe get an XL, just to be on the safe side. Forty-five shoes are good, and the jeans are just right. And yes, the further away the better.'

'What does it feel like?'

'The new clothes?'

'Being thrown out of home.'

I shrug my shoulders.

'I don't know,' I answer honestly. 'I've been thinking about it myself. For the time being it feels like a natural development of what came before.'

'You don't look particularly devastated.'

Sanni has finished eating and is dunking a tea infuser in her mug. I think about her words.

'I'm not really.'

The tea infuser clinks against her bowl of muesli. Sanni pushes it to one side, props her elbows on the table on both sides of the mug.

'Don't tell anybody, but the day I got divorced was one of the best days of my life.'

'I promise.'

'The best thing about it,' Sanni continues and runs the tip of her tongue across her lips, 'was putting him behind me. Saying that out loud feels almost criminal – the idea that putting somebody behind you means more than meeting them or the time you spent together.'

'It might feel like that,' I say, and assume that at this moment in time I am the one of us who has a better idea of what is criminal and what isn't. 'But I don't think speaking out loud is the worst thing a person can do.'

'I felt so free, so happy,' she continues. 'I wanted to throw a party.'

'Right.'

Sanni raises her eyes from her mug of tea and seems to return to the moment, to remember that she's talking to a man who turned up at her door in nothing but his underpants, covered in mud.

'I'm sorry,' she says. 'All I'm trying to say is that there's a positive side to everything.'

'I understand,' I reply, and I mean it. 'You're probably right. I just haven't had time to think of it like that. But if … if I'm not devastated, like you said, I'm certainly surprised.'

'You've got your whole life ahead of you.'

I frown at Sanni.

'Okay, that was a cliché,' she says. 'And it sounds corny, but that's the way these things go. I promise you, when you look back on this and think of Taina, you'll be glad it didn't come to anything more.'

'Anything more?'

'How long have you two been together?'

I tell her about our dating and our seven-year marriage. Which is now over. There. I've said it myself. But, of course, that's not the whole truth. This is more about … Sanni's phone beeps. She picks it up and looks at it.

'Asko,' she says. 'The guest has apparently landed in Helsinki.

That means he'll be in Hamina in a few hours. Asko says he'll text me when he needs me. You were saying…'

'At least three different things. I need to borrow a car. You'll have to keep me up to date. And I need those clothes.'

Sanni goes clothes shopping. When she gets back we head off to her brother's place to borrow his car. It gives me time to think about what I've said, to think about Taina, my marriage. It's true to say I'm not devastated. I've been plenty of other things: befuddled, enraged, jealous, revengeful, disappointed, angered, even nonchalant. But these emotions have simply passed through me; I can't seem to hold on to them anymore.

Does this mean I never really loved Taina in the first place? Of course it doesn't. Surely not. But the longer I think about it, the more uncertain I become. I stare out of the window. I've moved my car as close to the house as possible, only the back end can be seen from the road. I'd better not move around in the yard – there's too much of a risk I'll be seen, though Sanni's house is at the end of a quiet cul-de-sac. I've noticed the way information can move through this town faster than through fibre-optic cable. And besides, Sanni's house feels homely.

At first it feels somehow wrong to consider it more homely than my own home, but I soon realise that this too must change. If I continue to live, I'll move out of my house. Can I really call home the place where I saw my wife riding Petri in the back garden? I don't think so. The truth of the matter is that before long I won't just be dead, I'll be homeless too. Perhaps this should shock me more than it does. The fact is it barely moves me at all.

The good thing about death is that as it draws closer many things I used to think were important lose their significance. This doesn't happen the way you'd think or the way you hear people saying: that your loved ones become more important, that money loses its meaning, that the spirit of god (or God) and an appreciation of an eternal afterlife flickers into being. In my case my loved ones have become my enemies, the success of my business is now the most important thing of all, and the flame of eternal life is merely something that burns Sami to a crisp and glows like an ember, slowly simmering as it awaits us all. My own thoughts scare me. People don't know the depths of their own minds until they start to think about things like this.

Sanni's car pulls up in the yard.

The clothes are the right size. I don't know how it's possible. I don't think I've ever looked this relaxed and stylish: light-brown knee-length shorts, a red-and-blue checked shirt and a pair of black-and-white Adidas trainers. I look like an affluent tourist.

We set off to fetch the car. We don't speak on the way. I sit in the back seat so that I can lie down, out of sight if necessary. Once we get out of town I sit upright and look around. Sanni explains we'll take the longer route, just to be on the safe side. Asko's ex-wife, whom he visits from time to time and with whom he sometimes spends the night – don't ask – lives at the end of a road off the more direct route.

And so we drive along a stretch of dirt track, the landscape sloping off on both sides into large sandy meadows, some of which are now covered with undergrowth and small, attractive ponds. Young spruce trees grow along the shores and verges around the ponds. The ponds seem deep enough to swim in, the largest of them the size of several tennis courts. These small coves are like miniature versions of the paradise beaches in faraway countries. If I were still a boy, these sand dunes would provide the perfect setting for countless adventures.

The sky darkens, the wind gradually catching at the boughs of the trees.

Sanni takes a left onto an even narrower road. We drive along this track for about five minutes, until we turn right and find ourselves in a yard. We step out of the car and walk into a garden set between a wooden house and two smaller outbuildings, all painted yellow. The fourth side of the garden is open and faces the river. We are at the top of the embankment. A steep slope leads down to the river, which has almost entirely dried up after weeks of hot, dry weather. Sanni glances at me, looks me up and down and gives me an approving smile, content with how she has styled me.

Matti appears – from where, I couldn't say; perhaps from the gap between the house and one of the outbuildings. We shake hands. Matti is slightly older than Sanni, his eyes brown and intense. He has no hair at all and, like his sister, his build is similarly slim and sporty. He and Sanni have clearly already spoken about the matter, because we head directly towards the garage at the end of one of the outbuildings.

Matti is obviously sizing me up. It's perfectly understandable. He's about to lend me his car, and out here a car has a significance all of its own; people think of them differently from the way people in the big city do. Out here a car is something almost sacred – more sacred and more untouchable than … Perhaps I should reassure Matti: lending someone your own wife isn't without its problems either.

The garage door opens. It's not quite what I was expecting.

17

The Lexus is a sports-car model, and almost brand new. It is expensive, luxurious, top of the range. At first I'm horrified, then I realise that Taina won't pay the metallic-coloured car the slightest attention. On the outside it looks like any other small car. Only a closer examination reveals what it really is – that and the sound of the motor if I put my foot down any heavier than usual, as I did accidentally while pulling out of Matti's yard.

I pull the Hamina Baseball Club cap that Matti has lent me further down on my forehead: if Taina decides to look closely in the car mirror, I'm just a strange man in a strange car. That said, I doubt she'll be worried: I'm in Tallinn, nobody else is interested in what she gets up to.

Somewhere nearby the rain is already pummelling the earth with all its strength. I think of how I'm going to tell Sanni I'm dying. At some point I'll have to break the news to her. Even today she's mentioned all the big European cities, talking about them and our mushroom business in the future tense. At the same time both my kidneys are sore and sensitive to touch. The stasis can't last forever. Of course it can't. Nothing is permanent.

I see Taina.

She shrugs her large black sports bag from her shoulder and into the boot, then gets in the car. She reverses out of the driveway – our former garden – and the tyres grind the earth as she turns the car and drives off. She's dressed in a relaxed and stylish way, just like me.

And at that very moment, what has been forecast for so long finally happens: rain.

The first fat, aggressive droplets splash to the earth with the promise of more to come. Then they become denser and more regular. Soon the ground is black, the road gleaming, the lights of passing cars refracted by the water. Rain, finally rain. After days of close, muggy weather this is liberation, salvation, and not just because of its effect on the air. I can almost hear the mushrooms growing in the forest.

Taina's driving is calm and uneventful. Following her is easy, I think as my phone rings. I look at the name of the caller and answer it.

'Hello, darling,' says Taina. 'Are you already in Tallinn?'

I stare at the rear lights glowing red up ahead of me.

'Not yet.'

'Is it raining there too?'

'Pouring,' I say. 'I was just thinking this will do wonders for the mushrooms.'

'The timing couldn't be better. But you don't need to worry about things like that. Did you have a nice evening?'

Yes: I buried a man, crawled through the bushes and spent the night on a sofa.

'Mostly places I've been before,' I say. 'A few surprises along the way.'

'That sounds nice, dear. It sounds like you're still on the ferry. I can hear the engines and the rain in the background.'

'I'm driving in the rain. Listen, I forgot to mention this, what with everything else going on: Sanni has handed in her notice.'

Taina is waiting to turn left at the intersection; a passing car splashes a puddle of water up against her windscreen.

'Really?' she says. She doesn't sound like someone whose business has just lost one of its most important employees. 'Well, I'm sure she's given it a lot of thought and she's doing what she thinks is for the best.'

'I just thought that, because this is so out of the blue and comes at such a critical time, it might have quite an impact on our operations. The harvest is largely Sanni's responsibility…'

'We know where the mushrooms are,' she says abruptly, and perhaps even she is surprised at how quickly the answer comes out.

We're driving along the edge of the market square, slowly. In front of us are people either looking for a parking space or trying to get out of one. The traffic is essentially at a standstill. 'What I mean is, we don't necessarily need Sanni.'

'She might be moving to our competitor,' I hazard. 'The Hamina Mushroom Company. You know – Asko and his buddies.'

'I know, I know. I'm not worried about them. What can Sanni offer them? More of the same. That's not what we need now. And for the last time, darling, you're raving about work when you're supposed to be resting. I've got to go now. Have a lovely weekend.'

The rain falls like a silver curtain right in front of the car. We start moving again.

'Taina?'

'Yes?'

'I think something's happened between us,' I blurt out. 'Of course, I don't know whether it's been there for a while and I've only just noticed it, but that's the feeling I've got.'

Straight ahead, turn to the left, then edge to the right: Taina steers the car to the edge of the pavement, almost at exactly the same spot as I did when I visited the Seurahuone Hotel. I drive past her as she speaks again.

'Sounds like you really need this holiday, darling. Have a nice day. Talk soon.'

The Japanese arrive. A minibus pulls up in front of the Seurahuone. I'm not at all surprised to see Petri in the driver's seat. I watch as the group files out of the bus, and I recognise all of them except one. I assume this must be Shigeyuki Tsukehara. He is the same age and as stylish a gentleman as Kakutama, the man I know as the company director. Both are in their fifties, both are wearing a suit and tie.

Petri is running around with an umbrella, trying to protect the men and their suitcases from the downpour. This is not easy, because there are six men in the delegation and there seems to be some confusion with the suitcases. Petri dashes here and there, carrying pieces of luggage and holding out an umbrella. Eventually he gives up and stands on the spot in the rain. He looks as though he's just been swimming fully dressed only to find himself in completely the wrong place at the wrong time.

Taina is standing at the door of the Seurahuone. She exchanges air kisses with the men as they step inside the hotel. A moment later the street is empty and the men installed inside, doubtless the focus of Taina's welcome speech.

Petri is still on the street, giving the umbrella a feeble shake. Something about his demeanour seems to change. His shoulders slump, his frame narrows. He doesn't give the impression of a man who is about to make it big in the mushroom business through shrewd, innovative thinking. He remains standing in the doorway for a surprisingly long time, staring out at the rain then at his feet; then he turns and steps inside.

As I see it at the moment, there are three camps operating at once:

1) There is the business that I represent, which until a moment ago included Taina and Petri.
2) There is a new enterprise, spearheaded by Taina and Petri, which is attempting to steal clients from my business and create a market of its own.
3) There is the Hamina Mushroom Company: a new enterprise involving Asko (and formerly Sami and Tomi), who might, through Tsukehara, his new contact, be attempting to steer our collaboration in a completely new direction, leaving me and Taina and Petri to lick our wounds.

Rain patters on the roof of the car. An hour passes, during which I worry about the pain in my kidneys, have a spell of dizziness and, once I have recovered, wonder how best to instigate a relaxed, natural one-on-one conversation with Kakutama. Taina and Petri are inside the Seurahuone. I consider using the fire escape, which would involve climbing up to the roof. But the tin-covered roof, slippery from the rain, my physical condition and the fact that I don't know his room number discourage me from putting that idea into action. What's more, I recall what Taina let slip: *We know where the mushrooms are.*

Petri steps outside, returns to the minibus and starts the engine. Taina appears. She has swapped her clothes for waterproof Gore-Tex apparel and sturdy walking boots. Petri opens the bus door, Taina climbs inside, the door closes. Taina starts frantically waving her hands around.

Soon the Japanese appear too. They too are now dressed for the weather. I note Kakutama's bright-red, full-length overcoat, the only one of its kind in the whole delegation. Taina shows them to their seats. Her hands are moving more gently now, more slowly.

The bus leads us out of the town.

Taina may be a specialist when it comes to different ways of using mushrooms, recipes, tastes and the 'final product', as we call it in the business, but she's also experienced when it comes to traipsing through undergrowth in the woods. The same cannot be said of me.

We must be somewhere between the villages of Uski and Katti-lainen. We've driven out into the countryside, taking ever-narrower dirt tracks leading deeper and deeper into the forest, and I've almost completely lost my bearings. Because of the heavy rain, even the location of the sun in the sky is a mystery. As it turns off its lights, the minibus disappears from view. I switched off my own lights as we turned onto this final track.

It's a good thing the delegation is dressed in bright colours. I catch glimpses of them as they move through the forest terrain. The red coat is what I'm looking for. Eventually I spot it as it catches up with the rest of the group at the top of a small hill. I glance in vain at the passenger seat. I don't have a thin, waterproof summer jacket with me. All I have are the summer clothes Sanni bought me this morning. Kakutama's jacket flickers between the trees as he brings up the rear of the group.

Rain falls heavily from the sky. The air is warm and humid, the ground wet and squelchy. My brand-new Adidas trainers disappear into the undergrowth.

If moving around in the forest was arduous in the past, now it's many times worse. I look in despair at the distance between me and the rest of the group. Every step causes me to catch my breath and requires extra exertion. My stomach begins to ache, my ribs are sore – I don't know whether this is my kidneys playing up again or something else, something new – maybe my lungs collapsing. Every now and then I support myself against a fir tree and try to keep low to the ground.

The smell of the forest is thick and pungent, a curious blend of growing organisms and dead, decaying matter. Quite apart from being hard work, reaching the group is a complicated affair. I'm not entirely sure what direction I've come from or where I left the car I've borrowed. Sanni's brother will be thrilled if I tell him I've misplaced his Lexus in the woods.

The back of Kakutama's red jacket appears intermittently between the trunks of the pine trees, as though someone were flicking a light switch on and off. I struggle towards it, trying to keep out of sight as best I can. Taina is leading the group with considerable determination. The line of hikers must now be about twenty metres long; that's what happens in the forest. Eventually the terrain clears and we arrive at the edge of a logging area. A series of large boulders looks like the statues on Easter Island. I hop behind them, one after the other, and come a few steps closer to Kakutama with each new rock. I'm almost close enough that I could call out his name, but I decide against it.

There are two reasons for this: I can't take a big enough breath, and even if I could, shouting out wouldn't be a good idea. What's more, the others would hear me. Another boulder, then another. I'm not worried about the sound of my footsteps. The group is snapping dead branches and twigs themselves, and probably cannot hear anything but the sound of their own boots. Kakutama is within reach, but I have to be quick. I can't go for long stretches without stopping to take a good breath. As I step into a short ditch cut into the earth by one of the logging machines, an idea pops into my head. The ground has been churned up. I pick up a few suitable stones, take aim and throw.

The first stone misses its target, but Kakutama slows down and looks to the side, but not behind. Perhaps people can sense objects flying towards them even if they can't see them. I can't step out from behind the boulder because I don't want to reveal myself to anyone but him. And so I must make him – and only him – turn around completely and get him to notice me behind the boulder.

I throw another stone. It strikes almost right in the middle of the red jacket.

Kakutama lets out a squeal that is all too loud. I see him spin around. He looks the way frightened people in horror movies always look. The others start to turn too, so I have to drop to the forest floor, out of sight. I can hear loud conversation in Japanese and English. I recognise Kakutama's voice, then Taina's, and make out the words 'maybe' and 'bird'.

The ground is sodden and, given the recent stretch of warm weather, surprisingly cold too. The rain is even, constant and unrelenting. I can feel the cool and damp of the forest floor rising up my body as inexorably as water in a bathtub. The one positive thing about lying down is that it gives me a chance to catch my breath.

The rest of the group moves further away. Kakutama is still looking for something on the ground, maybe a bird, a small, stunned little creature. Again I wave my hands. Kakutama doesn't look up until I whistle. I can't quite imitate birdsong, but Kakutama raises his eyes in eager anticipation all the same, hoping to solve the mystery of the bird. He sees me instead.

Again he gives the frightened look familiar from horror movies, but only for a second. I thank my lucky stars when I see his expression change, first to one of confusion and then one of curiosity. He is about to say something, but I manage to hold a finger up to my lips. The freeze-frame situation lasts a few long, rain-filled seconds.

Once I am certain Kakutama will remain quiet without the help of my forefinger, I use the same hand to beckon him closer. He hesitates and glances back at his group, most of whom have already reached the other side of the logging area. I appreciate Kakutama's confusion, but there isn't much time. My hand is moving as though I'm whisking cream in the air. Kakutama nods and walks towards my boulder, each step a source of renewed anguish for me.

At the same time I realise what is now crucially different from our previous meetings: this time there is nobody with better English to help us communicate. My English is, if not quite that of a rally driver or a drunken tourist, then at best stiff, my vocabulary rather limited. Kakutama's pronunciation meanwhile makes it hard for me to understand him, even under the best of circumstances.

Kakutama has recovered from the shock. His eyes are curious and surprised, but friendly.

We shake hands.

The others must not know that we are talking, I say.

Kakutama nods.

What has happened? he asks.

It's a long story, I say. I need your help.

Your wife says you are no longer in the mushroom business.

Believe me, I am.

But your wife says you are not.

She is no longer my wife.

Kakutama looks at me, then glances towards the group wandering ahead, then at me again. I get the impression Kakutama has just put two and two together, and regardless of the language the result is the same. I can see in his eyes that he has just looked both into the past and the future, and returned to this moment with fresh understanding.

Why are you here? I ask, using my hands to make sure he knows that I mean this place, this forest.

Kakutama does not answer straight away. He is a businessman with decades of experience. He and I have done business together for several years. He has always been able to trust me. My pricing is fair and my product always of the highest quality. I never try to cut corners and I always keep my promises. Kakutama reaches a decision.

New matsutake, he says.

At first I don't understand what he says, though he only uses two words and I am familiar with both of them: *New matsutake.*

The moment of realisation is the same as if a doll's house that has been standing with its back to me, is suddenly turned round so that I can see all its rooms and furniture and … Taina's actions seem suddenly more understandable, though not more acceptable. A new genus. Of course. Sometimes answers are simple after all.

Thank you, I say. Then I compose myself in order to express my thoughts and objectives as simply and as concisely as possible.

I *am* in the mushroom business, I begin. I will make you an offer. This evening.

Again Kakutama looks over at the rest of the group.

You make me an offer, he says. I must go.

Kakutama walks off. He has no choice. The group has just disappeared into the forest on the other side of the clearing.

18

The bathroom is at once familiar and in some inexplicable way strange. My eyes flit from the door to the window, from the window to the showers.

The overall look is a combination of light blue and natural white. It's Taina's design. All the little knickknacks belong to her too: the colourful bottles, jars, tubs and boxes that fill the shelf space all belong to my ex-wife-to-be, who is now wandering through the woods with the Japanese. If she does spare a thought for me, she will imagine me either in a country across the sea or on another plane of existence altogether. Yet here I am.

I stand here naked and shave, probably for the last time in front of this mirror. Given the circumstances I feel remarkably well. I think it even looks as though I've lost a bit of weight. I look at myself sideways in the mirror. My stomach is still chubby and hangs miserably low over my hips, but perhaps now it is just a fraction smaller. My posture is better, my shoulders have returned to their correct height. I flex my arm, in the hope I might actually see evidence of some muscle in my biceps. I turn to face the mirror, fill my lungs with air and exhale slowly. Perhaps Sanni is right, I think.

I rinse away the remnants of the shaving foam under the hot shower. After my little adventure in the woods, this feels like a prize. I estimate I have about an hour, even if Taina decides to come straight home as soon as the Japanese are safely deposited back at the hotel. In all probability they are still examining a cluster of mushrooms deep in the forest, and Taina won't be home before my wet footsteps have dried.

A familiar radio mast helped me find my bearings in the forest. I realised where we were, where I'd parked the car, and approximately where the new genus of matsutake was growing. We'll find it when the time comes.

In the bedroom I take a bottle of aftershave from the bedside table. It is unopened and still in its packaging. I tear off the plastic wrapping and spray some beneath my chin and across my neck. I have two suits: one for work and one for special occasions. I take out the latter, put on a white shirt and a blue-and-green-striped tie. I get dressed and pack a bag with a few changes of clothes.

I don't imagine I'll need more than this. Not because I'm about to die – I am utterly determined to survive at least until the first harvest – but because by the time Kakutama and his colleagues return to Japan, Taina will know I am still alive and that I have been in town all along. By then we will have sorted out our differences, one way or another.

I look and smell better than I have done in years, though of course that's only my subjective opinion. I turn away from the mirror and look out of the window into the garden. The sky is still grey and leaden, but the rain has stopped for the moment. I wipe the bathroom clean, tidy up after myself and make sure there's nothing too obvious to suggest I've been here. I almost whistle as I walk down the stairs to the ground floor.

I'm singing by the time I get downstairs – a song by one of my favourite childhood bands; the heavier side of rock and roll. I don't know all the words, but it doesn't matter. I hear the guitar, pick up during the chorus and dance a few steps. I spin around once, twice. It makes me feel dizzy, but when I catch a glimpse of myself in the hallway mirror I know it's worth it. I'm in my stride, I'm an international gentleman – stylish, self-assured, and very definitely alive. I wonder where I have been all these years.

I grab my bag, throw it over my shoulder and give the place one last check: everything is as it was when I arrived. I open the front door, say something along the lines of 'You betcha, baby', and see Tikkanen standing beside the Lexus.

'Out with the old,' he says. 'And in with the new?'

I walk down the steps, pace towards him in my suit and open the car doors with a click of the key. I throw the bag onto the passenger seat and catch the scent of my own aftershave in the suburban air of our remote coastal town.

My initial enchantment has evaporated. It has disappeared with the wind whipping in from the sea and is finally dispelled by the police badge dangling round Tikkanen's neck. He nods at the Lexus.

'Going for an edgier, sportier look?'

As if he, a policeman, couldn't find out who the car belongs to. I'm convinced he already knows.

'I'm borrowing it,' I explain.

'What happened to your own car?'

'There's a problem with it,' I say, and it's true enough. The problem is that my wife would have recognised it.

'That's a sharp suit,' he says and sounds genuine. I'm beginning to see that this is Tikkanen's greatest asset in his job: he really is everybody's friend. 'You're not heading out of town, I hope?'

'Of course not. Are you following me?'

Tikkanen looks at me. 'I'm beginning to wonder whether it might be a good idea. Things seems to happen to you.'

I wait. I don't intend – in fact I can't risk – giving Tikkanen any more information than necessary. However, I get the impression he doesn't need it.

'We've already spoken about the disappearance of Tomi Alatalo,' he says, his eyes fixed on me. 'And also about his discovery. We've spoken about how his friends seem to think you are responsible for his disappearance. Interesting, I thought at the time, but I also thought this might just be a case of pure coincidence. That's life, isn't it? Then I receive a message telling me that one Sami Nevalainen is also missing. And before he went missing, he said he was going to meet you. Now I can't get hold of Nevalainen, you are dressed for the Milan Fashion Week and driving around in an expensive new car. What's more, you've just thrown a bag on the passenger seat that I guess contains a few days' worth of clean clothes. What do you think I should make of all this?'

I think about what Tikkanen has just said.

'A message?' I ask. 'What kind of message, and who sent it?'

'You'll appreciate I can't divulge that information.'

'I see. That means Asko,' I say and continue before Tikkanen has a chance to answer. 'Or worse still, you've received an anonymous tip-off.'

Tikkanen folds his arms across his chest. 'Are you saying you think such a claim is baseless?'

I don't like lies. I don't want to lie.

'It's not baseless in the sense that, as I understand it, both Tomi Alatalo and Sami Nevalainen have a certain antipathy towards me. And if I've understood correctly, that antipathy is fairly strong. But at the same time, I have no idea why they feel such antipathy. Not in the slightest. As far as I can tell, I've never done anything to upset them. As you know, I didn't even steal the sword that caused so much fuss and that seemed to start all this.'

'And we're back to the sword.'

'I didn't steal it.'

'Of course you didn't,' says Tikkanen.

The day around us is dark, the clouds like a thick, concrete mass; the rain will soon start sheeting down around us again like a wall of water. Tikkanen's last words are still hanging in the air, their meaning clear to both of us. He wants me to understand that he knows more than he's just said, more than his words suggest.

'So, where to?' he asks and nods directly at my tie.

'Business meeting,' I say.

'Here in Hamina?'

'I'm not going anywhere. The bag just has some more relaxed clothes – jeans, a T-shirt, that sort of thing.'

Tikkanen pauses for a moment. 'Important meeting?'

'You could say that.'

'And all the while your competitors keep disappearing,' he says and scratches his cheek. His beard forms a perfect square round his mouth; trimming it must be a dermatologically damaging procedure all of its own. 'That's quite a coincidence.'

I look him in the eyes. 'I didn't ask for any of this,' I say.

'I'm not sure we need to ask for anything in this life,' Tikkanen replies, and once again his voice is that of a friend: genuine, caring, sincere. 'Sometimes I think a lot of things happen without our asking for them.'

I can feel droplets of rain on my cheeks and on the top of my head. I raise my hand as if to demonstrate that I'm following the weather and that I've noticed the rain.

'Can I go?' I ask.

'Any time you like.'

I hear what he says, but I don't move immediately. Eventually I open the car door. 'Are you going to follow me?'

'Have you told me everything you know?'

We look at one another. I say nothing. I sit in the car, start the engine. Tikkanen remains standing beside his own car despite the onset of rain. I am careful not to put my foot down too much as I steer out of my former driveway.

The town is empty, the rain has laid a shimmering rug right across the square. There are no stalls in sight, only two bread vans seem to be open for business. Their hatches are propped open, and in the grey landscape the light glowing from inside them is like a roaring, enticing hearth. I can almost smell the fresh rye bread, almost feel the serrated breadknife in my hand as it cuts through the hardened crust into the soft, thick bread, almost taste and sense the dense, salty-sweet, buttered dough in my mouth.

Yet I know I can't eat rye bread.

I don't know whether it's because of my death and its assorted side effects, or my surprise encounter with Tikkanen and its psycho-somatic repercussions, or perhaps a combination of the two, but my stomach is full of tiny, burning needles, while my body as a whole feels the chill.

I'm looking behind me as much as in front. Nobody seems to be following me. Perhaps I've managed to bury all takers except for Tikkanen, and even his Polo is nowhere in sight.

As it seems I'm getting a headache in addition to my other complaints, I stop first at the pharmacy then the kiosk, and tank up: I drink some water and some Coca-Cola, swallow a paracetamol, followed by a mouthful of ice cream and chocolate. There are many advantages to this kind of diet: swallowing is easy, there's very little to chew, everything melts in my mouth, my headache abates and my general wellbeing perks up in an instant. In my case there really aren't any drawbacks to speak of: I probably won't have time to put on weight, my teeth won't decay, diabetes is the least of my worries, and the effects of my yo-yoing blood-sugar levels will be insignificant given how my body is being ravaged at the moment. And so I gobble up the chocolate bar as though it were bread, scoop ice cream into my mouth like porridge and wash it all down with Coke.

Then I wait.

It's not easy. At the moment it's the most difficult thing of all. It feels as though the minutes are being wrenched from me one at a time. Every second is a ticking, microscopic step towards the cliff edge. I don't like my thoughts and flick the radio on instead. I listen for a moment to a couple of presenters sparring with one another and switch it off again.

The minibus arrives, Petri behind the wheel. The group has spent all afternoon in the forest. Nobody minds the rain anymore; Petri doesn't leap out of the bus, let alone try to hold an umbrella above anyone. Now he remains sitting in the driver's seat while the others file out. Taina on the other hand is on the move: she guides the men from the bus and into the hotel, as though there was a risk her guests might get lost on the six-metre journey.

Once the men are all inside, Taina opens the passenger door and says something to Petri. He gets out of the minibus and walks round to the back. He carries a series of boxes – one, two, three – from the boot round to the back of the hotel, where the staff take deliveries.

I can guess, or rather I know, what is in the boxes: the new genus. Their own mushrooms for dinner, as Ilari, the frustrated reception- ist, told me.

I look at my watch. Taina has plenty of time to prepare whatever it is she is planning to prepare. She will take care of the tasting and charm the guests. That's fine.

The waiting doesn't feel excruciating any longer.

It'll soon be seven o'clock.

Dinner is served.

19

The dining room is beautifully lit: the electric lights are dim and warm, the candles carefully and evenly placed throughout the room. The dishes sparkle, the tablecloths dazzle white, the overall presentation is harmonious, complete with bunches of natural flowers. The restaurant seems to be closed to others. The guests have gathered near the bar at the far end of the room and are standing, holding glasses of bubbly. At a glance I can see that the champagne isn't cheap.

The entire Japanese delegation is here, all of them in smart, dark suits: the five men that I know and the one that I have never met. Taina, in a ball gown open at the back, is welcoming them with a speech. Petri is standing to the right of the group, in the darkest part of the room. He is wearing a suit and tie, and his dejected body language seems to suggest that he has chosen this far corner of the room deliberately.

Taina is standing facing the group, her back to me. She raises the glass in her hand. The champagne fizzes, her glass reflects the flickering of the candles, Taina's voice is excited and her words effusive. She is speaking in English, more with passion than with a full grasp of the grammar. She explains the evening's menu and speaks of a new age, of how exquisite tastes can bring people together.

Judging by the Japanese men's expressions, I guess that Kakutama has mentioned our meeting at least to Yuhara, the quality control officer. The two men are standing slightly aside from the others. They pay as much attention to my arrival as they would if I were simply returning from the gents. The others seem more taken aback. The logistics officer, Taketomo, the youngest of the group, whispers something to Okimasa, the marketing director with the bad skin, who is standing next to him. Hashimoto, the slightly hunched retail manager, puts down his champagne flute and looks anxiously around as though he is preparing for something, perhaps looking for the emergency exit. Tsukehara, the unknown man who, like Kakutama, is slightly greying, is the only one who smiles. Still, his smile isn't entirely friendly; there's something cool about it, with more than a touch of *Schadenfreude*. Petri has spotted me too and turns to look at the windows, behind which there is nothing but rain and an intensifying darkness.

Taina is in full flow and hasn't heard my footsteps. Her back looks tanned: in the soft lighting there's an almost copper sheen to her skin and her hair, which she has fastened in a bun. I stop an arm's length behind her.

Taina says a few more words before she notices the guests' eyes, all of which are focussed slightly behind her. You feel something like that in your skin before you really know what's happening. Taina pauses for a second or two before she glances over her shoulder and shrieks.

Though Taina's eyes are normally large, they seem to have grown all the more: she looks like an owl that has just been shot. Her mouth flies open, wine and spittle catching at the corner of her lips. The glass remains in her hand, but champagne sloshes over the floor and her black high heels.

'Good evening, everyone. And apologies for being late,' I say in my best English. 'Darling, everything is all right. My fever has died down.'

Taina doesn't seem to understand a word I say – at least that's what it looks like. Even a first-grader would understand my simple, builder's English, but the situation seems too utterly baffling. I take a step to the side, grab a glass of champagne from the counter and look out at the guests.

'I hope you all had a nice day in the woods,' I say and raise my glass.

After a moment's hesitation, the glasses begin to rise. Kakutama's is the first glass to reach clinking height.

'Soon we will all have a delicious meal,' I say and stand right next to Taina, so I am side by side with her, wrapping my arm around her waist. 'I am sure my wife has prepared a surprise for us. A great surprise.'

I give extra weight to the final sentence and reinforce it with my body language, all the while keeping my hand on Taina's waist.

Taina's eyes move from Petri – who has retreated into almost complete darkness in the corner of the room – to the guests, and finally to me. But she only gives me a glance. She has regained her composure, her mouth is closed, her lips attempting a half-smile. The hand holding her glass has steadied itself. Her body feels warm and robust against my own. I've almost forgotten what my own wife feels like.

The guests look anxious and expectant. I can understand why. Only this afternoon Taina has told them I am no longer in the mushroom business. Yet here I am. I am counting on our guests' politeness. They won't start asking questions right away, eager to know what is really going on. They are here to taste some mushrooms and possibly to cut a deal, and by then everything should be clear. Until that happens we can be polite to one another and see how the situation develops.

I give a short speech in which I welcome our guests to the most beautiful, most attractive small coastal town in eastern Finland, and explain that the rumours of my leaving the business are something of an exaggeration. I give particular thanks to my wife, who works night and day, putting both body and soul into the success of our business. Finally I apologise for a small change to the seating arrangements, as I would like to sit next to her. The guests appear to appreciate this, as they do everything else I have told them. There is an explanation for everything, we nod to one another in silent agreement.

Ilari, the man familiar from reception and one of the most valiant warriors in the battle against the world's printers, appears from the kitchen. We are ready, he says. He addresses his words to Taina, who manages to stammer out a thank you. Ilari disappears again, and despite the language barrier the guests seem to understand what is afoot, though of course they wait for confirmation from us. All eyes turn to Taina.

I kiss her on the cheek and whisper into her ear.

'I know you've killed me,' I say in Finnish and press another wet kiss against her cheek. 'And I know why.'

We look at the guests. They smile. My display of affection looked exactly as it was supposed to. Taina, on the other hand, looks like a woman who has just woken up from her worst nightmare only to realise that it was all true after all. I continue in English.

'My wife would like to invite you all to take your places.'

Taina, at once as stiff as a block of steel yet wholly malleable, eventually takes the seat to which I guide her, in the middle of the long table. I sit down with her on my right, Okimasa on my left and Kakutama directly in front of me. Yuhara is sitting to the right of Kakutama. To his left, in front of Taina, is our new acquaintance, Tsukehara.

As I have taken his seat, an extra place is laid for Petri at the end of the table. Nobody is sitting opposite him. If he ever decides to raise his eyes from the tablecloth, he will see the wall ahead of him, and if he looks to the side he will see the window behind which there is nothing but the rain sparkling in the light of the streetlamp.

Kakutama tells us about their day in the forest. It was fascinating, he says, exciting even.

Ilari pours glasses of white wine for everyone and explains that it is the driest of the dry, crisp and sharp, and that its long, rich aftertaste is the perfect match for the earthiness of our starter. I'm happy for Ilari. He sounds like a man who is now in his element, in a territory that he can control. We all need territory like that.

Taina hasn't said a word. She is utterly pale. I don't think I've ever seen her without some amount of redness or sun-kissed glow in her cheeks. I ask whether she would like to tell us something about the starter.

'What?' she asks in Finnish.

I repeat my question. By this point Ilari has begun serving bowls of soup.

'Soup,' she stammers in English.

Ilari sees that Taina is suddenly nervous and announces in beautiful British English that we are eating organic matsutake soup, whose rich taste comes not only from the rain-fresh mushrooms but from sprigs of local, organically grown rosemary and unprocessed cream of the highest natural fat content made from the milk of happy, free range cows (which doubtless have a healthy interest in philosophy, I almost add).

We thank Ilari, who seems deeply proud and content at being able to present the food to the guests. He disappears into the kitchen, his back as straight as a Roman column, and we begin to eat.

The soup is more delicious and more sumptuous than anything I have ever tasted before. The taste seems to please our guests too. After only a few spoonfuls we look one another in the eye, make a series of contented noises then clink our heavy soup spoons against the edges of our dainty bowls. Everyone except Taina, that is. She is sitting next to me, motionless, though it seems to me that she is constantly trying to inch herself further to the side. Perhaps only a millimetre at a time, but it's happening all the same, of that I'm certain.

'Is this the new genus?' I ask her in Finnish.

Taina's spoon stops between the bowl and her mouth, almost at chest height. At first she says nothing.

'Perhaps you'd like to tell us all about it?' I ask, again in Finnish.

For a moment I'm unsure whether Taina's hand has stiffened further. It has simply stopped in mid-air and doesn't seem to be trembling. The surface of the thick, creamy soup in the spoon is as still as the waters of a calm lake. Quiet, resting. After a moment's pause she slowly lowers the spoon to the bowl. She remains silent; the stiffness that a moment ago was in her hand has now moved to her face.

'How about I say a few words?' I suggest.

Taina does not reply. I don't know whether it is something to do with the candlelight or an after-effect of the shock, but she looks almost lifeless.

On the other side of the table Kakutama and Yuhara look across at me; both have almost finished their soup. I pick up a knife and clink it against my wineglass. Heads turn, and I stand up. I explain in English that I would like to say a few words about why we are all here today and that I will try my best to speak English, our shared language, though I warn them that I might need to explain some things in my native language, so I will use that too.

I see a few friendly nods and begin.

ENGLISH: Welcome, friends.

FINNISH: My dearest wife.

ENGLISH: Thank you for coming all the way to Hamina, and in such numbers. This is an honour that brings me great joy.

FINNISH: You are a whore. A devious, conniving whore.

ENGLISH: Success is about working together. We need one another.

FINNISH: When I saw your bare buttocks slapping against Petri's hips, I vomited.

ENGLISH: Working together means that each partner always does their best. For us this means that whenever we have a new product to offer, we tell you about it first, straight away.

FINNISH: And yet, as unfathomable as it is, the fact that you're sucking the delivery boy's cock isn't even the worst of it.

ENGLISH: Today you have seen – and, for the first time, tasted – the new genus, the new matsutake, which together we can turn into a great success. Judging by this soup, I have the courage to say that this is not only the taste of the most delicious mushroom in the world; this is the strong taste of success.

(Chuckles and nods of agreement.)
FINNISH: The worst is the deceit. And to crown it off, murdering me.
ENGLISH: Today is a celebration of our shared joy and future success. We can bring our cooperation together, make it even more effective. I have an offer that I would like to propose.
FINNISH: For all I care, Petri can screw you until your arse is so sore you can barely sit down. You can tie that brainless, walking penis to the end of your bed and live on nothing but cock if you want. It happens, and we can be forgiven for it. It's understandable.
ENGLISH: My offer is this: we will provide you with more matsutake, the very best matsutake, and we will begin expanding our operations in Japan together by opening our very own branch in Tokyo. I have just the person for such a job.
FINNISH: But the deceit, the plotting behind my back, is neither understandable nor acceptable.
ENGLISH: And what do I ask in return? Commitment. Monogamy. That we will be your only matsutake exporter for the next five years.
FINNISH: You should have told me. You shouldn't have murdered me.
ENGLISH: I sincerely hope we can shake hands on such a deal at the earliest convenience, hopefully this evening.

I glance around, then look at Kakutama sitting opposite me. He nods, raises his hands and claps. The others follow his example. We then stand up and shake hands across the table. The others continue to clap. We sit down.

All's well that ends well.

A sound, as though someone has let off a shotgun right next to my ear. A dull, ear-splitting thud followed by a volley whose power and force instantly exceed the speed of the noise that launches it.

Taina vomits.

For a split second, everything is airborne, like a bucketful of gruel that is quickly wrenched from mid-air into free fall and whose arch is longer and more impressive the more power and velocity is packed behind it. And everything is packed into this shower: the instantaneous thrust of Taina's robust upper body, something between the upper lift of a bench press and the final vein-splitting tug of a deadlift.

Her mouth opens wide, as it would in a dentist's chair – and with the same sense of agony. Her cheeks almost split, her gullet almost snaps in two.

The sound comes from somewhere at the bottom of her stomach and lungs. It is the most primitive of all human sounds, a mix of a war cry and the bellowing of a woman in labour, something so profound that it carries our thoughts to the birth of our species and beyond, to the big bang and the infinitesimal heat and pressure of the universe.

By now the fluid is already soaring on its inexorable jet-engine trajectory. Its apex passes the candles. But now it is followed by heavier liquid that drenches everything in its path and extinguishes the candles, plunging the table into darkness. It seems as though the liquid, surely exceeding the volume of Taina's stomach, gains added momentum as it travels through the air, and once it has crossed the table it finally crashes back to earth like a typhoon.

Tsukehara may have had time to see the oncoming tsunami, though he probably doesn't believe his eyes. He is sitting upright, his left hand in his lap, his right on the table. His soup bowl is empty for a second longer. His suit – a stylish, black jacket, a white shirt and sensuous, gleaming tie – are visible for a moment yet. Then suddenly they too are swept away.

Tsukehara's expressionless face is the first to disappear. His suit turns a light shade of brown, the colour of organic cream of matsutake soup. The bowl in front of him is filled to the brim. In the blink of an eye Tsukehara is transformed into a swamp creature, a prehistoric being with gills on its back, crawling forth from the primordial sea to begin life on dry land. That's certainly what his flailing looks like, as though he is concentrating solely on reaching the shore, on survival, on feeling land beneath his feet. His hands reach out for something to hold on to, something to offer him support. He writhes, wrenches, fights for his life.

The first wave is followed by another, but this time Taina's upper body moves sideways too and aims downwards. She is about to fall over, chair and all. And at the very second she hits the ground and expels another volley of vomit from her mouth, an identical shotgun is fired at the other end of the table.

Everybody turns, and those of us still standing and not yet covered in regurgitated soup watch Petri repeat Taina's performance. Petri has plenty of room at his disposal: the jet of bile stretches halfway across the room.

By this point we all begin standing up, moving away from the table.

Chair legs screech across the floor.

Someone screams.

A glass smashes.

Ilari comes running in.

Petri lets off wind from the other end, and possibly something else too.

The candles flutter, their flames wet and ragged.

I crouch over Taina and look at her face: pale and lifeless. I straighten up a little, turn quickly and see Petri on the floor. His expression too is familiar. I looked like that once my initial seizure was over and I had reached the bathroom to wash my face and look at myself in the mirror. There is no need for an official diagnosis; I know what is happening to Taina and Petri.

This is an exact repeat of my own initial symptoms.

20

Ilari has donned a pair of arm-length yellow rubber gloves, with which he is holding up the shell-shocked Tsukehara. I imagine Tsukehara is more dumbfounded than physically harmed. Still, his legs are like limp spaghetti, and Ilari has his work cut out trying to avoid Tsukehara's vomit-soaked clothes.

Taina and Petri are lying on couches in the foyer, Petri now without his shirt and in only his suit trousers. For some reason he seems to have pulled off his socks too. Ilari has given Taina two large terry towels, which she has slung awkwardly across herself as though she were enjoying a drunken evening at the spa. The acute and most powerful phase of the seizure is over for now.

We have left the dining room, which now both looks and smells like the site of a major drainage catastrophe. The smell of vomit catches in our nostrils, stings our eyes, rings in our ears, makes us gag and eventually throw up ourselves. The logistics officer Taketomo is still wiping his mouth with his tie.

I try to calm each of the guests in turn. I have told them many times over that this is nothing to do with what they have just eaten and that there is no need for them to be worried. I see that at least Kakutama is keen to believe me.

There is an explanation to all this, I say and look him in the eyes.

We are standing in the corner of the foyer near the reception desk, where there's a quiet spot for us to talk.

What is it? Kakutama asks.

I can't tell you, I say.

I leave out the fact that the reason I can't tell him is because I don't yet know the answer myself. All this time I have assumed, based on what I thought was logical thinking and supported by the evidence at hand, that it was Taina and Petri who poisoned me. Given what has just happened, that is probably not the case. Few people would first commit murder only to commit double suicide by vomiting themselves to death in public.

There is only one reasonable conclusion: they have been poisoned, just as I have, and in precisely the same manner. This in turn means that I must contact my doctor at once. I remember only too well what he told me about the initial phases of the poisoning.

I ask Kakutama for some extra time. In the same breath I assure him that the agreement we made only moments ago is still valid, and that I will respect the spirit of our agreement in full.

Is there something wrong with the mushrooms, Kakutama asks me, and his question is framed in a way that doesn't allow for half-truths or creative wording.

No, I say. The mushrooms are of the highest quality and they always will be.

Kakutama looks at me. He looks at me for a long time.

Very well, he says. I have trusted your word before and I will trust you now. We return to Tokyo on Tuesday. I hope that by then all this – Kakutama gestures towards the foyer, where Taina and Petri are sprawled across the couches moaning and Taketomo is standing shaking his head – that all this is sorted out and our agreement is clear.

I thank him, take out my phone and call my doctor.

'Has there been a change in your condition?' he asks.

'In my condition, no. But now there are two other people with identical symptoms.'

The doctor is silent.

'The very same symptoms?' he asks eventually.

I explain that I need his help and the antidote that he has spoken about, which he said might still work at this early stage. I tell him that the two patients will be arriving at the hospital in about twenty minutes and that they are to be seen by him and him alone.

'It's a good thing I'm only fifteen minutes away from the hospital,' says the doctor.

'No,' I reply. 'You are only five minutes from the hospital.'

But then: how hard it is to tell someone they will die if they don't do as you tell them. Or rather, telling them isn't hard; dealing with their reaction to the news is the problem. Petri jumps to his feet, rips a Yucca tree from its pot and hurls it at Ilari, who has just returned to his station behind the counter. He dodges the flying tree. Petri yells something that I can't make out.

It seems that all the tensions pent up inside him burst out at once: his deceit, his assistance in disposing of the body, his acute poisoning, his role as a sexual plaything. Taina watches this from her horizontal vantage point, her head raised. I allow Petri to bawl incomprehensibly, because I still have to break the news to Taina that she too is being taken to hospital to receive the antidote.

'Antidote for what?' she asks.

'Death,' I say.

It's essential that I get them both into my car and that I speak to them as soon as possible. Alone. The two principal reasons: I need information, and I still need to keep Tikkanen from getting involved in this matter. I have no desire to spend any more time with him answering cryptic questions in his stuffy office.

Somebody has murdered me, somebody is trying to murder Taina and Petri too. I can't help thinking – this is a brief but unavoidable thought – that I could just have left them to die. But Taina and Petri have been punished enough, I have reclaimed my mushroom business and I still want to get to the bottom of my own murder. For that I will need Taina and Petri's help. They must know something. I am sure of this, even though they themselves might not yet be aware of it.

Petri's state of disarray is acute, and his body is still bulky, though the sudden seizure has possibly weakened him somewhat. I must get him into shape to be driven to hospital. I ask Kakutama, Yuhara and the surprisingly healthy-looking Okimasa to help me. Ilari brings us a pile of white towels that we use to tie Petri up. In an instant he is a tight bundle of terry cloth.

Of course, Petri is still capable of making quite a noise, but for the most part this is nothing but a low growl in the background. Kakutama, Yuhara and Okimasa help carry Petri out to the car. We use one of the long tablecloths to tether him firmly to the backseat. I walk Taina out, put her in the car, and we drive off.

'Taina,' I begin. 'The same thing happened to me at the beginning of the week. The same symptoms, the same unpleasant series of events. Somebody has done this. Have you noticed anything strange going on recently?'

I sound like Tikkanen, of all people. I understand the fundamental impossibility of my question: I am speaking to a woman who has been planning a coup, who has deceived me, committed adultery and vomited over our potential business partners. I try to be more specific.

'Were you involved in poisoning me?'

Taina shakes her head.

'Do you know who poisoned me?'

Taina shakes her head.

'Do you know anyone who would want to poison you and the toy boy?'

Taina shakes her head.

'I was sure it was you who had done it. But now it doesn't look likely. You wouldn't poison yourself. You're not the type. After what's just happened, I wonder whether it's our new competitor. I don't think so. No, I'm certain they're not behind this. I've got, shall we say, enough first-hand knowledge of them that I know they are more interested in direct action. If they wanted to get rid of someone they would batter them or stab them with a sword...'

By now Petri is howling and growling. I decide to change tack. I keep my eyes firmly on Taina. I'm not worried about the traffic. It's evening and, after all, this is Hamina.

'The more I think about this, the more I realise we're an unlikely set of victims. I understood my own murder, when I thought you wanted me out of the picture. And from the perspective of our competitors, I can see the rationale in getting rid of us both. But what about the big baby in the back? Why him? He can't do anything; he doesn't know anything. This is something else – but what?'

Petri begins to bark like a dog. After that it sounds as if he starts to sob.

Taina wipes her face with a towel. 'I don't know,' she says, so quietly that I can only just make out the words.

'What don't you know?'

'Anything,' she says. 'All I wanted was … Am I going to die?'

'We'll see the doctor soon, and then we'll know. It's perfectly possible that you won't die.'

Petri lets out a lengthy, anguished whimper.

'I wouldn't do something like that,' Taina says quietly. 'Murder you, I mean.'

I don't know what to say. Of course it's nice to hear that my wife wouldn't think of murdering me. On the other hand, the very fact that she even has to mention it suggests that things haven't been going well in our marriage for a while.

'So,' I continue. 'Think carefully about the people around us. Who would have a reason to poison first me, then you and Boy Wonder?'

'Petri!' Petri pipes up.

Taina's expression remains impassive and doesn't betray in the slightest that she has heard the gruff howl from the backseat. Then she says something that I can't get out of my mind.

'Nobody knows about us,' she says.

'Who is us?'

'Me and…'

'Petri,' comes the cry from the back.

'Me and Petri and the Japanese visit,' she says. 'It's a secret. All of it. Nobody knew anything about it.' Taina turns her head slightly towards me. 'Then again, it turns out you somehow knew all along.'

I'm driving quickly and carefully, but not over the speed limit. The minutes and seconds are important. Rain patters against the windscreen, like a thousand small fingers rapping against a table.

'Are you absolutely sure you didn't tell anyone about your plans?' I ask.

Taina is silent for a few long, heavy seconds.

'I didn't even tell Petri everything,' she says eventually.

We pull up outside the hospital. I drive straight to the back of the building and park by the delivery bay as we have agreed. The doctor is waiting for us. Beside him is a woman whom, despite her civilian clothes, I recognise as the old-school matron who took my blood samples. I bring the car to a halt right in front of them. The doctor says he will need someone to help him. We extract a promise from Petri before untying him from his seat. There are tears in the corners of his eyes. Taina is full of questions for the doctor. The doctor won't promise too much, but says they both stand a good chance of pulling through. As he says that he looks at me.

I remain standing behind the closing hospital doors. The rain murmurs in the otherwise soft evening, and its sound fills the world as it falls around the small roof like three walls. Taina and Petri haven't spoken openly about their plans. But I have spoken openly about Taina and Petri.

21

The yard is empty, the ground softened with rain and dotted with puddles. The lamp on the wall of our mushroom production building illuminates only the front door, and even that only barely. I try as best I can to avoid the potholes filled with water. I can feel the rain on my face, on the top of my head, on my neck, my bare hands. The journey from the car to the front door is no more than fifteen metres, but already I'm soaked through.

Once inside I take off my suit jacket and wait for a moment. I flick the light switch on and walk to the point in the hallway where I was standing when the idea first occurred to me. This time the lights in the drying room are not turned on and the low, dull murmur of the machinery does not catch my attention or combine a second later with the hum of the surrounding world.

I turn on the electricity but do not start up the dryers. Instead I look at the log records. Nothing since last spring. Have I heard wrong? Am I barking up the wrong tree? I think for a moment, step into my office and boot up my computer. I wait for a moment and give the mouse a few clicks.

The dryers can be operated both manually and digitally. All digital use is automatically logged in the drying room program's own user profile and history. Even manual use, which is nothing more than pressing a sequence of buttons, is logged and registered by the program. In fact the use of all our electric devices, large and small, is logged in the company's energy-consumption management system, a complicated name for a simple program I installed about a year ago in an attempt to cut down on energy bills.

The dryer has its own number in the system, and that number appears on a few lines of the log details. It reveals that the dryer has been manually operated a total of eight times since the last official digital operation.

I return to the hallway and open the dryer door; the lights come on automatically.

The dryer is essentially a cross between a standard home oven and a shelving system for preserves – on a much larger scale. It is the height and width of a car and features dozens of separate drying racks. Everything looks exactly the way it should. I pull out about ten of the racks at random and check them. They are clean.

A thought occurs to me and I walk round to the side of the dryer. I turn the bolt holding the extraction fan in place and carefully remove the filter. It is about forty centimetres in diameter, new, bright white, and has clearly been changed only recently. This is careful work, I think as I fit the filter back in place. I walk back to the front of the dryer and take a few steps back. To the left of the machine I see what I have subconsciously been looking for all along.

Against the wall at the far end of the hall is a long counter, the end of which has turned into a tearoom for the staff – probably because there's a tap with running water. On the counter there is a coffee machine, next to that an armchair and a few barstools. Above the counter is a shelf with an array of mugs belonging to the staff, each with amusing or endearing texts. Next to a mug bearing the words 'World's Best Granddad' is a small tin, and in that tin a selection of biscuits.

If I'm not wrong, the appearance of the biscuits coincides with the first time the dryer was operated manually. I remember how happy I was when they suddenly appeared at the corner of my desk. I enjoyed munching on them with a cup of coffee as I took care of the company's paperwork. Whenever I asked where they got their rich, salty-sweet taste, I was told that the recipe was a secret and the conversation was changed – regularly and systematically – to the subject of women's wrongs, women's illogical minds, and how things should be in the eternal struggle between the sexes.

I hold the tin in my hands and the jigsaw comes together piece by piece.

According to my doctor, my poisoning was caused by nature's own toxins. Someone has gathered them and used our dryer to dry them. After this they have been ground to a powder and mixed with biscuit dough. The biscuits were baked and brought into my office. And I have eaten them.

There is only one more question.

Why, Olli?

Isoympyräkatu – the street which, despite being called 'Big Circle Street', does not form a full circle – comes to an end at a tight cluster of wooden houses. The oldest of the houses were built more than a hundred years ago, their foundations made of large boulders; some of them are wonky, some renovated, others falling to pieces. The house where Olli lives is something between the extremes.

A pale-yellow light, the old buildings wet from the rain, the narrow street and a few tall trees, their boughs as dark as the night, make the strip of road seem like a time machine. There is no evidence of the modern age. If I die right now and this is the last landscape I ever see, it will be impossible to say whether I died in 1946 or 2016, or whether this matters in the grand scheme of our passing. Plenty of people die all the time, and most of them believe they went too soon.

Judging by Olli's address and apartment number I estimate that he must have two windows looking out onto the street. Both of them are covered with closed Venetian blinds.

The garden is surrounded by a slatted wooden fence, and the gate is open. Olli's four-wheel quad bike is parked beneath a small shelter.

The garden is a mixture of mud and overgrown grass. Olli might be able to gather webcaps, hemlock, yew berries and fly amanitas, he might know how to harness them and cleverly poison people, but keeping his garden in order seems beyond his capabilities. In one of the windows looking out onto the garden the blind is not quite closed. At first I wonder whether there is a fire inside, then I realise it must be the television. The colour and lighting in the room is in constant flux. From the outside it looks like there is a disco going on.

I am about to ring the bell when I see the door handle gleaming in the rain. I try the door, and it opens gently. I hear the sound of the television, and it takes a moment before I recognise the show: *Who Wants To Be a Millionaire?* It seems Olli has other passions besides assassinating people.

The sound of the television is so loud that, though I can feel the hundred-year-old floorboards moving beneath my feet, I can't hear the sound of their creaking. The hallway is a short corridor that comes to an end at the toilet door. To the right there are two doorways. The darkened room at the front is presumably the bedroom, and the closer door, lit with warm light and filled with the sound of the blaring television, must lead to the living room.

On the television someone gives a wrong answer, the audience sighs with disappointment, Olli mouths something I can't make out. He is half sitting, half lying in his armchair.

The living room is tidy but slightly depressing. The furniture seems to be a selection of the kind of stuff people acquire when other people move house; the wallpaper and the waist-high panelling are a strange combination of English bungalow and Finnish sauna, the dome light hanging from the ceiling is fitted with a bulb far too strong, which reveals not only a spot of damp on the ceiling but every last ball of dust in the corners of the panelling and on the floor.

'Olli, would you turn the television down a little?' I ask.

Olli's hands fly up from the arms of the chair, his back straightens, his face seems to elongate, his mouth opens and his eyes are filled with questions. But he remains in his chair and continues to look like George Clooney, whose last film was a while ago now.

'Jaakko,' he says.

'Still alive,' I say and throw a biscuit into his lap.

He doesn't even try to catch it. He seems utterly frozen. The brown biscuit falls onto the front of his grey jogging trousers, where it breaks in two. Olli's head moves solely to look at the two halves. I'm not sure how long he has to stare at them before he understands what this is all about. I give him a few seconds to take it all in. Then I pick up the remote control from the table and switch off the television.

The silence seems to wake him up. He raises his eyes to meet my gaze. He looks exactly like the Olli I know: sincere, either slow or cunning – I still haven't worked out which – and somehow backward, despite all his apparent prowess with the opposite sex.

'I poisoned them for you,' he says.

Not quite the opening I'd expected.

'Them?' I ask.

'Taina and Petri,' Olli replies. 'They were at it like rabbits, screwing like…'

'Olli,' I say. 'You poisoned me first.'

For a moment he is silent. He looks me in the eyes, but still seems an open, honest man.

'I'm sorry about that.'

I am standing in a wooden house, looking at my murderer.

'You're sorry about it?'

'Yes,' he nods, again with deep sincerity.

'Well, that's all right then,' I say. 'Then everything's okay. You've apologised, so that's the end of it and I can go home to die now.'

I notice I am becoming agitated. I take a deep breath.

'Olli, for Christ's sake,' I say calmly. 'I really don't know what I was expecting. But I'd be lying if I said a simple apology makes this okay.'

Olli raises his shoulders. The gesture is presumably supposed to be a shrug, but it lasts so long that it seems more a sign that a moment of contemplation has ended in uncertainty.

'It was an accident,' he says. 'In a way.'

'How can you accidentally gather poisonous mushrooms, dry them and mix them into a sweet dough and roll them into delicious, little fucking biscuits?'

My voice rises towards the end of the question. Olli looks as though he is suddenly afraid of me.

'I was just experimenting to see if I could do something like that,' he says. 'To see how it … and whether anyone would eat them.'

'I fucking ate them.'

'You ate all of them.'

I shake my head.

'First you murder me, then you criticise my eating habits.'

Olli raises his hands in self-defence. 'No, mate, not at all. Everyone can eat whatever they want, everyone has the right to their own body, everyone…'

'Olli,' I say, as if to a dog.

We are both silent for a moment. Olli stares ahead, then glances at me from beneath his eyebrows.

'I was practising making them. The biscuits. I think I'd run out of options.'

'Options? What options? Either you don't bake anything at all or you bake deadly mushroom biscuits, is that it?'

Olli slowly shakes his head.

'I told you I've been divorced three times. I didn't want to get divorced, not once. The missus has always left me. I've been dumped. That's the truth. On top of that, I've been engaged six times, and every time I get given the boot. I've never dumped anyone. Nobody can deal with that. I certainly can't. The next one won't leave me. I'll feed her biscuits instead. I'll poison her. It's the only sensible option. The bitch will die while she's still happy – while we're both happy – before she has a chance to run off. It's a win-win situation.'

I don't know what to say.

'At least Taina and Petri got what they deserved.' Olli's voice is solicitous, angling for something.

Again I shake my head. 'They're in hospital,' I say. 'If the poison is detected early enough, the doctors might be able to stop it spreading.'

'But you wanted it to…'

'I might have said that, might have expressed my feelings in strong terms, but that doesn't mean I want this to happen.'

The surprise on Olli's face looks genuine.

'I thought you and me were on the same side.'

'How the hell can we be on the same side when you've murdered me and you're planning to murder other people too?'

Olli gazes in front of him. He seems to be thinking, either about my question or something else entirely. Then he looks at me again.

'Are you going to tell the police?' he asks.

'What would you suggest? Should we poison them too? And after them the rest of the people of Hamina? And when we get found out, everyone else in Finland? We'll feed people little biscuits until there's nobody left to find us out.'

Olli doesn't answer. He repeats the previous sequence of movements: first he stares right ahead, then glances at me surreptitiously. When he moves, I think he might try to attack me. But that's not the direction of his movement. Olli is trying to escape, to run away. By the time he's darted past me, and I realise I should run after him, he is already struggling with the front door.

Olli doesn't stop to put on his shoes. He yanks the front door open, leaps downs the porch steps and continues sprinting. At that same moment I gather my energy at the top of the steps, dive into the air and throw myself onto his back.

The rain is pouring around us, the earth is soft and wet. Our knees and elbows sink into the mud. Beneath us it feels like a soaked, lumpy mattress. We struggle with one another.

It seems neither of us knows how to fist-fight properly like they do in films, so we both try instead to get a firm hold on the other and wrestle him to the ground. But neither are we top-level athletes – far from it. What's more I have the added problems associated with my impending demise: I'm out of breath in an instant, gasping for air, the excess lactate in my bloodstream almost stops my movements altogether. The tie round my neck isn't the best wrestling kit either; I'm beginning to understand the benefits of Lycra.

We twist and turn, huffing and grunting, our movements slow. At times our faces are so close that we're breathing down each other's noses, at others we are almost standing up, wrestling on our feet, then we collapse again and roll in the mud. I can't see anything anymore. My eyes and mouth are full of earth, sweat and rain.

At one point we crash against the wall of one of the sheds. By the wall there is a pile of junk, including a plank of wood about a metre long. I manage to grab it as Olli wraps his arm round my neck.

He is behind me, squeezing and lifting so hard that it feels as though my neck could snap and my head could come away from my shoulders, and in the rainy night I begin to perceive a strange, bright light. I put all my strength into a single movement: I release my grip on his wrists completely, free up both my hands, take firm hold of the plank and bring it crashing to the side of my head with all the force I can muster.

The strangle hold round my neck loosens just enough for me to wriggle free. I turn and hurl the plank once more, this time to the side. The plank hits Olli round the ear. He raises his left hand to the side of his head as if to hear better. He is staggering from side to side, his legs unable to carry him, and reaches out left and right, trying to recover his balance.

This is my moment.

I turn, open the woodshed door, turn again, grab Olli by the shirt, and before he can coordinate his hands the better to grab hold of me, I wrench him with me, almost into a dance, and with a few pirouettes we are inside the woodshed. I release my grip, allowing him to drop to the concrete floor, and look around.

There is very little light: the remnants of a yellow glow from the solitary streetlamp, a glimmer of light through the open front door. I can't see anything but logs and other chunks of wood; no axe or other tools in sight. I leave Olli on the floor, step outside and close the door. For a moment I wonder how to fasten it shut.

I find the keys to the quad bike in a novelty whisky tin on the hall table. I start up the bike and pull it up in front of the shed. I carefully inch it right in front of the door, then jolt it forwards one last time. I switch off the motor. Olli can stay put.

The rain continues to murmur, and I am soaked through. As

I remove my hands from the handles of the quad bike, it feels as though I am letting go of my consciousness too. I wonder where my phone is – probably still in the car. I have to call someone to pick up Olli. The authorities. Tikkanen.

I realise I am walking, but I can't feel it. I am one with the rain, I am water pressing its way into the earth, losing my form piece by piece. I think I am dying, really dying, because that's what it feels like. I can't feel myself touching the car door; I don't even really know whether I have sat down inside or whether I'm still outside. I don't know whether I start the car or whether I simply sit there. Is this really a steering wheel around which my fingers are clenching or something else altogether? My eyelids droop, heavy. I am no longer on Isoympyräkatu, the street that isn't really a full circle, I am no longer in Hamina, no longer in a place where geography has any meaning. I am adrift, free, and at the same time connected to everything; at once weightless and firmly tethered to the here and now. I fly and float, glide and rest.

PART THREE
LOVE

1

Someone gently lifts the coffin lid. Just when I was comfortable and dead. Just when I was able to rest after all the exertion. It seems in this life people can't even die in peace. Someone will have something to say about that too. Perhaps this is one of the eternal laws of the universe: we never do anything right, and other people always know best about how we should do things, including dying.

Light swirls behind my eyelids, I am awake before I open my eyes. I have to blink for a moment before I can see anything. At first all I see is a gleaming light, a world of flashes. Shapes slowly begin to form: the large oak tree, the light-brown fence, the narrow road, the merry, yellow wooden house.

I take a few heavy breaths. I can't swallow, my mouth is so dry that I can hardly feel it; my throat hurts. The suit I am wearing looks and feels as though I've been wearing it while wrestling in the mud and the rain. If I take the worst hangover I can remember and multiply it by a hundred, this is the result. My left hand is twisted through the gap in the steering wheel and dangles on the other side. It feels numb. I find my right hand in my lap. The keys appear to be in the ignition. I don't really understand what I'm doing right here, right now. For some reason my first thought is of the quad bike: I've never driven one before. Then I remember everything else, and what I came here to do.

My phone is in the plastic trough between the seats. I pick it up and look at it, my hands moving too quickly. I almost faint. I try to open the window, but my left hand won't work. I use my right hand; the fresh air is like water, and I guzzle it down. I try the phone again.

Judging by the time and the amount of light it must be morning. Sanni has tried to call me six times. I didn't hear the phone ringing;

I was asleep. Or unconscious. She has sent me three text messages, the last of them only a few minutes ago.

Text number one: 'Jaakko, what's the plan? On the way to Ihamaa. Asko and Tsukehara apparently old friends. Something going on between them. All the Japanese with us. Something's happening. Sanni.'

Text number two: 'Jaakko, this doesn't feel good. Asko is staring at me. Tsukehara is raving in Japanese. I don't know what's going on. Weird situation.'

Text number three: 'Asko's coming.'

At the kiosk I pick up two litre-and-a-half bottles of Coca-Cola and down one of them on the spot. A vast quantity of the contents spills over my chin, my front and my tie, which I've already loosened several times. An ice-cold sugary drink has never tasted so good; now I know precisely what people mean when they talk about extinguishing thirst. My mouth has been as dry as an empty oven, but now it is awake. At first my throat almost gags, tries to cough the liquid back where it came from, before eventually coming back to life.

The rain has paused, the sky is dark and heavy. I drive as quickly as I dare and continue drinking all the while. The Lexus reacts when I press my foot harder against the accelerator. On the long, straight, empty roads stretching ahead my speed almost reaches two hundred kilometres per hour. I try to call Sanni. She doesn't answer. I check my direction on the phone. Google tells me it's eighteen minutes to my destination.

And they are long minutes. At the same time, I think and try not to think about what I've got Sanni mixed up in. If Asko's henchmen were prepared to do anything at all – and at the drop of a hat – what is their boss capable of? And what if Asko's staring at her because of what Sanni has just done, because she has told me what is going on? What will Asko do to Sanni? And what is going through the mind of Mr Tsukehara, his acquaintance whom Taina drenched in regurgitated soup? Has Asko already heard about the fate of Tomi and the sword? And if he has heard, how will that information affect him? If Asko and Tsukehara's plans are suddenly under threat, how will they react?

What *is* their plan?

I can't stop thinking about Sanni – her voice, her renewed enthusiasm, her beautiful living room, the way she has of teasing me. I think of her even when I think I ought to stop thinking about her. Especially at those moments.

I cover the rest of the journey in eleven minutes. Ihamaa is just a place name; it's not a village, not even a cluster of houses. At the spot where the map suggests Ihamaa is situated, there is only an oval clearing at the end of the track. Two vehicles are parked at the right-hand side of the clearing. One of them is a minibus. I steer the Lexus tight behind the minibus, get out and look around.

At first the situation seems hopeless. Then I begin to count the minutes back to Sanni's last message. I assume it would have taken the entourage at least five minutes to get ready and gather their things before setting off. That rules out the right-hand path, as the journey across the fields and the ditches to the other side of the forest is too long. I would be able to see them if they'd taken that route. So I cross the path and dive into the woods to the left.

The forest is a big place, but it is also quiet. If someone speaks even slightly louder than normal, you can hear it. If there is a group of people on the move, twigs snap underfoot, branches hit the person behind in the face and someone cries out; from time to time someone shouts in order to bring the group back together. I trudge forwards for a while, then stop and listen. Nothing. More trudging. Stop. Listen. Trudge. Stop. Trudge. Sto—

The sound of someone speaking a foreign language, combined with the fact that I'm about to step out into a clearing, makes me drop to the ground for cover. I don't know what Tsukehara is talking about, but he sounds like a man who means business.

I cautiously raise my head. It's a relatively large clearing, rectangular, and on further inspection it seems to be divided into smaller oblong sections. Narrow walkways run between each of the sections, and the group is gathered on one of these. They have formed a line and are standing with their backs to me. Only Asko and Tsukehara are facing in my direction. Sanni is standing slightly aside from the rest of the group. She is not looking at Tsukehara; her eyes seem focussed on the ground in front of her. Asko looks as though he is staring at Sanni, silently threatening her. I see something shiny glinting in the morning light, a long, gleaming implement in Asko's left hand, dangling and resting against his thigh.

It is Asko's turn to speak.

He speaks better English than me. Tsukehara translates into Japanese.

I'm beginning to understand what this is all about and why Asko has been so certain of his success.

The plan is ingenious. They can offer – at an unprecedentedly low price and in unprecedented quantities – organic matsutake grown naturally, right here in these woods. A product which is, in fact, none of the above. It does not grow in the woods but in this clearing; it is not natural or organic, because it is helped along using chemical fertilisers.

It is a scam, but Asko doesn't say this out loud. Be that as it may, I will say it out loud, because this is an insult, a personal affront to me; this is the denigration of an entire honourable profession, the deception of people and principles.

I lurch forward and rush into the clearing, straight towards the group, which has now turned to follow me.

The truth is, I don't know quite what I'm doing. But isn't that the nature of life – the moral of the story? At its best, most of life is simply practice – fumbling in the dark. But I have good intentions: now my primary aim is to protect Sanni. I don't want Asko's dagger or knife – I assume it must be one or the other, it doesn't look like a full-length sword – putting Sanni in any kind of danger. No, never again. I yell at the top of my voice as I hurtle towards Asko.

2

I've often heard the saying that we should live our lives as if we are going to die tomorrow. I believe I can go one better. I'm living my life right now as though I'm going to die right now. There is nothing to be afraid of. Life is new all the time, every minute is an adventure as branches snap beneath me, my feet thud against the ground, the forest seems to sway violently, and the primal roar coming from my throat frightens me most of all. Three litres of North-American sugar solution in my stomach, a suit stiff with clay and mud wrapped around my body and a pair of soaked, pinching fake-leather shoes obviously don't make for the optimal outfit for such an attack, but there's no stopping it now.

I can see from the group's expressions that this is not quite what they were expecting. Tsukehara looks as furious as a man can look without exploding into pieces. Kakutama is surprisingly calm – he has an almost satisfied air as he watches me lunge forwards. The others are caught in different degrees of shock and bewilderment, as questions quiver on their lips. Sanni seems surprised in a way that makes my heart flicker. I wasn't wrong about her.

And as for Asko – I've never seen him look like this before. If I said he had turned into a hunter, that would be to belittle him. Now he is a predator. A killer.

Asko barges through the row of onlookers, runs towards me and raises the knife in his hand. I don't understand how the blade can possibly become longer as his hand rises up, but then I see the hilt hurtling to the side. This is no run-of-the-mill mushroom knife. I crouch low to the ground and pick up a hefty pine branch. Perhaps it is through a synthesis of sugar, caffeine, adrenaline, love, anger and the profound, holy indignation I feel in attempting to defend a respectable mushroom business, but suddenly I move more nimbly than I have all week.

We approach each other like two jousters at a medieval tournament. Asko has clearly lost all self-control. He is allowing his anger to pour out of him unfettered. Good. I fumble for a firm grip on the pine branch and clasp it with all my strength.

Asko is approaching me as if he is in a Kung Fu film in which the action is shown in slow motion and every movement, down to the smallest gesture, is shown separately. I can see his furious, stiff face, the blade of the knife as it rises through the air, its glint, the tip of its blade as thin as a needle. If it hit me, it would pierce me like a balloon, slice me like an apple. Asko lunges; so do I.

And then, just like in the movies, both of us are in the air.

Asko's knife gleams as a sunbeam hits it; the steel flashes, reflecting the brilliance like a mirror. I grip the branch, thrust it forwards. The forest is soundless, the clearing like a silent room. The group of people behind Asko stand frozen, like statues propped in place. Asko grimaces, revealing his teeth. From my perspective his teeth behind the blade look like a shark's jaws. He might be about to shout something, but he is cut short.

The pine branch is longer than Asko's knife, and this simple fact settles everything. My pine branch strikes Asko in the groin with considerable force. Asko appears to double over in mid-air. The knife flies from his hand and sails past my face like a comet.

Just as decisive as the length of my branch is the grip with which I brandish it. That grip has all the strength that exists within me. The noise that Asko lets out is a mixture of a man struck by lightning and a man in the most extreme pain imaginable.

We fall to the ground. Asko curls into a foetal position and cups his hands to protect his crown jewels. Of course, this is only a gesture, an instinctual movement that can no longer alleviate the agony. He is still letting out a noise, but now it has changed in character. What was initially a howl of pain quietens to a weepy moaning as I crawl towards him and straddle him, putting my full weight across his body. He is no longer a threat to anyone. I am about to turn to face the group of people, especially Sanni, and perhaps give a victorious smile, when my plans suddenly change.

In a way Tsukehara's anger is understandable. He has travelled eight thousand kilometres in order to convince his partners to sign up to a new kind of mushroom-importing model with his business partner Asko, with whom he clearly has a long established history. Instead of success and esteem, he has been deluged in vomit, his plans have been ruined and his co-conspirator has been knocked almost unconscious. A man could get worked up over less.

Tsukehara's legs are swift, and his hands are like the wings of a small bird. He passes me and Asko, locates the knife on the ground and lunges into an attack. His eyes are so full of rage they are almost pressed shut, and he looks like he is weeping as he yells something. I don't have time to reach for my pine branch; I don't know where it is. Tsukehara is on top of me and is about to plunge the knife through my skull when the forest shudders, and to me it sounds as though several trees come crashing down at once.

Tsukehara freezes on the spot, then begins to slump to the side like a collapsing house. His hands clasp his right thigh, where a dark-red blotch is spreading through his trousers. Both Asko and Tsukehara are moaning; the gurgling, guttural sounds are deep and continuous.

Detective Inspector Tikkanen walks across the clearing towards us, a gun in his hand.

EPILOGUE

Sanni's hand is warm and delicate. For a moment it grips my own, then relaxes. She is about to fall asleep. The sun is rising, the clouds are white, like in a cartoon; the sky is an impeccable blue. I am content, I don't even feel the need to pull my stomach in. It would be pointless. She has seen me without a shirt on. She has seen me without trousers too. She knows what I look like; she knows who I am and what I am. I told her everything at the first opportunity.

First I had to tell Taina I wanted a divorce. Taina was still in hospital, but making a very good recovery. Our conversation didn't last long. I felt the need to say something positive too, so I thanked her for the food. I'll never forget how well I've eaten all these years, I told her. I left out the fact that those memories now come with a distinctly sour aftertaste, but even that pales in significance alongside all the gastronomic delights. And when, a few minutes later, I said that I guessed this was it, Taina simply nodded. She was keen to add that she and Petri would not be moving to Helsinki together. Petri wants to stay in Hamina, apparently. He hasn't said why, in fact he hasn't spoken to Taina since the incident. She assumes this must be because they went through too much together, too soon. To some extent I agree.

Asko was never officially charged with anything. But now that a decades-old murder case has resurfaced he has a hard time moving about the town. What's more, he is *persona non grata* in the mushroom business. He tried to trick his way into the business. People don't forget a thing like that. In the mushroom business that kind of behaviour is like murder; there's no statute of limitations.

Olli was eventually found in the woodshed. Tikkanen fetched him. Olli didn't resist arrest. He's getting married again; this time his bride is in good keeping at the Hamina women's prison.

Raimo has gently enquired what exactly happened to his sauna while he was helping his wife, who had come down with a case of the norovirus. He says he suspects there's something wrong with my ladling technique. It takes quite a violent throw to make a hole in the wall and snap the floorboards, he says. I told him I slipped. I haven't breathed a word about what's hidden behind the sauna. The grass grows quickly at this time of year.

And regarding that little matter: Sami is still missing. Tikkanen looked at me long and hard when, during questioning, I said I thought Sami was often a victim of his own emotions, that he could fly into a rage at the drop of a hat.

Suvi is no longer our temporary employee. Now she is our financial manager. I have never since brought up our conversation.

Tikkanen saved my life. I've thanked him on numerous occasions, and he has reminded me that I saved two people's lives with my quick response. It's true. I couldn't save myself. Well, maybe there's still time. Perhaps, though we die, we live on. Perhaps we leave something behind, a breath or a thought, something, anything.

Our business is thriving – better than ever in fact. Kakutama was especially impressed at how I was prepared to sacrifice myself for the sake of my business, how I put my life on the line to save our business agreement. He says he respects a man who, armed with only a pine branch, is prepared to resist an experienced man wielding a thirty-centimetre sashimi knife. I have congratulated myself on more than one occasion for managing to listen to Kakutama's account of the length and sharpness of the knife without fainting.

Sanni has brought me back to life. In so many ways. I want to take her in my arms, to thank her for everything. I want to tell her that I love her with all my strength, with every cell in my body. Of course, I will never recover, and I will die soon. But that is something we all have in common, even those of us who once imagined we would live forever.

Sanni opens her eyes. She smiles, looks me in the eye.

'Did you say something?' she asks.

I shake my head and gently kiss her scalp. She's asleep again soon.

The screen tells me we'll arrive in Tokyo in three hours. On the other side of the window the sky is blue as we fly towards the rising sun.

Acknowledgements

The Man Who Died feels like a turning point in many ways. After writing five very dark books – albeit all very different from each other – ranging from the dystopia of *The Healer* to the icy north of *The Mine*, I started to feel that I needed to change things up a bit. More than a bit, to be honest. I told my agent this. I think I also told him I needed to laugh a bit. His response: go for it.

So:

I would like to thank my literary agent Federico Ambrosini for his invaluable and incomparable support and feedback. I am very grateful to have him in my corner, so to speak. And on the subject of agents, I would like to extend my gratitude to everyone at the Salomonsson Agency, Stockholm.

I send my gratitude to the amazing Karen Sullivan of Orenda Books in London. She is a fearless independent publisher and an inspiration. She works harder than anyone I know. Thank you, Karen.

My most sincere thank-you goes to the one and only Harri Haanpää, the editor of this book (the original Finnish version, that is). This was my third book with Harri, and I think Harri has by now edited out one novel's worth of extraneous sentences. Harri, I thank you and your steadfast pencil.

Thank you also to the supremely brilliant David Hackston. Finnish is not an easy language, but you make it seem so. I'm privileged to be translated by you.

Thank you to West Camel for your fantastic and careful editing on the English version.

I want to thank my mother and father for giving me the love of books. I have the best job in the entire world, and I wouldn't have it without the bookshelves you put in our home a long time ago.

Finally, I wish to thank my beautiful, wise wife Anu. None of this would be possible without you. Thank you for everything. You are my heart and my home. May our journey continue.